Nicholas Royle, born in Manchester in 1963, is the author of four previous novels and more than a hundred short stories. He has also edited eleven anthologies of original short fiction. He lives in Manchester with his wife and two children. Currently he is adapting his fourth novel, *The Director's Cut,* for the screen. His website can be found at www.nicholasroyle.com.

Antwerp: A Novel

Nicholas Royle

Library of Congress Catalog Card Number: 2004100909

A complete catalogue record for this book can be
obtained from the British Library on request

First published in 2004 by Serpent's Tail,
4 Blackstock Mews, London N4 2BT
website: www.serpentstail.com

Printed by Mackays of Chatham plc

10 9 8 7 6 5 4 3 2 1

'Do you remember the Spitzner Museum at the fair? The sinister, somehow morbid atmosphere, the unusual aspect of this exhibition of wax figures in a context of joy, noise, light and conviviality? A link that still baffles me has been established between this strange but also beautiful museum and the surrounding joy'

– Paul Delvaux

'If there's one important thing in a film, it's the frame'

– Harry Kümel

'BELGIE IS DOOD' ('Belgium is dead')

– graffiti, Antwerp

for Kate

and to the memory of
Barry Burman (1943–2001)

CONTENTS

Part One

VENUS ASLEEP

DARK ENTRIES

The day Johnny Vos first laid hands on a woman's body started out like any other. Johnny took the PATH train from Hoboken, New Jersey into New York City. He listened to the song of the grinding rails and rushing walls, his mind's eye full of the last thing he saw before heading underground – the castellated Manhattan skyline, like Bruegel's vision of the Tower of Babel. He travelled on an empty stomach, as always. On arrival he would get coffee and doughnuts from a street vendor.

The two places – Hoboken and Manhattan – were only fifteen minutes apart by train, yet divided by the Hudson River and a state line. So near yet so far, was pretty much how Hoboken residents tended to think of New York. Some kids growing up in the New Jersey town were frustrated by Manhattan's tantalising proximity: they became resentful. For Johnny Vos it worked just fine. It meant he could lead a double life. One thing in one place, another in the other. So in Hoboken he kept himself to himself, was no trouble to his folks, head forever buried in some art book, but then he would skip school and take the train, sex-tourist with fake ID, tall kid with five o'clock shadow. He'd carry the price of a few beers and haunt the strip joints around Times Square and 42nd Street, where he would sit in the dark and watch from under the curled rim of a Yankees baseball cap. He preferred the Mets, but actually wasn't that bothered, and a Yankees cap meant you didn't stand out.

He was rarely challenged and on the few occasions when his fake ID had to be produced it was barely glanced at. Around Times Square and 42nd Street no one really cared. This was 1980. People gave a shit a lot less than they do today. Especially around Times Square and 42nd Street. Johnny Vos was seventeen.

He came out of the station on 34th Street and cut across to 5th Avenue. There was a used bookstore at 4th and 12th where the proprietor was happy to let people sit and read stuff. He had a good selection of art books and Johnny could pass a whole morning there. He regarded it as a form of education lacking at high school, where art class began and ended with Norman Rockwell. He gazed in wonder at Bosch's hallucinatory depictions of hell – a pretty good guess, he figured. His eyes were drawn to Grünewald, Friedrich, Ensor. He could tell the difference between the three Bruegels – Peter the Elder, Peter the Younger and Jan – he knew which one was cool and which two were not. The sense of history made him feel he belonged – somewhere, if not here.

He didn't pretend to be an expert, but he knew what he liked. He liked the old stuff. He was just looking at the pictures.

He checked out Rubens. The guy had seen some action. Johnny wondered if he'd used a different model each time. The thought was enough to make him look up from the book and check his watch. It was after 12.30pm. He always tried to leave it till at least one o'clock. It made him feel less seedy.

Without particularly hurrying, he covered twenty blocks in a half-hour. Ducking his head, he entered the Blue Zone at Broadway and 42nd. Waited while his eyes grew accustomed to the gloomy interior and his chest tightened in reaction to the smoke. Took a seat at the back. A waitress came by to take his order. On the wobbly stage, a girl with flabby thighs worked out a routine with leather chaps and a cowboy hat. It was tired stuff but it worked. Kind of.

Johnny got another beer, slipped lower in his seat. He figured three beers, maybe four, would be enough, but after two he felt no braver than when he'd boarded the PATH train. In his pocket was a matchbook with a handwritten address on the inside flap. He remembered how he'd felt when the girl, another girl in another bar, had written down the address the week before. He felt the same excitement now, mixed with a sharp anxiety. Watching the dancer on stage, he tried to convince himself this was enough, but he knew it was not. The writing down of the address had taken things a stage further. Where he was right now was not a place he could stay.

He left the bar and walked two blocks on unsteady legs until he reached a row of tenement houses. He was done rationalising and justifying. Too shy to work anything out with those girls at high school who might not have run away screaming, Johnny had got left behind. He missed the experiences his contemporaries took for granted, but soon was working on the basis that his own life was more adventurous, his world more real. He lived his life on the streets. This afternoon would be a rite of passage. No shit. But the nearer he got to the address on the matchbook, the more he wished he were dating Esther Balinski or Rachel Leibowitz, even with the compromise either would entail. He came to a halt outside the last house and examined a series of buzzers. He saw the one he wanted and leaned on it. Nothing happened. Johnny didn't even draw a breath.

Suddenly the door was no longer closed and a man had appeared. The man, only a few years older than Johnny, glanced at him and then was gone. Johnny caught the door and stepped into the hallway. The door snicked shut behind him. There was a sour smell. Something somewhere had gone off. A bare bulb failed to come on when Johnny pressed a switch. His breathing was shallow and wheezy. He thought about quitting but sensed that he'd never get even this far again. The stairs rose steeply. The effort and stress aggravated Johnny's asthma, but he couldn't stop now. On the first landing he scanned the doors to three apartments. Number six was ajar and Johnny could hear noise from within.

He checked the matchbook one last time and pushed open the door.

Once inside he could no longer hear the noise he'd been able to hear out on the landing. He could hear something else instead. A regular, muffled *thump-thump*, like a heartbeat amplified for effect on a soundtrack. It was a familiar sound, but he was too wired to work out what it was. Every object he saw, each sound he heard, it was as if he was sensing them for the first time.

He was in a narrow red-carpeted hallway. It was dark. Doors opened off it to the left and at the end. Coats were hung up on a series of hooks — a leather biker's jacket, threadbare woollen overcoat, denim bum-freezer with sheepskin lining. A cosy, warm smell came off them. Somebody lived here. A cheap Frieda Kahlo print, the artist's heart exposed, hung by the door on the left, which led to a tiny shower room with toilet. The shower head was dripping, but that was not the noise Johnny had heard on entering the apartment. He could still hear it and it was coming from the room at the end. He advanced slowly, aware of the wheezing coming from his chest. The wall beneath his finger-tips was warm and greasy. When he reached the end of the hall-way he stopped.

He knew what the noise was.

As he turned the corner into the room at the end, the first thing he saw confirmed it. A record spinning on a turntable, needle stuck in the run-out groove. He saw it by the light of a lamp with a beaded shade standing on a bookcase. The diffuse lamplight also fell softly on to the body of a woman in her mid to late twenties lying on the unmade bed in the middle of the room. She was naked and appeared fully relaxed, as if deeply asleep. Johnny held his breath and watched her, waiting for her to move as she sensed his presence. He didn't want to frighten her, but neither did he want to leave. A lump had formed in his throat. The tableau laid out before his eyes was the most beauti-ful thing he had ever seen. He'd seen this girl, Amber, before, of course, but partially dressed and in different surroundings. Here, in her own place, completely natural and totally naked, she was exquisite. She was lit like a nude in a painting, but not a Rubens or one of his contemporaries. The setting precluded any likeness to the Old Masters and the light was different. It was cooler, more modern, and the main difference was that painted nudes never aroused more than his aesthetic approval. The sight of Amber lying naked on her own bed aroused him in another way as well.

Taking deeper breaths, Johnny moved closer to the bed until

he was standing right by it. He saw what he hadn't seen before: that Amber's right arm wore a tourniquet around the biceps. The tourniquet was a belt and Johnny felt a twinge of sadness that it wasn't even leather. A syringe lay on the floor on the far side of the bed where it had been dropped. He looked more closely at Amber's face. There were purple shadows under her eyes. So she looked a little tired — so what? It wasn't an easy life. His hand came to rest on her forearm. He felt a tingle of electricity. Her arm retained a trace of warmth.

He looked at her body, gazing in rapt wonderment at her breasts, which rested on her ribcage but had not altogether lost their shape. The smooth skin around the nipples was the same golden colour as her hair, even if that colour was artificial, as evidenced by the soft dark furze nestling below her flat tummy. Her right leg was drawn up, the knee leaning over her left leg.

He held her wrist, but there was no pulse. He picked up an empty powder compact from the floor and held the mirror over her mouth, but there was no final whisper of breath to cloud the glass.

The heartbeat thump of the needle in the run-out groove seemed to grow louder. He walked around the bed and stared at the record, trying to read the label as it revolved. He couldn't, so he lifted the arm and the record slowed to a stop. It was a single: 'Dark Entries' by Bauhaus. Johnny moved the arm back over the record and placed the needle at the beginning. Dust, hiss. Then the track began with a howl of feedback and a fusillade of guitars. Bass and drums thundering like a stampede of wild horses. A strange, hypnotic male voice sang of a hovel, a bed, pain, neon lights, avenues of sin. Johnny sat at the bedside and held the dead woman's cooling hand. The urgency of the rhythm, intensity of the vocals. Something on the floor, half under the bed, caught his eye. It was the record sleeve. The front bore the name of the single and the band and an image: a female figure in a feathered hat, a human skeleton. Johnny turned the sleeve over. The reverse side featured a small, indistinct photograph of the band and a credit line for the picture: '*Venus Asleep* by Paul Delvaux'.

Johnny went back round the other side of the bed and sat down, holding the dead woman's hand as the needle once more went *thump-thump* in the run-out groove and the sky outside the tiny window turned deep red. He thought briefly about the man he had seen leaving the building. He tried to recall his face.

Part Two

DAWN OVER THE CITY

2

'T ZUID

When, as a young girl growing up in Zoliborz on the outskirts of Warsaw in the early 1980s, Danuta had dreamed of being in the movies, it hadn't been like this. There had been assistant directors juggling walkie-talkies, sound recordists weight-lifting booms, and glamorous stars walking the eternal tightrope between reality and illusion. The set had been overrun by make-up girls, hairdressers, carpenters, gaffers and best boys. Someone to say 'Action' or 'Rolling' or 'Quiet on the set, please'. She'd seen everything from early Andrzej Wajda to the Wachowski Brothers, and she thought she knew a bit about how films were made, but her dream was only ever just a dream and instead of arching her back on the Croisette at Cannes while a thousand flash bulbs popped and chummy voices called out 'This way, Danuta. This way, love', she wound up working the windows in the famous red light district of the Flemish city of Antwerp.

And that was how she ended up in the movies, after all.

There was no clapperboard, no bright forest of arc lamps, no catering van standing by. It wasn't that kind of set. It wasn't that kind of film. There was a director, one digital video camera, a few runners and three dozen extras hired by the hour from the Schipperskwartier, the sailors' quarter, the city's main red light district.

Danuta fished her watch out of the pocket of her long over-coat. It was almost 6am. If it weren't for the actors and runners,

Leopold De Waelplaats would be deserted. Danuta gathered that the town hall and police had granted permission for filming on the understanding that it had to take place on Sunday and be wrapped up by 6.30am.

Leopold De Waelplaats was situated on the city's fashionable south side, known as 't Zuid, halfway between the River Schelde and the inner ring road, the Amerikalei. On the square's south-east edge sat the great bulk of the Museum of Fine Arts, and on the south-west corner, diagonally across from where the director, Johnny Vos, had positioned his camera by the north end of the steps outside the museum, was Café Hopper. The proprietors of Café Hopper, where Antwerp's fashionable crowd would gather each evening, had agreed to let Vos have the use of the place for the duration of the shoot. Danuta knew how it worked: when the film was screened, Café Hopper would be acknowledged in the credits.

Most of the girls milling around waiting for the sunlight to pour into the square over the top of the museum wore coats hanging off their shoulders. A handful carried drapes and robes they would need in the shot. Danuta had a gold drape and a garland of pink flowers in her blonde hair, the blossoms carefully positioned to conceal her dark roots. Hannah, a friend of Danuta's who still worked in the red light district, Danuta having quit the Schipperskwartier for an Internet voyeur house close to the Grote Markt, wore a plastic tiara in her natural blonde hair and carried a gold-patterned tablecloth. The red rose tattoo on her right shoulder did not have to be concealed, since she would only be filmed from the left. Danuta and Hannah were nearest to the camera. Johnny Vos, his long hair tied back in a ponytail, stood between the women and his tripod, scanning the square for the runners, who were dotted about randomly. At a sign from Vos, they would gather the girls' coats, then cross back over the square to Café Hopper, where they would wait until the scene was done.

Danuta observed Johnny Vos as he anxiously checked his watch. A couple of blocks away she heard the grinding squeal of a tram. A moment later it entered the square and slowed to a halt. Passengers peered out of the windows, exhibiting disinterested bafflement at the unusual gathering. Then the tram was on its way and Danuta noticed that direct sunlight had finally entered the square at the far end of the museum steps. She looked at Vos, but still he waited. A few seconds later, the sun rose above the museum's façade, splashing into the square, and Vos nodded to the runners, who began to do what runners do. The girls took up their positions, handing over their coats and revealing their naked bodies to the first rays of sunlight. The few who had to carry robes did so, but most of the girls were naked.

Thirty metres behind Danuta, ten girls with robes draped over their left arms began to make a slow crossing of the square from the far side towards the museum. Danuta stepped on to her mark and glanced at Hannah, who was trying to hold her gilded table-cloth in place over the lower half of her body while leaving her large breasts bare and extending her left arm in an ambiguous gesture as she had been shown. Hannah caught Danuta's eye and they exchanged smiles. Danuta thought she was going to lose it as she wrestled with her gold drape, which had to conceal her left leg while exposing the dark bush of her pubic hair, then come up the side of her body and over her left arm, which she had to raise so she could clasp hands behind her head. Danuta looked round briefly to see several couples frolicking on the steps of the museum. The actor playing Paul Delvaux, the artist, whose painting *Dawn Over the City* was being loosely recreated in this scene, had started walking slowly towards the camera from the far end of the square, parallel with the museum steps. The only person in the shot who was fully dressed, he wore a charcoal-grey three-piece suit, starched white shirt and crimson-and-black bow tie like a red admiral that had settled momentarily at his throat. In his right hand he carried a palette, in his left a brush.

Aware of being watched, Danuta looked around. Hannah grinned on catching her eye. She nodded her head in the direction of Vos, whose spindly bare legs stuck out of the bottom of his shabby coat like the last two matches in a crumpled, much-thumbed matchbook. Danuta felt a brief pang as she looked at Hannah and was reminded of how much younger her friend was, despite the unselfconsciousness with which she exposed her body. She was never short of attention in the red light district, where the two had met. Because of Hannah's age she still retained a freshness that the older girls had lost. Danuta resolved there and then to get Hannah out of the Schipperskwartier before it was too late.

Johnny Vos was removing his watch. He slipped it into his coat pocket, then took off the coat and dropped it on to the ground behind the camera. He took up a position in front of Danuta, who was preceding the artist, and walked slowly into the left foreground. Hannah, a wash of thin hazy sunshine falling on to her magnificent breasts, the reason she had been chosen over Danuta to play the woman nearest the camera, gestured to Vos with her left hand. His own left hand moved away from his side as if either to reciprocate Hannah's gesture or to ward off her advance, but he left a gap for Danuta and the painter to occupy the centre ground unimpeded.

Once Vos had walked beyond the camera, unfazed by his own nakedness, he turned around and shouted 'Cut'. Danuta and Hannah and the other girls, required to process with stately, almost somnambulistic poise, relaxed; the actor playing the artist, like Vos, had walked out of shot. Instead of reaching for his coat, Vos went straight to the camera. He stopped the tape and played back the shot.

'Once more,' he said then, loud enough for the half-dozen or so women nearest to him to hear, among them Danuta and Hannah. 'From the top.'

With the retake completed to Vos's satisfaction, he gave a signal and the runners reappeared among the girls with their coats. The extras then gathered in Café Hopper for coffee and pastries. The guy playing the artist had disappeared, and Vos hung around near the door talking on a mobile phone. The café buzzed with an atmosphere of noisy camaraderie. The girls, many of them strangers to each other, were more relaxed than they might have been if grouped together on the north side of the city where they plied their trade.

Danuta leaned towards Hannah and asked her, 'So how is it going?'

'Good,' she answered brightly. Too brightly.

'Really?'

'Well . . .' She smiled ruefully.

Danuta knew that rueful smile. It was a smile that was written into the reflexive code of her own facial muscles. She touched the younger woman's arm. The smile faded slightly, but Danuta knew she'd connected. Grabbing a pen off a passing waiter, Danuta took hold of Hannah's wrist and wrote a number on the back of her hand.

'What's that for?' Hannah asked.

'Call me,' Danuta said. 'I'm your guardian angel.'

Johnny Vos entered L'Entrepôt du Congo at 12.35pm, ten minutes before the agreed time. He knew that the Englishman would arrive five minutes early, because journalists always did. They liked to get everything sorted out before their subject turned up. Pen, notebook, tape recorder, drink. But Johnny preferred to be there first. It was the way he liked to do it.

Only a handful of tables were taken. There were two single men, but neither looked the type, so he sat down at a table next to the wall on the left side of the room. A waitress smiled as she handed him a menu. He asked for a Rodenbach and told her he was waiting for someone else to arrive.

He looked around while waiting. In addition to the two other lone men, there were three couples and a woman on her own. She had to be waiting for someone, a man, he thought to himself. She was a handsome woman in her early fifties, dressed with casual style, the kind of casual style that costs a lot of money. Women like that did not eat in cafés on their own. Not in Belgium, not in America, not anywhere. It was a universal law.

Johnny's Rodenbach arrived. He took a sip of the gleaming, dark, sour beer and placed the glass carefully on the table, then glanced at his watch. It was 12.40pm. He half-turned so that he could see the door. It opened and in walked a man in his late thirties, dark wavy hair, light blue eyes. He was wearing a quilted leather jacket over a slate roll-neck pullover. He looked English; he looked OK. Glancing around, his eyes locked on to Johnny's. Johnny stood up and the two men shook hands.

'Frank Warner,' said the Englishman.

'Johnny Vos.'

They sat down and Frank ordered himself a beer.

'Looks good,' Frank said, admiring the dark brew. 'It's one thing the Belgians do better than just about anybody.'

'You've been before?'

'Yes, but not to Antwerp.'

'Me neither,' admitted the American.

'So what made you choose Antwerp as the setting for the film?'

'Is this the interview?' Johnny asked, taking a packet of cigarettes and a book of matches out of his jacket pocket.

Frank laughed. 'Sorry. Getting ahead of myself. There's no rush.' He shook his head as Johnny offered him a cigarette. 'I mean,' he added, seeming less sure of himself, 'unless you're in a hurry. You must be on a tight schedule?'

'No problem,' Johnny said through a cloud of acrid smoke.

The waitress asked if they were ready to order food.

Johnny ordered the pasta with red pesto and, seeing that Frank was hesitating, advised him to have the same.

'I suppose you are doing a lot of interviews?' Frank asked.

'This is the first.'

Again, Frank seemed wrong-footed.

'How's work on the picture going?' he asked.

'Aren't you going to use a tape recorder?'

'I won't misquote you,' Frank assured him.

'All the same.' Johnny stared him down.

Frank took a Sony microcorder from the pocket of his leather jacket and placed it on the table.

'So, how's it going, or is it too early to say?'

'We filmed our first big scene this morning,' Johnny said, sitting back in his chair and looking away from Frank. An unbroken series of mirrors ran around the interior of the café at eye level, just below the windows. As Johnny talked about the scene they had shot that morning, he casually examined his reflection. His long, dark brown hair was streaked with grey highlights. It could do with a wash, he noted. A couple of days' beard growth. Eyes the colour of the Rodenbach. He became aware of the Englishman watching him in the mirror and met his gaze for a moment before turning his head back towards the table. 'So I guess I couldn't have wished for a better start,' he finished.

'It was one of Delvaux's paintings?'

'*Dawn Over the City*, 1940.'

'It's an unusual approach in a biopic, isn't it?' Frank asked. 'Bringing to life the artist's works in a way he never would have done in his lifetime.'

'I'm showing what existed inside his head.' Johnny spread his palms outward as if explaining to a child. 'That's what I regard as the job of the biographical film. The rest is just research.'

'Why not just show a montage of his paintings instead of using live actors? Isn't it all just a bit too David Hamilton? A bit soft porn? Aren't you objectifying women?'

'What the fuck does that *mean* – objectifying women?' Johnny said as the waitress arrived with the pasta. 'It's bullshit,' he said. 'Women *are* objects, no more so and no less so than this bowl of pasta, this glass of beer. We're all objects, me and you included. You know who's closest to the camera in the scene we shot this morning? Me. Butt naked. That make me an object? So I'm an object. Who gives a shit?'

Johnny shook his head, looked away. The café had filled up. Only one of the lone men was still unaccompanied. The stylish woman in her fifties had been joined by a younger man wearing a designer fleece. That figured, Johnny thought. Designer fucking fleece. They were talking animatedly. Johnny contrived to catch her eye in the mirror. On the wall above the bar was an old black and white photograph of King Baudouin that dated back to the days when the Congo was still a Belgian colony. It was unusual that any bar or restaurant in Antwerp – such as L'Entrepôt du Congo – gave its name in French.

'Delvaux was francophone,' said Frank, as if reading Johnny's mind.

'He settled in Flanders, on the coast, and the Flemish welcomed him,' Johnny responded. 'It's a lot cheaper and easier to film here than in Brussels. The bureaucracy . . . Plus, this is the land of my people. Vos, Johnny Vos. It's not a French name.'

'Your antecendents were Flemish?'

Johnny nodded as he pushed his plate aside and lit another cigarette.

'It's not a big deal,' he continued, 'the whole language-split thing. The French-speakers tend to stay in Wallonia and the Flemish-speakers stay in Flanders. Brussels is a special case, of course.'

'What do you think of the recent success of the Vlaams Blok?'

The Flemish nationalist party, the Vlaams Blok, advocated the forced repatriation of immigrants.

'I'm a filmmaker, not a politician.'

'Thirty per cent,' Frank pressed him. 'Thirty per cent of the vote here in Antwerp. Does one out of every three people here really support the extreme right?'

'As I said, I am not a politician. I thought we were supposed to be talking about the movie?'

Frank paused, looked at his empty plate and moved his fork through ninety degrees.

'You're right,' he said. 'I'm sorry. Let's talk about the film. What drew you to the subject matter? Why *this* film?'

'It doesn't feel like I ever had a choice. The subject matter chose me.'

'You've been interested in Delvaux how long?'

'Since I was a kid.'

'What happened?'

'What happened? Nothing happened. I saw one of his paintings. Guess you could say I was impressed.'

Frank nodded, thought for a moment.

'How did you go about casting the women's parts? I mean the women in the paintings.'

'They're hookers. I went to the red light district. Next question.'

'You seem to be drawn to prostitutes. What's the attraction?'

'Would you have put the same question to Alan Pakula after he made *Klute*?'

'I'm just looking for a common thread between this movie and your last one.'

'Guess you found one.'

The waitress stopped by.

'Would you like to see the menu?' she asked.

'Yes,' said Frank.

'No,' said Vos. 'I have to be somewhere,' he muttered, gathering cigarettes and matches together.

'That's a shame. We were just getting started. Perhaps we could grab five minutes when I visit the set?'

'Call the production office,' Vos said as he got to his feet. 'Great lunch.'

3

LAST HOUSE ON THE LEFT

There were seven girls in the house on Moriaanstraat, and fifteen digital video cameras. The owner called it the Last House on the Left, despite the fact it wasn't. The reference to Wes Craven's 1972 video nasty was lost on the girls who worked there, with the exception of Danuta, who'd seen the film on second-generation pirate video. The Last House offered the girls no privacy, but it was dry and warm and, most importantly of all, rent free.

Danuta was tired and needed to sleep, but a German TV crew making a documentary about Internet porn had been granted access to the house and they trailed from room to room, trying, unsuccessfully, to get the girls to do stuff on camera – to touch each other or leave the door open while going to the toilet. Because even those girls who knew a little German refused to speak it, the language used was the elliptical English of the inter-national sex industry, which at its most basic consisted of three verbs – fuck, suck, come – and a bunch of numbers, as well as 'yes' and 'no', but mainly 'yes'. Danuta was Polish, as was Maria; Helena was from Romania; Marie and Denise were from Ireland, via Amsterdam, where they'd both worked the streets; Katya was Russian; and Nana was from the Democratic Republic of Congo. They felt a degree of comradeship that transcended racial differences and they all spoke English well enough, in fact, to share each other's problems. They had adequate Dutch when English wouldn't do, which was rarely.

The German TV crew comprised four: the camera guy, the sound guy, the lighting guy and the guy who asked the questions.

'So the cameras are running all the time?' asked the guy who asked the questions.

'All the time,' replied Eva.

Eva was the owner's assistant and house manager. She was around most of the time, checking the cameras, getting them fixed when necessary, even running errands for the girls, who liked and trusted her.

'When users log on, what do they see?' asked the TV guy.

'They see what you see. This house. The girls.'

'Where are the cameras?'

'Everywhere.'

'Everywhere?'

'What part of "everywhere" do you not understand?'

Eva didn't take any shit, not from anybody.

'So, when they sleep? When they go to the toilet?'

'You seem to have a thing with the toilet. The cameras are always there, always running. Could be there's no one looking, but the possibility is always there. The girls know this. It's not a problem for them. It's their job, OK? They earn a living.'

Katya, the Russian, who was sitting in front of one of the computers, called Danuta over. There were three computers in the house that were permanently connected to the Internet. Members could send emails, even chat with the girls online, if the girls felt like it.

'A message for me?' Danuta guessed.

Katya nodded. 'It's that guy again,' she said. 'What does he want?'

Danuta double-clicked the message.

```
Subject: Out again
From: jan7230@freeze.com
To: danuta@lasthouse.com
```

Where have you been? You go out, I don't know where you go.
I miss you. You are the most beautiful thing in my life.
Watching you sleep sometimes I feel faint. When you go out,
it is like a light being switched off. Janx

Danuta clicked on reply.

That is very kind of you. Where do I go? Just out. If we all spent all our time in the house we would go mad. And the members would not appreciate us so much. Dx

She pressed 'send', then checked through the in-box to make sure she hadn't missed anything. The messages were meaningless to her, but if any of the girls did anything to upset a member, such as failing to reply to a message, it could rebound on them directly. One girl had already been kicked out of the house for telling a member to fuck himself up the arse with a greasy spatula. Sideways.

'I'm going to the bedroom,' Danuta said.

'I'll come with you,' Katya replied.

The girls tended to feel they enjoyed greater privacy in their shared bedrooms. It was an illusion, because there were cameras in every room, but you could at least be apart from the other girls and, in the case of this particular afternoon, the German TV crew. If they managed to forget the cameras, which they had found they had to force themselves to do in order to cope with day-to-day life, then the bedrooms were the only place for a private talk.

'Did you ask?' said Katya as soon as the door was closed behind them.

The single black eye of a camera watched them from a wall bracket high up in the corner of the room.

Somewhere on the outskirts of Wolverhampton an insurance analyst, single since the beginning of the year, was beating off to the sight of two women alone together in a bedroom.

'Yes, and he thinks he will need you. There's another big scene coming up.'

Danuta lay down on her bed, on her side, facing Katya, who perched on the edge of her own bed.

'That's good,' said Katya. 'Thanks for asking.'

'No problem.'

A bored IT engineer in some blighted suburb of Liège murmured softly at his screen as he studied the two girls.

Danuta realised she was staring straight into the lens of the

camera, which was angled down in such a way that it stood a
good chance of catching a stray gaze. She looked away, irritated
but trying not to show it. It occurred to her that nothing would
please anyone watching right now more than if she and Katya
were to start kissing and touching each other, but it wasn't that
kind of a deal. At least, not so far. The house hadn't been operational that long. Danuta had been there the third longest at two
months. The members frequently asked, via email, but the owner
had yet to instruct the girls to perform acts upon each other.
Danuta had no doubt that at some point he would, but, until that
happened, they would continue to do the other stuff: lift their
tops on request, perform aerobic routines in the nude, sit on
glass-topped tables, and so on. That was bread and butter to them.
That was what they did, or they wouldn't be in the house.

The girls had all come to the house directly from working the
windows in the red light district, where it was most girls' aim to
do ten men in a day. Ten men at fifty a time made a good wedge,
but they rarely managed that many and, in any case, the pimps
would take a big cut. It was possible to earn nothing one day and
very little the next. Some of the girls worked in the peep shows
or got into porn to supplement their income. The Last House
sounded like a good alternative when Danuta heard about it. But
it was early days. Anything could happen, and probably would.
Danuta's view was that it was best to be prepared for the worst.

'That guy,' Katya whispered, turning away from the camera,
'the one who sends you the messages – does he talk about himself?'

'No.' Danuta was whispering, too, and she had turned her
back to the camera. 'All I know is his email address. Jan something. Could be his name. Might not be. But I don't want to
know, you know?'

Jan had been emailing Danuta exclusively for a fortnight.
There would be at least two emails a day and an online chat every
other day. Having a regular client was not entirely a new experience – there had been a few familiar faces when she and the
other girls had been working the windows – but it was different
when the visual traffic was one way. Jan could watch her, whatever she was doing, whenever she was in the house, while

remaining hidden behind the anonymity of email. Jan was probably not his real name. Of course, you didn't necessarily know a
client's real name in the red light district either, but you could at
least take a good look at them, through the window, and assess
the level of risk. The members were faceless, ageless, nameless.
The one thing they weren't was sexless.

Back downstairs, Danuta was welcomed by Eva with the news
that she had another message. Danuta was surprised to see not
Jan's address but that of Johnny Vos, the director. She opened the
email.

```
Subject: Filming
From: jvos2000@headburst.com
To: danuta@lasthouse.com

We might need your friend, the Russian girl, if she's still
interested. I'll need to see her first. Kind of like an audi-
tion. Can you bring her to my hotel? Call me.
- Later. Johnny Vos.
```

Danuta clicked on 'reply' and emailed him back, saying that
she would do so.

'Katya,' she called out, looking up from the machine. 'It's on.'

Katya smiled and thanked her.

The German crew backed into the room. Maria followed
them, talking to camera.

'I left the red light district,' she was saying, 'because I never
wanted to be there in the first place. I came to Antwerp to be a
waitress. But when I get here I am told the waitress job no longer
exists. If I want I can work in peep shows, or be a prostitute. I
have no money, I have to work. I have no choice. I should never
have left Poland, but once I leave, it is too late to go back.'

Danuta had heard Maria's story before. She'd heard all the
girls' stories before and they were fundamentally the same. Lured
to Antwerp under false pretences by men posing as restaurant
owners or employment scouts, young women found themselves
sucked into a world of fear and uncertainty. Many of them stuck
with it because they could see no alternative. A small handful

found the work suited them. Many more did not and soon suc-
cumbed to the false promises of easily obtained drugs, thereby
locking the chains that had been effectively placed around their
ankles and throwing the keys into the Schelde.

Danuta had been persuaded to come to Antwerp by her
boyfriend, Mustafa, a Turk. She had known him for only three
weeks in Warsaw when he said he was going to Belgium and suggested she accompany him. She would easily find work, he
insisted, which she could not locate in her hometown. They'd
been in Brussels a day when he said there was a chance of some
work in Antwerp. A half-hour train ride, he said, pressing against
her to emphasise his point, then backing off and looking around
as if she weren't there. She went to Antwerp mainly because she
was unhappy and work was the one thing that she thought might
help her escape her unhappiness. Money, independence. Mustafa
returned from a meeting, however, and said he'd been let down,
but there was some other work, on the north side. Bar work, he
said. She went to look at the bar. It was nestled between two rows
of blue- and red-lit windows on Falconplein. As it was early, not
all of them were occupied, but some were, and the girls in them
looked tired and drawn beneath their make-up.

Danuta took the bar work. The first day, she began at ten-
thirty in the morning and didn't get off till nine at night. She had
noticed people passing by the window all day, but it was only
when she got outside that she realised they were all men. She
joined the throng, slowing down to walk at their speed, which
had about it a kind of forced insouciance, a false nonchalance.

Only one sound was louder than the incessant shuffling:
women tapping on the glass with their rings. They did it insis-
tently, as if unaware, stuck inside, of the volume of the noise and
how it carried over the streets of the red light district and
beyond. It was like the Geiger counter's uncanny death-rattle.
The moment any man turned and made eye contact with one of
the girls, even for a split second, the response was instantaneous.
Rat-tat-tat-tat. Rat-tat-tat-tat-tat.

Being among the men but apart from them, she was able to
see something about them that perhaps, had she already been on
the other side of the glass, she might not have seen. They circled

the red light district like sharks, but their eyes were sad and furtive. If the women, on the other hand, were bait, they did at least appear to realise it and with this self-awareness came power.

Danuta had let Mustafa lead her into this world, but now, her eyes opened, she chose to stay, in order eventually to escape. She made faster progress than Mustafa had intended, choosing her own pimp, a pocket-size Russian mafioso who seemed well connected, but not to Mustafa, who was reduced to trying to buy Danuta's time. 'Go away,' she hissed. 'I'm working. This is what you wanted. You should be happy.' He did leave, but came back with three other Turks — squat, dark men with mayhem in their eyes. All the girls in the red light district carried mobile phones. At slack times they slouched against their partition walls talking to each other on their mobiles. Danuta had been there long enough to get a mobile, but not long enough to make any friends. She called her pimp's number, but it was busy. Mustafa knocked on the glass, the three Turks standing behind him like a Greek chorus. One of the men stepped forward and jabbed his elbow sharply into the window. His hand groped inside for the lock, fat fingers fluttering with surprising grace. Danuta watched as he climbed in, followed by Mustafa and the two other men. They represented an instantly threatening presence in the narrow booth, moving forward bulkily, forced by the narrow dimensions to switch to a two-two formation. Danuta retreated and it suddenly seemed to her as if she were outside herself watching. As if she were a camera bracketed to the wall in the top corner of the room. Or as if she were even more remote than that.

She watched Mustafa grab hold of her arm and shake her. A hand slapped her cheek and she started swaying. The wall rushed to meet the side of her head. Dark shadows closed in and within seconds the picture was lost. Momentary crackle of static and then nothing.

Maria was still narrating her own similar story to camera when Danuta's mobile rang. She ducked out of the room to take the call. When Danuta came back, Maria had finished her story and the TV crew, apparently having called a halt, were packing up.

'Something wrong?' asked Katya, seeing Danuta's dazed expression.

'That was the police,' she said. 'I've got to go.'

'Where to?' Katya asked. 'I'll come with you.'

Danuta nodded. Katya told Eva they were both going out and she didn't know when they'd be back. The girls were meant to restrict the amount of time they spent out of the house, but Eva sensed the urgency in Katya's voice and, in any case, if it came to it, the girls trusted Eva to take their side in any major disagreement with the owner.

In the back of a cab on the Ring, Katya asked Danuta what it was all about.

'I don't know,' she said, skin pulled taut across her forehead. 'The police rang me. They found my number somewhere. They wouldn't tell me where, or what it was about.'

She looked out of the window, fighting back emotion. The cab drifted east, beyond Centraal Station towards Zurenborg, rolling to a standstill under the railway bridge that separated Draakplaats from Tramplein. Danuta paid the driver and the women got out. Just before the bridge, a cobbled road led up towards the level of the railway and Antwerpen-Oost station. Two disused water towers dominated the left side of the little road, dwarfing nearby houses. Enormous cylindrical structures built in the contrasting brown and white brick pattern that had been a characteristic of Belgian architecture since the late nineteenth century, the towers were topped by vast iron drums with conical bases. They resembled giant golf tees.

At the base of the water towers were gathered a dozen plain-clothes policemen, a man with a mangy-looking dog on a piece of string, three police cars and an unmarked vehicle with a detachable blue light on the roof. One of the policemen, a tall, broad-shouldered man with untidy blond hair, moved away from the group and approached Danuta and Katya.

'Which one of you is Danuta?' he asked.

'I'm Danuta. This is Katya, a friend.'

The policeman's blue-eyed gaze took in Katya, then returned to Danuta.

'Detective Dockx. We found the body of a woman. Your

mobile number is written on the back of her hand. The writing is faint but legible.' He paused, waiting for a reaction. 'Does this place mean anything to you?'

'I've never been here before in my life.'

'It's likely the dead woman was a friend of yours,' Dockx said. 'You had better prepare yourself.'

'Can she come with me?' Danuta asked, holding on to Katya's arm.

Dockx considered the request and nodded his assent.

The other men stepped back to allow Danuta and Katya to enter one of the two water towers, with Dockx leading the way. They followed him up a vertical iron ladder. Tiny rust flakes floated free as their feet brushed the steps. At the top they climbed on to a wooden platform. The walls were bare brick, the floor rotting boards and exposed joists, across which they had to pick their way with care.

'She was found by the guy who lives in the other tower,' Dockx was saying. 'In fact, it was his dog that found her. Mind your step.'

Dockx crossed the platform to where a threadbare blanket lay humped on the floor. As Dockx knelt down beside the blanket, his knee joints protested. He took hold of a corner of the blanket and pulled it back to reveal the head and shoulders of a blonde woman in her early twenties, a red rose tattoo on her right shoulder. Unlike Danuta's, the blonde hair was genuine. Caught in the hair was a scattering of white crumbs, substance unknown but too granular to be scurf. The skin on the face was waxy and tinged with grey. Dockx reached under the blanket for the dead woman's right arm, which he lifted out carefully with the intention of showing Danuta where her mobile number had been written on the back of the hand.

'Can you tell me who she is?' the policeman asked.

'Hannah,' said Danuta. 'Hannah Witowski.'

Dockx replaced the blanket and led the women back to the iron ladder. By the time they reached the bottom of the tower, two MPVs had joined the police cars and were disgorging forensics personnel in paper suits and face masks.

'Why don't you let all the tarts in Antwerp traipse through

and take a look?' one of the newcomers said to Dockx in Flemish, as he came alongside.

Dockx merely glared at him, but another, shorter man, with a shaved head and a thick black goatee, stepped forward and said, mildly, 'Fuck you, Willinck. We've got our job to do.'

Dockx took Danuta and Katya aside, followed by the man with the shaved head and goatee.

'This is my colleague, Detective Bertin,' Dockx told the two women.

Dockx and Bertin asked Danuta a series of questions about Hannah and anyone she might have known.

Katya hadn't known Hannah well. She knew that Danuta was closer to her, that they had both been working as extras on the Delvaux film and that Danuta had been trying to fix her up with a place in the house. Hannah had been working the windows in the red light district for three months, after coming to Antwerp from Gdansk.

Danuta told them about the film and its director, Johnny Vos, whose email address and phone number she passed on, but she omitted any mention of the Last House or her efforts to secure Hannah a place there.

'How was she killed?' Danuta asked Dockx.

'We can't disclose that kind of information,' Bertin answered for him.

Dockx said they would definitely need to contact Danuta again. Bertin added that they already had her number. It could have been a joke, but his eyes betrayed no humour. Dockx offered them a ride, but they declined.

Katya held Danuta's hand in the cab. When they got back to the Last House there was another email for Danuta.

Subject: re: Out again
From: jan7230@freeze.com
To: danuta@lasthouse.com

I missed you. Janx

4

BONAPARTE DOCK

Even before spending his first night there, Frank knew he had made a mistake in selecting the *St Anna* 'boatel'. For some reason, he had expected a floating hotel to be something more than a converted cross-Channel ferry, but that was pretty much what it appeared to be. He cursed the guide book for its recommendation, thinking it highly unlikely the writer had been within a nautical mile of the vessel.

The room was not a room, but a cabin, which he should have expected, but for some reason hadn't. The window was not a window, but a porthole, nauseatingly close to the waterline. The cabin did at least have power points and a phone jack. Frank's first meeting with Johnny Vos had not gone very well. He was determined that the second would go better. He knew enough about Vos and his previous work – there had not been a great deal of it, after all – but was not so well informed on the subject of the new movie. He knew a little about Delvaux – born 1897, died 1994; conversant with surrealism if not exactly a surrealist; specialised in nudes and architecture (classical Roman, contemporary Belgian), trains and trams – but not enough to begin to understand why Vos wanted to make a film about him. So Frank woke up the iBook and went online.

There was tons of stuff. Jpegs of Delvaux's paintings in virtual museums; links to actual museums both in Belgium and around the world. Fan sites stuffed with comment, eulogy, even poetry.

Dissertations, academic papers, transcripts of talks. Near the top of the list was the Paul Delvaux Museum in St-Idesbald, a little place on the Belgian coast. He checked out the museum's site, wondering if Vos had been up to the coast to take a look. If his first movie was anything to go by, the American tended to take his research seriously, despite his disparaging tone during the interview. *The rest is just research.*

One site included thumbnail images of Delvaux's work. The paintings possessed a weird hallucinatory beauty, and it quickly became apparent that the female nude was the artist's main pre-occupation. One of them, *The Spitzner Museum,* showed a topless woman walking past a mysterious group of fully dressed, professional men. Spitzner cropped up a great deal. Frank refined his search and discovered that the Spitzner Museum had been a kind of travelling sideshow that Delvaux visited as a young man in the 1920s or 30s when it was a temporary attraction at the Midi Fair in Brussels. Among the exhibits was a Sleeping Venus, a supine mannequin, its chest engineered to rise and fall mechanically, simulating breathing. The Sleeping Venus made a great impression on the young artist, influencing both his subject matter and his mood. He sketched the museum, inside and out, including numerous onlookers and the mechanical figure itself, which he painted as a sleeping woman. In a variety of other settings he painted women either asleep or lying down, or apparently sleepwalking, usually at night, bathed in moonlight. The women would be either naked or partially dressed, the atmosphere invariably dreamlike.

From one link he learned that the actual Spitzner collection had been donated to the Sorbonne in 1997.

As he was in the process of quitting out of the browser, Frank noticed a link to www.spitznermuseum.org. Thinking it might be worth a quick look, he relaunched the application.

Frank then spent an uncomfortable half-hour clicking through dozens of images of human deformity and graphic injuries and skim-reading some unpleasant but morbidly fascinating copy. It was an online freak show, rotten.com with pretensions. He bookmarked it, then checked a few favourite sites to lighten his mood. There was no mention of Johnny Vos on either

Film.com or 24 Frames Per Second; the Internet Movie Database listing was the same as it had been the last time he'd looked, naturally, featuring just the one film, *American Nightmare*. He entered the title in the search field and checked it back the other way. IMDb listed a few other films with the same title. The only one he'd seen was Adam Simon's intelligent documentary about horror films of the 1960s and 70s.

From IMDb, he went back to the search engine, typing 'Johnny Vos'. Links to online video stores, amateur review sites, the listing on IMDb. A link to CNN Europe caught his eye and he clicked on it.

It was only a small item, but he spotted it straight away.

Murdered prostitute linked to movieland

Belgian police have revealed that Hannah Witowski, a 23-year-old Polish prostitute active in Antwerp's red light district, had been working as an extra on a film being shot in the city by US indie director Johnny Vos. Witowski's body was discovered in a disused water tower close to Antwerp East rail station. A videotape found with the body contained a recording of *Monsieur Hawarden*, the 1968 debut film by Belgian director Harry Kümel. more . . .

The Eurostar train left London Waterloo on time, trundled through an overcast Kent and dipped into the tunnel before emerging into the bright sunshine of northern France. Its speed increased swiftly until the train appeared to be flying above the surface of the earth.

As the announcement was made over the PA, that the train had reached its maximum speed of three hundred kilometres per hour, Siân put aside her magazine and looked out of the window. She realised, with an abrupt sensation of light-headedness, as she watched bright splashes of green flash past the window, that she felt happy. For the first time in as long as she could remember, she felt something at least in the same area code as euphoria. Brussels and the connecting train to Antwerp were only two hours away. She felt as if the distance between her and Frank were being narrowed in more than just the geographical sense. Frank might not realise it, but she did. Frank, after all, didn't know she was coming.

He had wanted her to come, originally, despite her antipathy towards Johnny Vos, antipathy based on her conviction that the American was a misogynist. She had watched his first film, *American Nightmare*, in a poky New York theatre surrounded by supposed cineastes who talked all the way through the screening. Sitting beside her, Frank laughed knowingly at film-world references that went over her head. He chuckled grimly at scenes in which she could find nothing funny. What did it mean for cinema — indeed, for society — if the torture, mutilation and, finally, almost mercifully, the execution of young women became a laughing matter? Was the fact that they were prostitutes supposed to excuse the graphic violence and degradation? Or was it the fact that the filmed events were based on a true story?

Siân had tried to work out what had got to her more deeply: the film itself, or Frank's insensitivity to her feelings. As soon as the credits rolled, she got up and left. She knew that Frank always stayed to read the final acknowledgements, and, whereas normally she found this an endearing habit, it needled her that he didn't make an exception on this occasion. She waited for him outside, sulkily trudging up and down, but when he joined her he neither apologised for the film's excesses, nor asked for her opinion. Instead he talked excitedly about his own responses, which were entirely positive.

'Did you *see* the way he used light and dark?' he gabbled. 'Heaven and Hell imagery like *Jacob's Ladder.*'

He glanced at her too quickly to notice her expression, otherwise he might have caught on and attempted to backtrack, but instead he kept on. He babbled. He jabbered. He blathered and wittered, and still didn't stop to think. Eventually Siân had to raise her voice and they had a row in the middle of the street, which ended with Siân storming off and them remaining separated for the whole of their last night in New York. It had only been a short visit anyway, so the incident effectively soured it for both of them, which was a shame, since the trip had been conceived as a way to help them get over some complicated stuff that had been going on.

Back in London, the merest mention of Vos's name or the slightest reference to his film in the presence of Siân and Frank would be enough to bring the temperature in the room down a swift ten degrees. When the news broke that Vos was to shoot a film in Belgium, Siân hoped that Frank would give it a wide berth, and maybe he would have done if he hadn't been approached to write a piece about it for one of the broadsheets. Frank had gone freelance after three years as a staff writer on the film magazine where they had originally met. Now that he was out there again, pulling in a feature commission here, a couple of reviews there, Frank tended to take whatever he was offered. Which was how he justified the decision to accept the Johnny Vos job. 'We need the money,' he'd said. Siân knew that if he'd heard the line in a film, he would have denounced it as a cliché. But the truth was they did need the money. She knew that. Yet she also knew that Vos was tainted. He'd spoiled their trip to New York. Whether he was a misogynist, his work pandered to the prejudices of women-haters.

Frank had asked her to book a few days off and come with him to Antwerp. She'd told him to fuck off and, not unreasonably, he had. So now she was coming to tell him she was sorry and to see if they couldn't finally put New York and the rest of that stuff behind them and move on.

The train slid into the Gare du Midi silently, gracefully, almost majestically. It certainly beat messing around on boats, Siân thought, or schlepping in from the airport.

As Siân stepped on to Belgian soil for the first time, a man was walking his schnauzer on the empty wharves by the Schelde in Antwerp, forty miles north of Brussels, when he spotted a suspicious object bobbing in the wake of a passing freighter. The man called the police, who advised him to keep the object in sight until they arrived, which they did within five minutes. A brace of cars turned up, but no police launch, so two of the uniformed officers commandeered a tender from a craft moored nearby and rowed out into the channel.

Two other officers had remained on the wharf. 'What made you think you should call us out for this?' one of them asked the man, revealing his scepticism that the call-out was worth the interruption to time spent sitting on his arse.

'I don't know,' the man said apologetically. 'I thought I could see something – hair or fabric, or something . . .' The man's voice tailed off uncertainly.

'Seaweed,' the officer retorted. 'Or rope. Anyway, we'll soon find out.'

The other officer knelt down and stroked the schnauzer, but the dog scrunched up its heavy brow and snapped its whiskered jaws, catching the officer's hand. The policeman withdrew, swearing. It was only a nip, the greater injury being to his pride. He was about to reprimand the man when the radio in one of the cars crackled into life.

The voice on the radio could be overheard saying, 'Call for an ambulance. Get on to the morgue.'

If anything, the first cop now appeared even grumpier. He could see overtime looming. The second cop, scowling, made the necessary calls. The witness stroked his dog as he watched the tender returning to the wharf. The Schelde was very wide at this point, four hundred metres or more, and the officers were having to battle against the current. One rowed while the other was bent double inspecting something in the bottom of the little boat. When they reached the wharf, both men looked shell-shocked. The dog owner strained for a glimpse of the body as it was man-handled from the boat to the shore. One of the policemen had wrapped his jacket around the lower half of the body, but the man saw enough to be able to tell his wife, when he got home, that it was that of a young woman, well put together, lips painted bright red. She couldn't have been in the water longer than a couple of hours, he guessed. There had been something tied around her neck, some kind of bag or package, weighed down with an object unknown.

By the time Siân had reached Antwerp and taken a cab from Centraal Station around to Bonaparte Dock, the body in the Schelde had made the early evening news. Frank, by now, had the

TV on, tuned to a French-language station broadcasting from Brussels. He had the sound turned up and couldn't find the remote to lower the volume when he opened the cabin door to find Siân standing outside. They embraced, but the reunion was intruded upon by the blaring of the television, from which there seemed no escape in the tiny cabin. The waters outside the port-hole, moreover, were those in which the woman's body had been found, give or take a few hundred metres.

The body had been identified as that of Katya Egorova, 26, a prostitute who had arrived in Antwerp from Moscow within the last six months and had been living lately at an address in Moriaanstraat.

The watertight package that had been recovered along with the body, the reporter announced in French that Frank could just about follow, had contained a pre-recorded video cassette of a film, *Les lèvres rouges*, a cult movie by Belgian director Harry Kümel.

'This follows the earlier discovery of the body of another prostitute, also with a video of a film by Harry Kümel, *Monsieur Hawarden*,' the reporter was saying.

'It's gone mad here,' Frank heard himself telling Siân in a state of some excitement. 'Two prostitutes murdered within days of each other, one of whom was an extra on Vos's film, and both bodies discovered with videos of films by Harry Kümel.'

'Who is Harry Kümel?' asked Siân irritatedly.

While Frank could see it wasn't the way Siân would have scripted their reunion, he couldn't help being caught up in the unravelling story.

'This film, the one they've just found, *Les lèvres rouges*, was released in the UK as *Daughters of Darkness*. It's a kind of lesbian vampire movie – 1970, 71, something like that.'

'What about the girl?' Siân asked. 'What about the woman's body? You know, I mean, was the video found with the body, or the other way around? I can tell which *you* think is more important.'

They stared at each other across the tiny cabin, Siân's eyes full of reproach, Frank baffled and slightly cross. On the TV, the pic-ture had switched back to the studio, where the anchorman was now turning to the female arts correspondent to ask, 'So, who exactly *is* Harry Kümel?'

5

WESTMALLE TRIPEL

'Kümel's made half a dozen films,' Frank said, raising his voice so that Siân could hear him in the noisy bar. 'He's a well-known and respected figure in Belgium and is known to critics around the world, but has never become a household name abroad, possibly because he's not made that many features, and they've tended to be quite different from each other, or perhaps because much of his output is simply too strange for popular taste. How many of these beers have we had, anyway?'

They were in a jazz café on Melkmarkt drinking Westmalle Tripel. A standards trio was playing on a little stage at the end of the bar.

'A few,' said Siân.

'Yeah, well, where was I? Harry Kümel. His first film, *Monsieur Hawarden*, was a period thing, black and white.'

'When?'

'What?'

'When was it made? This film. *Monsieur* . . . whatever.'

'I don't know – 1968? Anyway, Rutger Hauer was in it, or he would have been, but his part was cut.'

'Why?'

'I don't know. You want to know? I'll tell you what: I'll ask Harry when we get together.'

'Is that likely?'

Frank raised his eyebrows. 'It's a small country.'

'Your phone,' Siân said.

'What?'

'I think you'll find your phone is ringing. Better take advantage if you've bothered to charge it up for once.'

'Ah.' Frank clamped the phone to his ear but couldn't hear a thing over the music. Miming to Siân, he started to climb down from his stool, fell off instead, picked himself up and stumbled outside to take the call.

When he came back, somewhat sobered up, Siân had ordered two more Westmalle Tripels. The beers stood on the bar in their tall, scooped glasses, a declaration of intent. The amber-hued beer as rich and aromatic as honey. The first mouthful gave you a buzz, while the sting was the kind of hangover to which any sane person would prefer death. They were on their fourth glass each.

'Who was that?' Siân asked.

'Wrong number.'

'Right.' It was far from being the first time Siân had heard the joke, but after a few beers it was almost funny. 'I hope you haven't got to go,' she said.

'It was the guy I'm doing the Johnny Vos piece for,' Frank said. 'He's been talking to the news editor.'

'And he said that Johnny Vos is a misogynist prick?' Siân suggested. 'A pornographer who fancies himself as an arthouse director? That's hardly news.'

Frank could handle this kind of stuff when it was clear that Siân was having a go, but not trying to start a fight. She signalled this with a look. To call it a smile would have been stretching it. It was a look in the eye that could have evolved into a smile in a quarter of a million years. The Westmalle Tripel helped. Frank was relieved they had managed to take a step back from the gulf that had opened up between them on the boatel.

'You're right, that's not news,' Frank said, raising his glass to his lips. 'At least, not to you. I think it might be to anyone with a serious interest in film, however.' He drank deeply from the Westmalle.

'What was he like,' Siân asked, 'when you met him?'

Frank looked at her, thinking about how to answer, but thinking slowly because of the beer, and half-distracted by the jazz in

the background, and, frankly, dazzled by her beauty. Frank knew
that Siân liked it when he complimented her, which, in turn, was
one of the many things he liked about her. No false modesty, no
indignant remark that looks were unimportant, no fuckedupness
in that crucial regard. He said she was gorgeous – it made her feel
good – she said thank you – end of story. It didn't matter whether
she was gorgeous or she wasn't. Frank said she was and she liked
it. He got a kick out of making her happy and they both knew
that it worked the other way round as well. So what was the
problem? He'd forgotten. They'd not been getting on. All that
complicated stuff. New York. Johnny Vos.

'You see that guy over there by the door?' Frank asked, low-
ering his voice and leaning closer to Siân.

'Yes.'

'I *think* that's Jan Bucquoy.'

'And Jan Bucquoy would be . . . ?'

'Only one of the best-known Belgian film directors. *The
Sexual Life of the Belgians*. Ring any bells?'

'And you reckon that's him?' Siân sounded sceptical. 'He just
happens to be having a drink in the same bar as us? Does he
know who *you* are?'

'As I say, it's a small country. On the way here I thought we
passed Anke De Boeck in the street. I didn't say anything
because I wasn't sure. But I bet it *was* her, actually. You know, the
actress?'

'You can *be* somebody in Belgium,' Siân said mockingly.

'Even if it's somebody else,' Frank remarked, looking gnomi-
cally into his glass.

'Yeah, right. Tell me about Johnny Vos.'

'To be honest, he was a bit of a cunt,' Frank admitted. 'Sorry,'
he added quickly, recalling her standard response to his use of the
cunt-word a fraction too late. 'Although it could well have been
me getting off on the wrong foot. I cocked it up. We never really
relaxed and he had to go after a while. I'm going to see him
again.'

'So what did the news editor have to say? Anything important?' Siân remained on the ball despite the beer.

'The girl they pulled out of the river was all set to work on

Vos's film. She was going to be one of Delvaux's women. In the paintings. An extra, like the first girl.'

'Those poor girls,' said Siân.

They fell into a brief melancholy silence.

'So Vos knew them?' Siân asked after a while.

'I don't know.'

'He must have done. The first girl was an extra, the second was going to be.'

'He's using a lot of extras. He doesn't necessarily have much contact with them, if any.'

'The police'll want to talk to him,' she pointed out.

'I expect so,' he agreed, downcast.

'They might arrest him.'

'Why should they do that?'

'For boring the arse off people,' she suggested. 'Crimes against cinema. Or just for being a difficult interview. When are you due to see him again?'

'I was going to call his production office tomorrow.'

'Production office? His hotel room, you mean?'

'I don't know whether to react to that or go for a piss,' Frank said. 'Actually, I think I'll react to it *by* going for a piss.'

Getting up, he steadied himself with a hand on Siân's shoulder. He leaned over the table and delicately moved two red curls, tight as fusilli, away from her eyes.

'How long are you going to stay?' he asked her.

'Well, at least until you get back from the loo.' She smiled again. 'After that, we'll see. We don't have to decide now, do we? You do *want* me to stay? I'm kind of assuming you do?'

'Well, now you're here,' he said, 'you might as well. I haven't finished telling you about Harry Kümel.'

'Mmm, can't wait.'

They left the jazz café around one, just as it was beginning to get busy. In London, if they went out, they were generally home by midnight. There were places they could go and stay later, but the Troy Club on Hanway Street would always remind them of the bad times, of poor old Angelo, the film despatch clerk who lost his way somewhere along the line, and of what had happened to

Frank's other friends, frustrated arthouse director Harry Foxx and
sexploitation king Richard Charnock, of the whole scandal surrounding Iain Burns. It would always remind Frank indirectly of
Sarah. His wife had been dead more than fifteen years, but some
wounds never heal.

Angelo, Harry Foxx and Richard Charnock had not actually
been particularly close friends, but there had been a certain intimacy between them and Frank, the kind of intimacy born of
working together on a project that was ill-conceived and, in ret-
rospect, a gross error of judgement. In the early 1980s, the four
aspiring directors had filmed the suicide of a terminally ill man –
Iain Burns, a cinema projectionist – whom they had befriended.
The film had disappeared, but, within a few days of the shoot,
Frank's life was turned upside down by another disappearance,
that of his young wife, Sarah. Her body was found a week later
by a man out walking his dog. Bodies, without fail, are found by
men out walking their dogs. It's an occupational risk of owning
a dog. Walk the dog enough times and eventually you'll trip over
someone whose school photograph is paperclipped to the front
of a missing person's file. Sarah's body was found in undergrowth
beside the towpath of the Grand Union Canal in north-west
London. She had been hit by a car, then taken there and dumped.

Heading north from Melkmarkt brought Frank and Siân to
the red light district. The transition was brief and distinct. One
minute they were passing shops and solicitors' offices closed up
for the night, the next they were surrounded by full-length
narrow windows strip-lit blue, red, ultraviolet. A young
woman standing, sitting or perched on a stool behind each one.
The streets around them were no longer empty of all but a few
stragglers like themselves, but thronged by silent, shuffling men
window-shopping.

'We might bump into your director friend,' Siân said sarcastically.

'He's certainly spent some time here,' Frank admitted. 'Where
else would he find two dozen female extras happy to appear
nude?'

'Drama colleges, filmmaking workshops, the university. Just
off the top of my head.'

'The university? You'd rather he use vulnerable eighteen-year-old girls away from home for the first time?'

'At least they'd *be* eighteen,' Siân countered. 'Half of these girls have yet to see seventeen. Lured here from Eastern Europe and the Far East. As you so rightly say, away from home for the first time.'

They had stopped and turned so that they were looking at each other. When Frank found himself bereft of a suitable response, as he so often did in these arguments, Siân turned and walked on, leaving Frank staring not into space, but straight into the sad, dark eyes of a Vietnamese girl who looked about sixteen going on thirty.

Rat-tat-tat-tat, went her rings on the glass. *Rat-tat-tat-tat-tat. Rat-tat-tat-tat-tat.*

The following morning presented Frank with a hangover the like of which he hadn't experienced since an occasion three years previously when he'd drunk two bottles of particularly vile red wine at a party in Wimbledon, vomited spectacularly in the host's kitchen sink, then lost consciousness until he awoke six hours later curled up in his own empty bath still fully dressed, and promptly vomited again. The resulting headache had never been equalled in its severity and relentlessness – until now.

And this time he had another problem – a dilemma. Siân had come a long way to be with him. She had made a gesture. Sure, she hadn't warned him, but that was part of the gesture. It would have been less grand if she had. She had come and he was glad that she had come. But at the same time he had a job to do.

In fact, now, he had two jobs to do.

He still had the piece to do on Vos, plus there was what the news editor had asked him to do. File a piece for the main section of the paper on the two murdered prostitutes and their connections to Vos and, indeed, Kümel, then – yes, *then*, rather than before – dig around a bit, see how much of a story there really was. A bit of snooping, in other words. He had no news experience, but it was work and work was money and, as he was always saying to Siân and she was just as often repeating to him, they needed the money. The hundreds of interviews he'd conducted

with actors, writers, directors would be some prepara
prided himself on doing a bit of digging where they wel
cerned, never settling for the superficial.

He lay awake in their narrow bed, the dirty grey water of
docks lapping at the hull in time with the pounding in his head.
He watched Siân breathing as she slept on. He gazed at her bare
freckled shoulder and remembered their drunken, affectionate
lovemaking of the night before, only a few hours ago, yet it
seemed like a dream. He wondered which one of them had fallen
asleep first, or if they had been lucky enough to drift off together.
His mind moved on, trying to figure out what to do, but coming
up against a brick wall. There were two imperatives: he had to do
the news story, as it couldn't wait and he'd agreed to do it, but he
had to be with Siân and appear to be making her his top priority. There was too much to lose otherwise.

Siân made it easy for him. While they were having breakfast
in a café just south of the red light district (even at that hour of
the morning, a third of the windows were occupied, although
business looked to be slow amid the empty streets) Siân asked
Frank for the second time when he was going to see Vos.

'I want to come,' she said. 'Can I come?'

'What?'

'I'd like to come along. I'd like to meet him. See what he's
like.'

'You want to come along,' Frank said neutrally.

'Yes,' she said brightly, as if it were the most natural thing in
the world, which it plainly wasn't.

'You want to come along on a job,' he said, his voice level, 'and
meet a man for whom you have had nothing but bad things to
say since you saw his first film.'

Siân nodded and smiled as she picked up her coffee cup.

'What makes you think, Siân, that I would compromise myself
professionally to the point where I would permit myself to be
accompanied on an interview by a person who has let it be
known,' Frank said, 'on numerous occasions, that she has con-
tempt for the subject of the interview?'

'Oh, don't be such a pompous prick, Frank,' Siân snapped. 'If
you don't want me to come, that's too bad. I'll go shopping or

something. That's what girls do, isn't it? I'm sure I can find a way of filling my time.' She replaced her coffee cup, started rummaging in her pockets for a tissue. Suddenly she was brisk. Frank didn't like Siân brisk. Brisk was bad. Brisk was what Siân did when she wanted to distance herself from him, when he'd offended her. Brisk was a sign that he had some ground to make up.

Frank didn't have much choice.

He phoned the number he had for the production office. It was an unfamiliar number, probably a Belgian mobile. The call was diverted to an answering service. Frank left a message. Would somebody please call him back to arrange a second meeting? He didn't hold out much hope.

'The only other thing I can think of,' Frank said, 'is to wander down to Moriaanstraat, see if we can find out where the Russian girl was staying.'

That, it turned out, wasn't too difficult. Moriaanstraat was short and narrow and crawling with the media. A lone police officer stood guard outside number six.

Frank craned his neck to get a view of the upper storeys. He caught sight of a pretty black girl at one of the windows on the second floor. She had raised the blind and was peering down into the street.

'Look.' Frank nudged Siân.

'It must be a brothel,' Siân said.

'But we're outside the red light district.'

Moriaanstraat was a minute's stroll east of the Grote Markt and the cathedral. The red light district was ten minutes' walk to the north.

'Exactly. It's the best place to situate a brothel if you don't want people to know what it is,' Siân argued. 'They said on the news that the girl in the river was a prostitute. They both were.'

'Look, we're not going to get much joy here, are we?' Frank said. 'Why don't we get a drink over there – ' he pointed to a bar – 'and keep a lookout?'

'Whatever.'

They settled into a space by the window from where they could watch Moriaanstraat. Frank imagined a litre bottle of sparkling mineral water, chilled so that it beaded with condensation the moment it was taken out of the fridge and set down on the bar. He pictured a tall, narrow glass filled with ice and a slice of lime. The ice cracking with the quiet thunder of a glacier settling as the water was poured in. He dreamed of tipping the glass to his lips, the rim subtly bevelled, the cold water making the inside of his mouth tingle as it seeped in. He could almost sense the fresh bracing taste of the water on his dry tongue and anticipate its restorative fizz getting to work on his hangover – refreshing his breath, rehydrating his ravaged brain and sinuses, soothing, calming, treating and curing.

'What would you like?' asked a waitress.

He regarded her in silence for a moment.

'A beer,' he said. 'Westmalle dubbel.'

Ordering herself a cappuccino, Siân raised an eyebrow. 'It's barely midday,' she said.

'Hair of the dog.'

The place was quiet. A young blonde woman with dark roots occupied the next table on her own, her fingers fidgeting with an empty glass.

'What about Johnny Vos?' asked Siân.

'I'm waiting for him to call back,' said Frank.

They both looked out at the street. Frank was aware of the girl at the next table shooting them sly glances.

'This is good,' Frank said, holding his glass up to the light. The beer was the colour of burnt sugar, its thin bubbly head like demerara. There was the faintest of fruity tangs, but it was a long way from the cherry beers and fruit-flavoured lambics, which were like drinking sherbet dissolved in Coke. 'I won't be able to drink English or American beer ever again. We come from a culture where the only feature of 90 per cent of the beers available to us is their shitty aftertaste, if they have one at all.'

'So now you're a beer writer,' Siân commented.

'Depends who's asking,' Frank quipped. 'If it's the food editor, then yes. Vos could be the peg. Compare and contrast American and Belgian beers. Actually, there's a brewery in Brooklyn does a dark beer not unlike this. Brooklyner Dunkel-Weisse. Something like that.'

'Vos is from Hoboken, New Jersey, isn't he?' Siân said.

'Birthplace of Frank Sinatra.'

'Did you know there's a Hoboken in Antwerp?'

'No, I didn't know that,' he admitted. 'Whereabouts?'

'To the south-west. Outside the ring road, but not that far out. I saw it on the map.'

'Well, fancy that,' Frank said.

'Please?'

Frank and Siân both turned round.

'I'm sorry,' the blonde woman said. 'I heard you talking about Johnny Vos, the film director.'

Frank and Siân exchanged glances.

'Yes?' said Frank.

'Do you know him?' The woman had an accent. Eastern European.

'Vaguely,' Frank said. 'Why?'

The woman glanced out of the window towards Moriaanstraat, anxiety scratched across her brow.

'I know him too,' she said. 'I'm working with him.'

'Working with him?'

'Yes.' Her hands fidgeted under the table.

'You must be an actress then?' Frank said, his body angling forward. He felt Siân lay her hand on his arm. 'Or a technician. A runner, perhaps?'

Suddenly the woman tensed, her eyes wide.

'What is it?' asked Frank.

She didn't respond, so he followed her gaze and saw that she was staring at a taxi that had stopped close to the top of Moriaanstraat. There was a man sitting in the back, but whether he had just got in or was about to get out was not clear. The street was too narrow to permit parking, and with the police nearby the cab would not be able to wait for long.

The blonde woman looked down, turned away, as if she didn't want to be seen.

'What's the matter?' Siân asked. 'Are you in trouble?'

Frank was staring at the taxi, trying to make out the passenger in the rear seat.

The woman had become agitated. She turned away from the window altogether.

Siân looked at Frank, who was frowning after the now departing taxi.

'What?' she asked.

'It couldn't be,' he said, half to himself.

'What?'

'Unless I'm going mad,' Frank said, 'that was Wim De Blieck sitting in the back of that cab.'

'Wim De Blieck?'

'Yes, you remember. You must remember. The guy who came and asked us all those questions after the whole Iain Burns thing blew up.'

'Came and asked *you* questions, you mean. I had nothing to do with Iain Burns, did I? Anyway, it can't be him.'

'Why not? He was Belgian, wasn't he? Maybe he came home.'

'But what's he doing here? And why was *she* so unhappy about seeing him?'

They turned to look at the woman, but she had gone. She was halfway across the street before they spotted her. Frank followed. The waiter thought he had a runner on his hands and had to be placated by Siân, who slid a couple of notes across the counter. Frank, meanwhile, was still thirty metres behind the woman when she reached the doorway of the house on Moriaanstraat. She showed ID to the cop on the door and slipped inside. Frank stopped, wary of becoming tangled up with the police. Siân caught up.

'Just let her go,' she advised.

'She's gone,' he said, looking up at the house, its windows all screened by shutters or blinds.

Frank's mobile rang.

The call lasted a minute or two, although Frank spent most of that time listening.

'Wrong number,' Frank said, after the call was over.

'Ha ha.'

'It was Vos. He wants to meet.'

'Has he been with the police?'

'He's been with the police.'

'He wants to get round you,' Siân remarked. 'He wants you to print the truth. The truth about Johnny Vos. The great artist, falsely accused. And you'll do it.'

'We need—'

'—the money. I know.'

By mutual intuited consent, they wandered away from the house on Moriaanstraat.

'Where and when?' Siân asked.

'Now. Well, half an hour. Across the river.'

'The left bank.'

'The Linkeroever.'

'How are you going to get there?'

'Don't you mean, how are *we* going to get there?'

'I don't want to cramp your style.'

'I work better under pressure.' He smiled at her. 'There's a foot tunnel. Let's go.'

The St Anna Foot Tunnel was one of the most cunningly concealed facilities in the whole of Antwerp. Signs pointed in its vague direction as you walked south down the right bank of the Schelde, but at no point were you advised to cut back inland. The first time Frank had gone looking for it, he had walked for almost half an hour. The waterfront views had been interesting, but not that interesting, and the tunnel entrance had eluded him.

Only by venturing off the St Michielskai and diving into the warren of streets behind it did he come upon the entrance to the foot tunnel, hidden in a pleasant, leafy square besieged by antiques outlets and junk shops. By not calling attention to itself, it made itself special, almost as if it were a natural tunnel, a hole in the ground that just happened to lead to the other side of the river.

The antiques shops were quiet. The signs said they were open, but business was slow. Siân had a thing about antiques shops: she couldn't walk past them. Frank was halfway across the little square to the tunnel entrance when he realised Siân was no longer with him. He stopped, looked back and saw her standing outside a shop at the east end of the square. He walked back and stood alongside her. She was looking at the contents of the window, yet appeared distracted. Frank looked into the window, too. He saw an art deco lamp, a flugelhorn, a set of poker dice, several sepia postcards, a shop-window mannequin. Something about the mannequin – a bust, female – bothered him, but he couldn't say what it was. He turned again to look at Siân.

She looked pale. He noticed a little smudge where she'd mis-applied her eyeliner and suddenly the full force of his feelings for her gusted inside him, taking him by surprise. He felt tears spring to his eyes and instantly blinked them back. His body tensed. He looked down, then up, craning his neck, and caught sight of something for the first time – a security camera monitoring them implacably from a bracket fixed to the wall.

'Let's go,' he muttered, his voice broken and gruff as he took a final look at the unsettling mannequin bust.

Siân allowed herself to be led. As they approached the entrance to the foot tunnel, he was reminded of a corresponding journey in London. They'd taken the Central line, then the Docklands Light Railway to Island Gardens, where they'd got off and walked the short distance to the Greenwich Foot Tunnel under the Thames. They'd taken the ramshackle lift down to the level of the tunnel and walked hand in hand under the river. Frank remembered an overwhelming feeling of safeness, both with regard to Siân and in general. The sense of the huge shift-ing mass of the Thames above them had heightened the feeling. He had felt, in fact, as if their relationship were as watertight as the tunnel. Nothing could assail them, not after what they had been through together, and not after what he had been through on his own, before meeting Siân. She had saved him.

Frank had found his wife Sarah's death impossible to come to terms with, in part due to its horrifying circumstances. It was fifteen years before he dared treat a woman as a human being again, rather than as an object for his gratification. He saw plenty of women, often concurrently, but trusted none. Siân was the first one who made him feel he was able to break the routine if he wanted to. But it was far from straightforward. When the film of Iain Burns's suicide re-emerged shortly after Frank and Siân had got together, it was clear that the fallout and scandal would either destroy them or make them stronger. Fortunately they withstood the pressure, but they were not invincible and they almost cracked at the sudden reappearance in Frank's life of one of the women he'd been seeing around the time he met Siân. Yasmin called and left messages on the machine, messages that Siân heard and had the tact to ignore, at least for the first week. But when Siân picked up Frank's phone and found herself speaking to Yasmin, she lost it, tearing the line out of the wall and yelling at Frank, who walked out of the flat, falling back on his old ways. Confrontation and Frank had never got on.

He hadn't even reached the end of the first block when his mobile rang.

'Keep walking,' Siân said, 'and I'm gone. You'll never see me again.'

Before Frank could answer, she'd hung up.

He stood in the middle of the street, unable to move in either direction. Eventually, he returned to the flat.

'I'll get the number changed,' he mumbled to Siân when he was back inside.

'Maybe it's time to look for somewhere new?' she said.

They had always agreed that it was temporary, her moving into his flat in central London, and that they would find somewhere more suitable for the two of them.

They found a place to the north near Manor House that was big enough for both of them and all their stuff. Siân had some items of furniture that she had inherited and wanted to hang on to. They bought a two-up-two-down on the Harringay Ladder and let the spare room to a graphic designer with a sculpted goatee, baggy combats and the smallest mobile phone in the world. When he moved out to a flat-share in Hoxton, they decided to convert the spare room into an office for Frank, taking a gamble that the dedicated space would increase his rate of production.

Frank wrote his BFI Modern Classic on Harry Foxx's 1993 film, *Nine South Street*, and worked every freelance commission he could get. Siân stayed on as picture editor at the magazine where they had met. Life went on and began to look as if it might be OK again, but they went to New York, where their chance encounter with Johnny Vos's film *American Nightmare* screwed things up again.

'If a mere film can threaten our relationship,' Siân had asked, 'what kind of shape is it in?'

'A mere film, *a mere film!*' Frank had retorted, as if he'd long suspected Siân valued people and relationships over celluloid.

They chose the escalator over the lift. An antique of wood and rubber, it moved at a rumbling crawl that allowed them to study the well-maintained wooden frames lining the walls, the brass lock of each one polished until it shone. Used to the increasingly vulgar escalator panels on the London Underground – split-beaver ads for West End musicals, tits-out bras by Swedish fashion chains – Frank and Siân were surprised to see so many of the cases empty, while others contained faded photographs of the tunnel's construction, or discreet, tasteful, low-key ads for small businesses on the Linkeroever.

The tunnel itself was long and straight, tiled to head height, where a black line marked the transition to a painted (in parts peeling) surface. Two lines of stone flags were laid either side of a central unbroken series of floor panels, mirrored on the ceiling by regularly spaced fluorescent strips. It was perhaps three metres wide, 400 metres in length.

As Frank and Siân increased the distance between themselves and the right bank of the Schelde, they grew smaller and the details of their appearance were lost in silhouette as light seemed to swell around them. There was a final flare and then they were gone and the tunnel was empty.

Part Three

THE NARRATOR

6

BLODIE BELGIUM

When I saw the scrum outside the Last House on Moriaanstraat, I didn't immediately register the presence of a police officer, but I asked the driver to move on nevertheless, since I don't much like big crowds. The driver responded. Through the rear window I could see a blonde woman running across Korte Koepoortstraat towards the house. Even at that distance I recognised Danuta, one of the two Poles. I was used to having only indistinct glimpses of her. She didn't tend to linger under the gaze of the camera. She was less accommodating in that regard than some of the other girls in the Last House. I had been meaning to have a word with Eva, about Danuta, for some time.

A man appeared, crossing the road in apparent pursuit of Danuta, but I was too far away by now.

The taxi skirted the red light district, and I felt its not unfamiliar pull, but I requested that the driver head towards the Ring.

After Eva had called me to tell me about Katya turning up dead in the river, I had tried calling her back on her mobile, but the call went straight through to the answering service, which was why I had decided to drop by in a cab. Not a good plan, as it turned out. She must have been too busy with the police and reporters, although I was confident she'd have given little away to either bunch. Eva was reliable. I'd first come across her in the Diamond Quarter and sensed it would be advantageous to maintain contact. When I had the idea for the Last House, I called her. It wasn't strictly her sort of thing, but then neither were scruples, which meant she could be flexible. I made sure I offered the right kind of money and she jumped into bed, although not literally. Not yet.

Technically, I still shared my bed – and my house and part of my life – with a beautiful but haunted Englishwoman called Penny Burns, the widow of a cinema projectionist, Iain Burns, who had gone missing, then apparently committed suicide in London. I met Penny when she came into my jeweller's shop in Felixstowe, a mournful, misty port on England's Suffolk coast, to sell small lumps of Baltic amber that she had picked up off the beach. There had been something about her, some magnetic loneliness, some unspecified longing that had appealed directly to me. I discovered that her husband was missing. In any real, practical sense she had given up looking for him many years previously, but the look in her eyes showed that she hadn't stopped either scanning the horizon or poring over the pebbly beach at her feet, as if she might find some trace of him in either place. She saw nothing in between. I don't think she focused on me once in all our initial meetings. In spite of this – or perhaps because of it – I became entranced by her. I took to following her, watching her from a hotel room across the street from her house, even calling her at home on invented pretexts. I pursued her with some determination, I have to admit, until she eventually softened towards me.

When her missing husband's likeness appeared in the newspapers and it was established that the mummified body found wrapped in a 16mm print of Nicolas Roeg's *Bad Timing* on a demolition site in central London was his, Penny looked to me for support, and she got it. I took her to London, stood by her through the formal identification procedures and other encounters with various authorities, and when we were through with those I took her back to Felixstowe. Our relationship was already close by this stage and it became closer still. Penny asked me to move into the house she had shared with Iain Burns. Naturally, I put up some resistance to this, since it felt more than a little like trying to slip my feet into a dead man's shoes. But Penny had cast her spell over me. She asked me to clear out her attic, which meant handling a lot of Iain Burns's stuff. She didn't even want to see it.

I handled a lot more of his stuff, in a non-literal sense, when

I went to see the film reviewer, Frank Warner, and Angelo, who still struck me as the weird one of the group despite what had come to light about Harry Foxx and Richard Charnock. I interviewed Frank and Angelo, and managed to piece together, for Penny's benefit, what exactly had happened to Iain Burns. She was quite clear about wanting to know. She wanted what the Americans – and increasingly the rest of us – call closure.

I suppose I was bound to worry that if I was taking the place of the deceased, as I appeared to be, I might be falling into some kind of unintentional trap. Could his disappearance have created a template for any man who allowed himself to get close to Penny? That lost, longing look in her eyes, could it have been there all along, since before she knew Burns? There was no way I could know the answer to that. I had to trust my instincts, which on the one hand warned me to steer clear, but on the other reminded me that I was not going into this blindfolded. I knew everything that had happened and all I had to do was prevent it from happening again. I was not, after all, Iain Burns. I was another man entirely. I was Wim De Blieck.

I suggested to Penny that we decamp to Belgium, the only other place I could call home. Her initial reaction was one of surprise. I suppose I hadn't told her very much about myself, but then she hadn't asked. If we talked about the past, it was mainly about hers. I assured her that if we slipped across the North Sea – taking a ferry from Felixstowe would mean we didn't even have to travel via London, which for Penny had been for ever soured – we would be in a better position to start afresh. Journalists, who had been hassling Penny since the news broke about Burns, would not know to follow us there. We would be wiping clean our tracks. Dogs cannot follow a scent through water.

Penny could see that the argument made sense and there was nothing keeping her in England. For all her fifteen-year search for her missing husband, she was a pragmatic and unsentimental woman. To whet Penny's appetite, I took her on a day trip across to Zeebrugge, while the ferries still operated that route, then on to Bruges. Making an early start and booking on the last ferry back, we managed to see the sights, take a boat trip on a canal. I allowed Penny to see me looking relaxed and apparently feeling at home. I laughed and joked with the crews, exchanged informal chit-chat with waiters and bar staff. I created the impression that this was a country where we would be safe, comfortable, at ease. She didn't have any particular hang-ups about independence, despite having been on her own for so long, perhaps because the search for her husband had actually *replaced* her husband in her life. *I* now appeared to have replaced *that*. What might happen to her if I ever went away was not something I dwelt on.

Following the trip to Belgium, Penny became impatient that we make our move. Indeed, she could no longer relax in the house. I would catch her standing at the window, staring at the rundown hotel across the street, the one where I had booked a room back in the very beginning in order to observe her comings and goings. She took to wandering back down to the beach and staring, no longer at the tidemark in search of amber, but out to sea, as if straining for a glimpse of the Flemish coast.

But I couldn't move just like that. I had valuable assets to consider; organising a move to Belgium would take time. Given that my family, such as it was, had operated out of the Diamond Quarter in Antwerp, that was clearly where we should go. My antecedents were long gone, but I hoped that my name – plus membership of the Diamond Bourse in London – would open any doors that stood in my way. Most business in the diamond world is done on handshakes and verbal agreements, even deals amounting to millions of dollars. Trust is fundamental. Family – and other contacts – count for a great deal.

As far as closing down the UK business was concerned, I had to make sure all accounts were balanced and any repair jobs completed and returned to customers, so that no one had any reason to pursue me across the water. A clean break. It was what we both needed.

I decided to sell everything off bar the diamonds. Once in Antwerp, I would specialise. I had, of course, specialised in Felixstowe, but concentrating on amber was never going to generate sufficient turnover, so I'd kept a general stock as well. Now it was time to get rid of it. I called in a couple of spooks from Hatton Garden. They spent an hour and a half in the shop sweeping whole trays of trinkets into bags. The figures were so small, they added them up in their heads. My stock was old-fashioned. People didn't want this kind of stuff, except once a year, Christmas perhaps, when they'd buy any old rubbish.

The Hatton Garden boys asked to see the diamonds. I said I didn't have any. I saw one of them glance through into the back room. The angle afforded him a pretty good view of my desk lamp and its twin daylight tubes.

I showed them the amber instead, told them to give me a price for the whole collection, which they did. I weighed the figure in my head, sure I could do better if I shopped around. These characters were scrap merchants. But I agreed and they took the lot, even the pieces Penny had brought me. I reasoned that she didn't need them any more, not now her husband's body had been found and buried. She'd sold the pieces to me, in any case, so they were mine to do with as I saw fit, even if I *had* always held on to them. Out of all the amber I bought off all the women like Penny, my Amber Girls, who found lumps of the stuff on the beach and brought it to me, I had kept Penny's in reserve, vowing never to sell it. I'd sold other pieces, but not Penny's.

I sold it now. Clean break. Time to move on.

But I kept the diamonds.

They paid me on the spot for everything else, in cash. It wasn't a significant sum, it wasn't even a fair amount, but I didn't care.

'Are you retiring, then?' the Hatton Gardeners asked me.

'On this?' I waved my pathetically thin wad at them. 'Hardly a nest egg, is it?'

I didn't tell them what I was doing, where I was going.

They shrugged and left. I went into the back room, where Penny and I had first talked, where she had told me about her endless search for her missing man, and I took out my packets of diamonds. It was still early; there was plenty of light from the sea-facing window. You shouldn't sort diamonds in artificial light, nor in direct sunlight. Ideally, you would have a north-facing window and a daylight lamp. An east-facing window, such as I had, meant you sorted your diamonds in the afternoon, or you pulled down your blinds and relied on the lamp.

I worked for two hours, firstly sorting out those that were eye-clean from those that were not. Then I worked with the loupe to separate the stones according to the standard classification system. Diamonds, in common with amber, contain inclusions, but of a different kind. In a piece of amber you might find a scrap of bark or an insect, whereas inclusions in a diamond are naturally occurring imperfections in the carbon, tiny specks or smears that tend to be either white or black. According to convention, the classification of diamonds depends on the four Cs: colour, clarity, cut and carat weight. They forgot to add a fifth: cost.

The colour is determined by a number of things, among them the density of nitrogen atoms present. Clarity depends on the number and nature of any inclusions. So far, it's a question of nature's provision, although a clever cut can conceal Very Small inclusions. The cut is all important. The goal is to cut the stone in such a way that the light goes in and is reflected off as many facets as possible before coming back out again. Cut it badly and the light can get trapped in the stone, making it appear dull and lifeless, thereby reducing its value. The biggest single determining factor relating to the value placed on a stone is its carat weight. With a hundred points to the carat, a stone of ninety-seven points is worth significantly less than one that hits the scales at one carat. A customer with his wits about him will choose stones that fall just short of a carat, because to the naked eye they look just as big but cost considerably less.

The clarity scale goes from P (piqué – inclusions visible to the naked eye), through VS (Very Small inclusions) and VVS (Very, Very Small inclusions) to IF (Internally Flawless). A lot of my stock was VS1 or VS2, with a good sprinkling of VVS1 and VVS2. I worked until the light began to fail. By the end of the afternoon I had confirmed that I owned enough diamonds to make it feasible I should be able to set myself up in business in Antwerp. I knew, however, that I would have to start small in order to avoid attracting attention, and the cash I'd accepted off the two characters from Hatton Garden would cover little more than immediate expenses.

The London Diamond Bourse is located at 100 Hatton Garden in an anonymous, modern building that looks bland from the outside and scruffy within. Swiping my security card, I passed through the floor-to-ceiling turnstile and crossed the lobby to the stairs. I never take lifts if I can help it. The trading floor of the Bourse is on the second floor, behind more turnstiles and security checks. Most of the people who pass you as you negotiate the various interiors of the Bourse are carrying thousands of pounds' worth of stones. Serious dealers have their suits specially made with deep inside pockets. Most, but not all, are Jews. Hasids are common. I felt slightly out of place and was aware that other members were looking at me. I had not been a regular visitor to the Bourse, by any means, but had kept my membership renewed.

I passed beyond reception on to the trading floor itself. The trading floor was somewhat tatty. It had had a lick of paint since my last visit, but that wasn't saying much. I hadn't been there in over fifteen years. The room appeared at first to be L-shaped. Long white tables, regularly spaced, adjacent to the three walls benefiting from natural light. I walked to the end of the shorter wing and turned left into a small cafeteria. For a building containing more diamonds per square foot than any other space in London, it was surprisingly low key. A Stamford Hill transit caff for millionaire minicab drivers. If they were to put out an announcement advising the owner of a Volvo estate that it was causing an obstruction, everybody in the place would be on their feet.

I got a coffee from the counter and sat down at an empty table in the canteen area. Most tables, in truth, were empty. After 2pm small groups would gather to play cards, chess, backgammon. House rules disallowed such games before two.

Maybe half a dozen deals were being done in the whole place, big black hats paired off across the wide white tables. Scales, daylight lamps, electronic calculators. Haggling, negotiating. Handshakes. Amounts scrawled on blotters. Ninety days' credit.

I still had a key to one of the lockers along the back wall. I opened it and had a look through the stuff I'd left there. There were safety deposit boxes in the basement. These lockers, on the other hand, were not intended for valuable items. Which also meant no one would expect them to contain any. It was risky, but I've never objected to a low level of risk.

I knew I couldn't walk back into the place after fifteen years and expect to start dealing diamonds just like that. My purpose on the first visit was to show my face.

I stayed in London for a few days and hung out at the Bourse some more. I was surprised by how quickly I was accepted back into the fold. By the end of the week I was chatting with other members and one of them, a charming, ancient Jew with a voice like mud sluiced through gravel, gave me a name. When he extended his hand, I couldn't help noticing the faded number tattooed on his wrist.

I telephoned the name and we set up a meet for later that day, at the Bourse. He was looking for VVS2s and VVS1s. IFs, even. I told him I had plenty, which was partly true. I did have plenty of VVS stones. I also had one stone that looked IF under a 10X magnification loupe, but in fact wasn't. It was a crafty cut, deceptively shallow. If I showed him the stone at the beginning of our meeting, he would be bound to spend an age inspecting it. If I waited and only brought it out once I'd won his trust, my bet was he'd go for it. The price difference made it a worthwhile gamble. If he rumbled it, all I had to do was act surprised and be grateful to him, compliment him on the sharpness of his eye.

The name curled up and sat in the palm of my hand. We shook on a deal that favoured me. Who cares if you have to wait ninety days when you're talking that kind of money? And the icing on the cake? He gave me a contact in Antwerp. Everything was beginning to shift into place.

The following week, Penny didn't ask where I was going and I didn't tell her. I spent three days in Antwerp preparing the ground. I met the contact, who seemed like someone I could do business with. I looked into rental properties and selected something small on Sint-Jozefstraat. The sale of the shop in Felixstowe happened a lot more quickly than the agents had predicted, so that we didn't need to wait ninety days for the diamond money to come through. By the end of that week everything was ready. I wondered if Penny might prevaricate, now that the fantasy was set to become reality, but she could be ready to go inside twenty minutes, she said. Her house had sold within hours of going on the market. Her buyer was in no hurry to move in, but she was more than ready to get shut.

As soon as we were settled in the house in Sint-Jozefstraat, I looked for signs of improvement in Penny, but found none. The hoped-for light failed to appear in her eyes, no spring enlivened her step. She remained a window-watcher, a street-spectator. One day not long after we had arrived I was returning to the house after making some calls in the Diamond Quarter and I crossed the Stadspark. I saw a woman who resembled Penny sitting on a bench, but she looked too mad, too depressed, too much like a bag lady, minus the bags. Then I realised it *was* Penny and I was shocked. I stood at a distance and watched her for several minutes, while she didn't move, just stared into space, and I wondered what I should do.

I did nothing, apart from walk on behind the bench where she was sitting and return to the house. When she got back I asked her, innocently, where she had been.

'Around,' she said apathetically.

The next day I followed her. I left the house at 10am, saying goodbye to Penny as normal, but then I waited at the bend in the street until she appeared, turning left out of the house. I backed into a doorway to allow her to pass – she stared straight ahead, but her eyes were blank – then I followed her at a distance of thirty metres. She took a zigzag route to reach the Stadspark, where, instead of finding a bench, she stopped briefly to watch the geese before walking around the edge of the lake and leaving the park on the east side, which took her directly into the Diamond Quarter.

She walked past numerous jewellers' shops. Once or twice she would stop and look in a window, but I didn't get the impression she was looking for anything in particular, nor in fact that she was really seeing the displays for what they were. At one point, when I was watching her from across the street and she slowly turned round, I was worried that she had caught sight of me in the reflection, but she continued to turn. A Hasid rode past on a motor-scooter, his black hat replaced by a helmet. She watched him go by, then continued staring down the street long after he'd gone, before finally turning back and resuming her walk. She approached the Diamond Bourse – one of four in Antwerp – and I wondered for one light-headed moment if she might turn and enter the building, but instead she walked on.

The raised train tracks leading into Centraal Station were on my right, diamond dealers operating out of flimsy, box-like premises folded into the arches below. Window displays here were rudimentary, vestigial. The stones could even be fake, like plastic flowers in a florist's. The sort of people who window-shopped here wouldn't be able to tell the difference. Penny crossed the street and I hung back slightly. A train rattled into the station overhead. At the end of the street, where it fed into Koningin Astridplein, Penny turned right. She walked across the front of the station and I realised where she was going.

I waited until she had paid and gone through the gate, then I bought a ticket and followed her through into Antwerp Zoo. I looked around for Penny and couldn't immediately see her. I kept looking, but she had vanished. She could easily have taken one of at least two directions, possibly three, but the paths inside the zoo are all curved and, close to the entrance, there's an abundance of shrubs and bushes. I wondered if I'd fallen for an elaborate deception. But what would have been the point? I wasn't carrying any stones. And what would be Penny's motivation? *I* was her rock.

Antwerp Zoo is one of the oldest and best-loved of city zoos. It works hard on behalf of animals threatened with extinction and is famous for its okapi breeding programme: 75 per cent of okapis in captivity around the world have Antwerp blood in their veins.

I found Penny in the reptile house. She was standing in front of what appeared to be an empty tank, which it occurred to me was not a bad metaphor for her life. Looking across a divide to something that wasn't there. But then I saw the snake. Camouflaged and perfectly still, it would have remained invisible to me if it hadn't been for Penny.

Antwerp Zoo used to be known for its 'cold barriers'. Instead of being kept behind glass, the snakes were separated from the public by a twelve-centimetre-wide refrigeration zone. The cold barriers seemed to work well during the day – visitors filed through the reptile house and the snakes kept their distance – but were not always so efficient when the zoo was closed. Handlers would occasionally enter the reptile house in the morning to find some snakes on the floor and others straddling the cold barriers, chilled to the point of immobility and needing to be warmed up to get them moving again.

I closed the gap between myself and Penny until the distance between us was the same as that between her and the snake. If she'd been able to zoom in on the snake's black eye, she might have seen me reflected in it.

I debated whether or not to make my presence known to her, and decided against it. They say you should never wake a sleep-walker and that was what she most closely resembled. She was sleepwalking through her life. I backed off silently and made for the exit. Even if I'd decided against waking Penny during this episode, I wondered if I should adopt the same policy, or a different one, in general. If I wanted to, it would be within my power to jolt her out of her torpor. But what would I gain by doing so? What might I stand to lose?

Questions, but no answers.

I left the zoo and walked aimlessly across the top of the Diamond Quarter, then found myself heading in the direction of the river. Because the angles in Antwerp are skewed, because the river doesn't flow from south to north, but from south-west to north-east, and all the little roads leading to it veer accordingly away from the map's grid, it's easy to wander off course when attempting to navigate using your sense of direction. The geography works against you.

The whole country is skewed – and no wonder. Opposing forces are tearing it apart while simultaneously converging on the capital. The line that runs across the country, separating Francophone Wallonia in the south from Flemish-speaking Flanders in the north, passes to the south of Brussels, an enclave of a city where 80 per cent of the population speak French.

Belgians – real Belgians who have always lived here, rather than slippery customers like myself who have lived abroad, gaining a little perspective before coming back – will tell you that the issue of the language split, the cultural divide, is overplayed. That no one here is that bothered. It's only outsiders who make a big deal of it.

If that's the case, why do people throughout Flanders glare at ignorant tourists unfortunate enough to address them in French?

Why did right-wing extremists Vlaams Blok score 33 per cent in elections in Antwerp in 2001? Wallonia – and most of Brussels – is being pulled towards France, while Flanders feels the tug of Holland to the north. This despite the fact that there are fundamental differences in temperament and character between both different sets of common-language users: the Dutch think the Belgians are cold and insular, while the French regard the entire nation as a joke, and seem to treat the Francophone community in particular as a convenient scapegoat. But those who do so should beware.

When the trunk and arms of a woman were found wrapped in a bloodstained sheet in Regent Square, London, in November 1917, a trail of evidence led to French butcher Louis Voisin, living and working in London at the time. The sheet bore a laundry mark, IIH, and there was a scrap of paper with the words 'Blodie Belgium' scrawled on it. The laundry mark was traced to a missing person, thirty-two-year-old Frenchwoman Emilienne Gerard, who lived close to Regent's Park. In her lodgings police found bloodstains and an IOU signed by Louis Voisin.

Voisin, who lived nearby, received a visit from the police, who found him in the company of another woman, Berthe Roche. They also found more bloodstains in his kitchen and, in a cask hidden in the coal cellar, the head and hands of Mme Gerard.

The Blodie Belgium note had been Voisin's idea. He thought it would confuse the police in the event of its being discovered with Mme Gerard's remains. Once they had him in custody, the police gave Voisin pen and paper and asked him to write the words 'Bloody Belgium', which he did, but he repeated the original spelling mistake.

Voisin was hanged at Pentonville on 2 March 1918, a victim of his own combined ignorance and arrogance.

But people will always generalise, and the Belgians are without doubt a peculiar nation, for the simple reason that they have no real sense of national identity. There's no sense of pulling together for the common good of all Belgians, apart from the touching but ineffectual efforts of the royal family. The government is riddled with corruption. Inefficiency is rife in the upper strata of civic authorities. It was the failure of the police to get their act together that allowed unemployed electrician Marc Dutroux, in the mid-1990s, to inaugurate a collection of young girls in specially constructed cells in his Charleroi basement.

Because of the skewed orientation of the streets, my wander in the direction of the river brought me, unawares, into a part of the city I hadn't seen in a long time. When you're not used to it, the experience of walking through the red light district is like being the soft silver ball in a pinball machine, as your eye is drawn first this way, then that, from one side of the street to the other. The women look at you in a way that women normally don't. You learn what it is to be an object. Walking through the tiny warren of restaurant-lined streets behind Brussels' Grand' Place is similar – hawkers importuning you, their eyes rolling as they extol the attractions of their mountains of rubbery squid, lobsters pink as porn, barnacle-encrusted clams – but different. In the red light district the threat is closer to the bone. What the women want from you is harder to give. Money I can part with. Self-awareness is a different matter.

Some of the men who wander through the red light district gaze appraisingly at the goods and are completely indifferent to the looks the women give them. Nothing fazes them. They cannot be shamed. Others are furtive, preferring to look without being observed. I found these men easier to understand. After all, if you watch unobserved you cause no offence. You upset no one.

Whatever the circumstances, watching unobserved will always provide greater pleasure. Watch children at play without their knowing they are being watched and their innocence, their lack of self-consciousness, is beguiling. You are fortunate to witness what would still be taking place if you were not there to see it. It is a position of some privilege. Standing on the edge looking in. Taking part, but without others' knowledge.

I entered a bar that was lined with shelves stacked with videos, face out. I ignored them and stepped up to the bar, ordered a beer. I didn't particularly want a beer, but it is a ritual: you buy the beer, drink it standing at the bar, or checking out the videos, then you buy some tokens, which you spend in the video kiosks and peep shows towards the rear.

I took my tokens and entered one of a dozen empty booths

grouped inwards around a circular bed that is enclosed and hidden from view until you enter a booth and place a token in the slot. The screen rolled up and the bed began to revolve, the woman lying upon it to gyrate in what she imagined was a provocative, sensual display. Her breasts and genitals remained on view, while her flabby midriff was ill-concealed by a loose wrap. Nothing aroused me in her display as much as the pitiful attempt to hide what she regarded as her imperfection.

The bed had executed perhaps six complete revolutions when the screen started its slow rumble downwards. I pocketed my remaining token and left the booth. As I walked through the red light district I kept seeing the face of the woman in the peep show, the way her eyes swivelled to remain focused on my window as her bed revolved. Someone had told her to maintain eye contact with the punters. Someone who didn't understand the mechanics of arousal. Someone whose concept of eroticism meant they were in the wrong business.

The red light district petered out a couple of streets shy of Bonaparte Dock. Several boats were moored around the side of the dock, including, on the west side, a floating hotel, the *St Anna*. I watched the slate-grey waters lapping at the vessel's hull for a minute before walking away from the dock towards the river. It's a good stretch across to the Linkeroever, the Left Bank, between 350 and 500 metres. A long, narrow dredger was making slow progress downstream, laden to the gunwhales and sailing low in the water. The tide was rising, which slowed her down even further. I watched until she had sailed out of the frame, up to the bend in the river and around it. Then I allowed my gaze to drift back along the far bank until it snagged on the outline of the King Baudouin Monument close to the ground-level building of the St Anna Foot Tunnel.

Part Four

THE ANXIOUS CITY

7

LE ROI TRISTE

Frank and Siân turned right out of the tunnel buildings and had to shield their eyes against the sudden glare. The river was in front of them, sunlight cascading like minted coins on to a carpet of shattered glass.

'That'll be it,' Frank said, pointing to a dark, angular shape 200 metres away.

Johnny Vos had told Frank he would wait for him by the King Baudouin Monument. Frank checked his watch. They were on time. He took Siân's hand and they walked at a relaxed pace towards the monument.

'I hope he's more civil this time,' said Frank.

'Perhaps he makes allowances for ladies,' Siân deadpanned.

Frank shot her a look, but she was gazing at the river. He hoped she wasn't going to cause any trouble.

The monument was a wall facing the Schelde, as blank, for the most part, as a cinema screen, but running across the width of the structure at eye-level was a series of photographs of the former king on official duties at assorted points in his reign. Baudouin, who had been monarch from 1951 until his death in 1993, had been popular with the Belgians, many of whom credited him with holding the country together. His interest in social issues had engendered widespread sympathy.

As well as the photographs there was a rough-hewn statue of

the former king that reminded Frank of the melting wax figures and bread-head sculptures of Marc Quinn.

Sitting on a low wall perpendicular to the monument, smoking a cigarette, was the American director.

As Frank and Siân narrowed the gap, Vos flicked his cigarette butt to one side and composed an elongated frame with his hands, using his forefingers and thumbs. Through it he squinted at Siân as she approached.

'Amazing,' he said. 'The likeness is incredible.'

Frank and Siân exchanged a look, each curious to ascertain if the other knew what Vos was talking about.

'Look up,' he said, still framing her with his hands. 'Raise your head, just slightly.'

Siân found herself complying with the request, despite its coming from a man whom she had been expecting, if not intending, to dislike from the moment they met.

Siân did look up, tilting her chin towards the top of the monument. Vos's eyes slid down her face and over her body. Frank stared pointedly at Vos, his own eyes narrowing into flinty chips.

Vos was the first to speak, addressing Siân. 'I guess you know Delvaux's work, right?'

She looked down at him. Frank now looked at Siân.

'No. Not really. I mean, Frank's shown me one or two.'

Vos looked at Frank for the first time, but Frank had turned away to observe the skyline across the river.

'Likeness to whom?' Siân asked.

The director turned his gaze back to her.

'*Evening Beauty*, 1945,' he said. '*The Echo*, 1943. Any number of Delvaux's paintings from that period.'

Siân didn't say anything. She looked briefly at Vos, then at Frank, who finally spoke.

'This is Siân,' he said. 'She's a picture editor.'

There was a silence, but Frank was wary of introducing Siân as his girlfriend. It wasn't the G-word that would bother her; she wasn't – thank fuck – one of those women who insisted on 'partner'. It was more the connotation of being an appendage, rather than someone with her own reasons for existing. Sometimes Siân was cool about it and sometimes she was not. Since the meeting was potentially volatile anyway, he decided not to risk it. Instead he mentioned the film magazine where they had met and where she still worked.

Vos merely waved that away and continued as before, listing Delvaux paintings.

'Maybe I'm wrong,' he said, 'maybe you're later. Delvaux only really used one model from 1966 to the end of his life. *The Blue Sofa, Chrysis, Homage to Jules Verne* – they're all the same girl. Danielle Caneel. Maybe you're her.'

'What do you mean, maybe I'm her?'

'I mean maybe you look like her. Although maybe you could *be* her.'

Another uncomfortable silence ensued, during which Siân held Vos's gaze defiantly before eventually looking away into space between the American and Frank.

'Caneel,' Frank said. 'Isn't that—'

'No, that's Caneele with an "e",' said the director dismissively. 'Séverine Caneele.'

Siân frowned.

'She was in *L'humanité*. Bruno Dumont's second feature,' Frank explained. 'Non-professional actress. Amazing perform-ance, but not enough to save the movie.'

'I kinda liked it,' Vos remarked.

'The dead girls . . .' Frank said, switching the subject '. . . the police interviewing you – all this is going to set you back on the film, isn't it?'

Vos took out another cigarette and lit it.

'Because of the way I work,' he began, 'I'm not really tied down to a schedule. I don't have sound guys and lighting guys hanging around. I do pretty much everything myself. Two, three runners on a big shoot is all I need. Plus the performers, of course. That's the beauty of this technology. You can dispense with all the unnecessary garbage and just make the film you want to make. That's how I work. Essentially,' he added, 'it's how all visionary directors want to work, but few can, because they work within the system. I have never worked within the system and I never will.'

'What did the police say?' Frank asked.

Vos and Siân both looked at Frank, each obviously surprised by the question.

'Frank,' Siân gently admonished.

'What?' he asked, all innocence. 'What did they say, Johnny? If you don't mind my asking.'

'I got nothing to hide,' said Vos, pulling deeply on his cigarette a couple of times, then throwing it in the direction of the river. 'They asked me to outline my relationship with the dead girls – to account for my time – when did I last see either of them? That kind of stuff. It was a more easygoing interview than *our* last one,' he added, looking at Frank.

'So what *was* your relationship with them?' Frank asked.

'The first girl, Hannah Witowski, was an extra on the movie. Katya Egorova was looking forward to being an extra, but she didn't make it.'

'The way you work, you probably know everybody, even the extras. You do pretty much everything yourself, as you say, including, presumably, drafting the extras.'

'Hannah was in the first scene for about two seconds. Katya hadn't even started. She was going to be in the next big scene.'

'Another Delvaux picture?'

'*The Anxious City*, 1941.'

'But you met her?'

'As a matter of fact, no, I didn't. She had asked if she could be an extra and I decided that for *The Anxious City* I needed all the extras I could get, so I got word to her to say yes, she could get a day's work, or a half-day's work, whatever. But I never met her. She was due to come meet me, so that I could take a look at her and make sure she wasn't totally wrong for the scene.'

'But you definitely met Hannah. She was in a scene you shot. And as for Katya, she was coming to meet you and never made it?'

Vos took out another cigarette. He seemed on edge, but the cavalier attitude he had shown in their first interview was softening.

'That's about right.'

'Surely that makes you a suspect in the eyes of the police?'

'Guess that's why they wanted to interview me.'

Vos looked away, directing a how-stupid-is-this-guy grin towards Siân.

'Doesn't that freak you out,' Frank asked, 'assuming, of course, you had nothing to do with their deaths?'

Vos met Frank's stare with a level gaze.

'Sure it freaks me out.'

There was an uncomfortable silence, broken only by the drone of a freighter passing downriver against the tide.

'On the other hand,' Vos continued, 'I'm not freaked out, because both these girls were linked to me, however indirectly. The police were bound to want to talk to me and bound to regard me as a suspect. They wouldn't be doing their jobs if they didn't. Fortunately, I know nothing will come of it, because I'm not involved.'

'Did you contact the police yourself when you heard about Hannah?'

'No, they called me.'

'So, someone else told them?'

'I guess so.'

'Who do you think did that?'

'One of the other girls?'

'Girls?'

'Extras.'

'A friend of Hannah's?'

'I guess.'

'And the second girl, Katya, she had not yet worked on the film?'

'We established that.'

'The scene you were going to do with her, was it going to be the next scene?'

'Yes, but she would have been one of plenty of extras. That's why I called her, because I needed so many, and I knew she wanted to do it. For these girls, it's something different, you know. I'm not saying it's glamorous, but I guess it beats working the red light district.'

'Doesn't that point of view represent something of a change of heart from the Johnny Vos who directed *American Nightmare*?'

'Only if you believe I set out to glorify prostitution in that

movie, which obviously I did not.' Vos rubbed a hand across his
stubbly chin. 'You did *see* the movie?'

'We saw it in New York,' Frank said, 'on its release.'

As Johnny's eyes flicked to Siân, Frank realised he'd unwit-
tingly dragged her into the exchange.

'So what did you think?' asked the director. He didn't put a
name on it, but he was looking at Siân.

'What did we think of it?' Siân said, ever the politician, playing for time. (Frank noticed the 'we' and was glad for it.) 'Frank
seemed to rather like it,' she said, 'whereas I thought it sucked.'

Frank's mouth dried. Johnny smiled, but the smile was a little
lopsided.

'You wanna elaborate?' he suggested.

'I would, but it just seems terribly boring to go on about how
misogynistic it was. How cruel and callous and dispassionate a
view it put across. Don't you think?'

At the same time as fearing meltdown, Frank grudgingly
admired Siân's forthrightness.

Johnny looked as if he was getting some kind of kick out of
the exchange of views.

'Surely the important word there,' he said, 'is "dispassionate".
Sometimes you have to take a step back.' He paused, looked as if
he was about to add something, then didn't, but continued to
stare at Siân.

Frank watched a small craft heading upriver, moving a great
deal faster than the freighter going in the opposite direction,
thanks to the tide. He felt irritated at being excluded and cross
with himself for feeling it. It was petty, yet Vos had a particular
way of looking at Siân that was beginning to get under his skin.
As he tracked the small boat's progress, he wondered if it was Vos's
charm or Siân's apparent susceptibility to it that really bothered
him.

His trip to Antwerp wasn't turning out how he had planned.

8

INSTITUT JOSEPH LEMAIRE

If you head out of Brussels on the N4, passing through the top of the Forêt de Soignes, leaving Tervuren and King Leopold's famous Central Africa Museum to the north, you'll soon come into Overijse. Don't stop. After a turning on the right to Tombeek, take the second road on the left. Pass under what remains of a square archway and drive on, taking, naturally, the right-hand lane of this incongruous, overgrown avenue leading into the forest. It's evening, just getting dark. Pass the first track on the right and wait for the second. As you turn into it, your headlamps light up the hedgerow, scattering insects and tiny animals, which run for cover. You make silent progress up the narrow lane, extinguishing your lights, and come to a halt on a patch of muddy gravel, leaving enough room to open your door so you can get out.

You take a miner's lamp from the back of the van and walk around the wire-mesh fence towards the clear area you can make out between the trees. The lamp is not switched on. You don't need it yet. You know from experience that using the lamp while there is still some daylight will only serve to make it seem darker. You're also conserving the batteries, just in case.

You come upon the clearing suddenly. It's the size of half a football pitch. You walk to the centre of it, watched only by the ragged lines of trees standing on three sides. Long grass scratches at your trousers, brambles catch in the laces of your shoes. The moon climbs slowly across the sky, almost full. The land where you are standing would have been cleared decades ago to provide a pleasant outlook for the occupants of the building that squats on the fourth side of the vast space. A hundred metres long, four storeys high, complementary curves of glass and concrete – a company headquarters or an office building with ambition? Private sanatorium or government facility? Whatever it was, it now stands empty. The story of ten, fifteen years' decay is scrawled across the building's façade. Loose tiles, smashed windows, peeling paint. Runoff trickles from broken gutters, trailing mossy slime on white walls. Crows clatter in and out of gaping metal window frames. The passing seconds are marked by water dripping from rotten ceilings into reflective lakes on corridor floors.

An overbearing sense of solitude pervades the building. It reeks of abandonment. The concrete steps up to the main entrance have been split by persistent weeds. The main glass doors, although not locked, are wedged shut. The adjacent plate glass window, having been smashed at some point, provides a convenient entrance.

When you try to remember it later you jumble everything up. The order in which you see things is lost, but the building's former function soon becomes apparent. There are interminable corridors slippery with X-ray films. Endless doors opening on to patients' rooms, doctors' offices, empty labs. White surfaces glowing in the moonlight – enamel washbasins, peeling walls, official letterhead. Not just letterhead, but letters typed, signed and presumably never sent, unless these were copies. But why should they be copies? Why would they make and keep copies and then leave them scattered over the floor of the institute when the facility shutdown?

INSTITUT JOSEPH LEMAIRE
1900 OVERIJSE – TOMBEEK
Tel: 02/687.70.56
687.73.83

The text of every letter was the same, the language French.

Dear M or Mme X
  The results of your test show that you have a pulmonary

condition that requires further treatment. Please make contact with
the institute at your earliest opportunity.

And handwritten above the salutation of every letter was the
same single word: '*Décédé*'. Deceased.

You pick one out at random. Dated 12 March 1978, it's
addressed to a Madame Y in Houdeng-Goegnies. *Décédée*.
Another, dated 13 May 1978, to a Monsieur R, avenue Emile
Max, 1030 Bruxelles. *Décédé*.

You pick up two of the X-ray films from the corridor floor
and stick them up in one of the few unbroken windows, as if
examining them on a lightbox. The moonglow makes the ghostly
images appear to hover in the air. White ribs and spinal column.
Black bellows of lungs, hyperextended, on one film, by emphy-
sema, while, on the second, white threads suggest plural plaques
or pulmonary fibrosis. Difficult to make a certain diagnosis, but
in the late 1970s both were still symptoms of tuberculosis. The
Joseph Lemaire Institute was a TB clinic. You imagine that merely
by handling the films you have contaminated yourself with
bacilli. You take a handful and rub them on your face, as if to
make sure.

At the end of the main corridor on the ground floor, a round,
high-ceilinged space accounts for the curves you noticed from
outside. A wheelchair, crushed in some terrible accident but still
resting on its wheels, sits in the middle of the raised circular floor.
Graffitied messages run around the wall under the windows. In
florid Gothic black script, with spelling mistakes: 'Het leven van
ieder wraakzuchtsmens is een labyrint met in het centrum zyn
DOOD!' – life for vengeful souls is a labyrinth with death at its
centre. And, underneath, in simple blue capitals, in English:
'GARFIELD I DEEPLY IN LOVE WITH TULMA'.

On a store cupboard door near by: 'TBC IN THE HOUSE'.
Tuberculosis. In the house. You like the description of this place
as a house. All these rooms and corridors, all this available space.
Like a hotel without staff. A place to stay.

On the first floor the messages read: 'The place to die', 'Today
is a nice day to die', 'Way to Hell'. One floor up: 'Kill frenzy',
'Fuck you'. On the third floor, the word 'Entrance' has been

written with an arrow pointing to a yawning lift shaft, cables creaking within.

You climb the remaining stairs up to the fourth floor, or what remains of it: a deep balcony, shattered observation terrace, windows leading out on to the first part of the roof. A vertical ladder to take you to the very top. By now night has its indigo backdrops in place, a fringe of burnt orange trailing over the horizon in the west, towards the southern suburbs of Brussels. The flat roof, on three different levels, is extensive. A pincushion of RTBF TV and radio masts, picked out with red warning lights, bristles on a patch of higher ground 200 metres away to the south. Planes track silently overhead, having taken off from Zaventem. Arcane silver graffiti glimmer in the moonlight. The institute is hemmed in on all sides by woodland.

A place to stay, for a while. For yourself, at least. For others, an eternity.

Beneath your feet, on the wall of a balcony on the next level down, is a spray painting of a vengeful-looking cartoon girl and the warning: 'L'oeil du diable est sur vous. Mais elle vous aime aussi.' The eye of the devil is on you. But she loves you, too.

You find the use of the feminine personal pronoun interesting.

Re-entering the building from the roof, you begin to patrol the corridors, broken glass crunching underfoot like ice on a canal towpath. The endless procession of doors reminds you of the Gauquié-Hôtel, Oostduinkerke, where you had spent the winter, and you think about your friends who are no doubt still there. The Gauquié-Hôtel was in better nick than this, but there's no reason why you shouldn't stop here for a while. Make some new friends. Move on.

You go down one flight, then turn through 180 degrees to descend the next. The winding, the steps, the sense of forever going down but never reaching the bottom. The act of placing one foot in front of the other on the next step down. The mesmerising repetitiveness of it.

In 1978 you were fifteen. Former Italian premier Aldo Moro had been shot dead by Red Brigade terrorists; in football the host nation had won the World Cup in Argentina; and Harry

Kümel's *The Lost Paradise* was a major hit at cinemas throughout
Belgium, both in Wallonia and Flanders. You went on a trip from
the children's home in Charleroi to the Butte du Lion at
Waterloo. The steps up and down the monument seemed never-
ending. The thumping heat of the sun relentless. You had climbed
to the top and beheld in a stupor the majestic sweep of agricul-
tural land that was the battlefield. Your head had begun to spin
with the effort required to remain standing, with the press of
the crowd, with the sense of the battle taking place right there if
not then. You negotiated the steps down in a dazed funk. The
other children had gone on ahead, as usual. You didn't fit in,
had no confidant. They only spoke to you if they spotted an
opportunity to take the piss. As you neared the bottom of the
steps, you found your way out, via the visitors' centre, blocked by
a woman in a wide-brimmed hat. Whichever way you tried to
get around her was obstructed, either by the woman herself –
though she wasn't big, she seemed to take up a disproportionate
amount of space – or by the men in dark suits and dark glasses
who stood in close attendance. You waited behind her on the
stairs for a few moments, but the moments became elastic and the
wait began to seem endless. She was speaking in Spanish to a
tourist with a camera around his neck and you couldn't figure
out why a crowd of people should have gathered to watch.
Eventually, irritated and increasingly claustrophobic, you tried to
force your way past the woman while muttering your excuses,
but found yourself pressing against her from behind to get
through the gap. Immediately the men in dark suits started to
move and the woman turned to present a mask of outrage. You
saw it only for a split second because suddenly one of the dark-
suited men had come between you and her and was staring down
at you. Just as you were thinking to yourself that the woman must
be someone important, another woman who was standing
watching nearby hissed incredulously, 'It's the Queen! It's the
Queen!' And all the other children from the home, who had
appeared in the crowd on the other side of the semi-circle that
had formed around Queen Fabiola, laughed and laughed and
laughed, and then everybody else began to laugh as well until
the only people who weren't laughing were the stony-faced

secret service men, the haughty Queen and your miserable wretched self.

You reach the ground floor of the Lemaire Institute and start again. Never make rash decisions. You need somewhere for the time being, but you know from experience that wherever you stay tonight will become your space for the duration. Marking territory. Once you make the first exchange – fragments of dreams leaking out of your head, in exchange for information, traces of the past, institutional memories travelling the other way, two-way traffic – you'll be unable to switch. You'll both possess and be possessed.

On the third floor, room 318, a single word sprayed on the door in red: 'PARANOIA'. Your room. Centre of operations. You push open the door, move inside. Immediately to your right is a row of three washbasins. Windows line the far wall, one of them bearing an illegible graffito in fuzzy green. Something, some creature of the night, has had a half-hearted go at the wall on the left; it remains intact, but the floor is covered with debris, among which you spot a single playing card: the joker. You pick the card up. Using a pin prised from a mildewed notice board, you fix the playing card to the outside of the door in the middle of the gap between '318' and 'PARANOIA'.

9

COGELS-OSYLEI

After originally threatening to spend her time in Antwerp shopping, that was in fact what Siân ended up doing while Frank went off to do his next interview. Antwerp, it seemed, according to the people who knew these things, was the latest fashion capital of Europe. The Sunday papers had been full of it before Siân had left London. The Antwerp Six. Designers Ann Demeulemeester, Dirk Bikkembergs, Dirk van Saene, Dries van Noten, Martin Margiela and Walter van Beirendonck. Old story? Of course. The features pages wouldn't touch it otherwise.

So, while Siân made her way to Dries van Noten's Het Modepaleis, Frank took a train one stop out of Centraal Station. 'Get off at Berchem,' Harry Kümel had said. 'It's easier to find a temporary parking spot there.'

Centraal Station was in turmoil. The magnificent dome was partly closed off, passengers rerouted via various obscure cut-throughs and emergency-lit passageways. In front of the station a chunk of Koningin Astridplein was sectioned off while gigantic machines gnawed away at the earth. Within, numerous lines were out of use, all services leaving from two platforms. Frank boarded a train due to depart in six minutes. He stood by the door and punched in Kümel's number on his mobile, which, as usual, was almost out of juice.

'I drive a silver-grey Citroën C5,' the director said. 'Licence plate number—' The signal suddenly faded. Frank looked at the phone; the battery hadn't quite run out. He put it back to his ear. '—never mind,' Kümel was saying. 'Silver-grey Citroën C5. There are not many C5s around.'

Frank didn't have a clue what a Citroën C5 looked like, but Citroën was something to go on, and silver-grey narrowed it down still further. He realised he was a little nervous about getting into a car with a possible murder suspect, but clearly he couldn't be that high on the list, not while Johnny Vos was still walking around a free man. Plus, Kümel was a known public figure with half a dozen films to his name. Frank had seen a few of them: *Daughters of Darkness* (1970), the film on the videotape found with the Russian girl, Katya; *Malpertuis* (1971), starring Orson Welles as the grizzled patriarch of an accursed house of innumerable floors and interminable corridors; *Eline Vere* (1991), a big-budget adaptation of a nineteenth-century Dutch novel; and two of the three half-hour films that made up the light-hearted erotic compendium *The Secrets of Love* (1986).

Daughters of Darkness was a late-night favourite, often described as a 'lesbian vampire flick'. Set in out-of-season Ostend, it starred Delphine Seyrig as the Countess Bathory. Frank had always thought that fans of lesbian vampire flicks, were they to seek out the movie, would actually be quite disappointed. As a genre film it was low key. But if, instead, you kept Alain Resnais's *Last Year at Marienbad* in mind, *Daughters of Darkness* had more resonance – the settings in grand hotels, the delight in ambiguity, the cool European sensibility, the question marks over identity and past events, and the fact that both films starred Delphine Seyrig. In *Daughters of Darkness* she recreates a look and even, at one point, a particular provocative pose from *Marienbad*.

The rubber-trimmed doors snapped shut and the train edged out of the station. Down below to the right, the gaudy metallic shopfronts of Pelikaanstraat contrasted sharply with the refined stonework of the four-storey Diamond Bourse. On the left-hand side of the train, men bent their backs laying the new lines coming into the station. Within three minutes the train pulled into Antwerpen-Berchem and Frank prepared to get off.

He made his way to the rear of the station and descended the steps to street level. Several cars were parked by the side of the road and all of them were silver-grey. None was a Citroën, as far as he could tell. He checked his watch and paced up and down. He took out his mobile and checked that, too. No calls, no messages and very nearly no battery. Perhaps Kümel wouldn't show. Maybe he was just in the act of bagging up a video of *Malpertuis* in preparation for his next victim.

Just as it occurred to Frank that no one had yet said how Hannah and Katya had been killed, another silver-grey car swept into a space by the side of the road. Frank clocked the Citroën's double-circumflex decal and ducked to get a look at the driver. He'd seen one picture of Kümel in an online directory of Belgian filmmakers, a snapshot taken a good fifteen years ago. It was impossible to tell if this was the same guy, but he looked to be in the ballpark age-wise and had the relaxed confidence of a man who'd known a certain degree of success. Dark glasses concealed the director's eyes, so that his face, when it turned towards Frank, remained blank.

Frank climbed into the car and offered his hand.

'Hello, Harry? Frank Warner.'

Kümel took his right hand from the gear stick and returned the greeting. With his left he tugged the steering wheel down, pointing the car's blunt snout back into the stock car rally that passed for traffic in Belgium.

'They should have built the international terminal here,' Kümel said, unexpectedly.

Frank looked at him, waited for him to go on.

Without turning to look at Frank, he continued: 'Instead of digging up Centraal Station. So much upheaval. They should have chosen this one instead. It's close enough to the centre. It's part of the city.'

'You've lived in Antwerp all your life?' Frank asked.

'Yes.'

'You were born here?'

'Born here and lived here all my life.'

'Is it a dangerous place?'

'Dangerous?'

'These murders . . .'

'Two women. Prostitutes, I gather. I was not aware they had ruled out suicide.'

'What about the videos? *Monsieur Hawarden*, *Daughters of Darkness*.'

'Maybe they didn't like my films. I would say it's quite likely *someone* doesn't like my films.'

'Have the police spoken to you?' Frank asked.

'Of course,' Kümel answered straight away, glaring at a driver approaching from the right, who, quite rightly, was not going to concede the right of way. The Belgian system, which, in most cases, prioritised vehicles coming from the right, meant that half the cars on the road at any one time had dented front wings on the right-hand side. It added a whole extra thrill to the business of being a passenger.

Frank waited, but Kümel was too shrewd to be lured into idle talk by the old silence routine. He was cautious, self-contained, quick-witted: a good hand in any game.

'Look at these places,' Kümel said, peering up through the windscreen. 'Built 100 years ago in a panoply of styles. Art nouveau, neo-Renaissance, neo-Gothic, neo-Byzantine, *Jugendstil*. The combination is unique.'

Still trying to get his head round 'panoply', a word he couldn't remember ever having heard in direct speech before, Frank looked out at the streets through which they were driving. Lined by three- and four-storey, ornate buildings with turrets and balconies, lodgements and floral motifs, columns, busts and mosaics, they were, he had to concede, deeply impressive.

'Where are we?' Frank asked. 'Still in Berchem?'

'Cogels-Osylei. Are they not extraordinarily beautiful? Look!'

'Yes, they're beautiful.'

'You've seen *Providence*, of course?'

'Of course.'

Providence, an elegant puzzle of a movie starring John Gielgud and Ellen Burstyn, was another Alain Resnais film and a favourite of Frank's.

'He shot part of it here.' Kümel gestured at the grand buildings. 'Exteriors. Alain's a friend of mine. No, rather an acquaintance. I helped him with the locations. I didn't like Mercer's script, though. Found it too . . . literary. *Marienbad* is that too, and so is that superb, unequalled masterpiece *Muriel*, but they "admit" they are literary and intellectual, while Mercer cannot decide which is which. Typical for an American intellectual.'

'I remember being shocked by the autopsy sequence. The way they opened the rib cage. It looked . . . I don't know . . . *real*.'

Frank felt embarrassed by his inability to think of a more apt word. The Belgian director spoke better English than he did.

'So do these houses, don't they? They look like the real thing. The genuine article. But they're not. They're all for show. It's all a façade. The houses are falling to bits.' Kümel turned to glance at Frank as he swung the Citroën by a bus depot. 'What you see is not necessarily what you get. Do not – as I am sure you would not – place too much trust in appearances.'

Not knowing how he should respond, Frank remained silent as he watched the gloriously mismatched houses slip past the car. Now that he knew that Resnais had filmed parts of *Providence* here, he couldn't see these streets as anything other than a film set. The houses were stage flats, two-dimensional boards propped up at the back. Their windows were tricks, optical illusions suggesting depth where there wasn't any.

'It's like no one lives here,' Frank said.

'People do live here,' Kümel responded. 'They are no longer family homes, of course, but are divided up into apartments. In the 60s the whole *quartier* was very nearly bulldozed, but the people protested, as people will always do,' he added, with a tired, dismissive wave, 'and the buildings were saved. See here,' Kümel directed. 'Twelve devils.'

He pointed to a row of carved black demonic figures above a doorway on the left. Frank tried to zoom in and focus on just one of the evilly contorted faces, but the car was picking up speed again, heading out of the fantasy enclave, back into the real world.

They sat across from each other at a table outside a café on the Left Bank by the St Anna Strand, an artificial beach, sand shipped inland from the coast. Kümel, his expression still concealed behind dark glasses, stirred a milky coffee. Frank, meanwhile, had ordered a Westmalle Dubbel, it still being too early in the day for the tyranny of the Tripel.

'This place—' Kümel indicated the Left Bank with a sweep of his arm – 'nobody comes here. Nobody at all. Look around you. It's deserted. Always has been and probably always will be, at least until they build a bridge over the Schelde. Antwerpers – it's not that they're snobbish, but they never come here.'

Frank did look around. The café terrace was one of three facing the river. Only one other table was occupied, by two boys in leather jackets and tight jeans. Germans, by the look of them.

'What about at the height of summer?' Frank asked.

'Sure,' Kümel conceded, 'these places start to fill up, but it never gets busy. All this open space, this greenery, and no one uses it.'

Frank looked back at the German couple. They sat across a table from each other, one staring at the river, the other at his drink. Yet their lips were moving. Frank looked at Kümel. Of athletic build, he dressed young for a man in his early sixties, in drawstring pants and a T-shirt advertising the Rotterdam Film Festival.

'A small number of people live here,' Kümel was saying, 'in these tower blocks behind where we are. But even they don't come here. It's a ghost town.'

'It's so cool.'

'It's just like a ghost town.'

Trefil Arbed's former nail factory and wireworks, five kilometres out of Ghent next to the railway line by the Schelde, had been closed for ten years or so by the beginning of the new millennium, and had been a top target for graffiti writers at least half of that time. Eddy Verhaeghe and Wim Vermandel, neither one of them yet fifteen, had skipped school to come here, having heard tales about the place, even seen pictures in *Graphotism* and elsewhere. They knew that some of the older boys at school had been out here writing their tags, spray-painting their pieces and dubs. They wanted to see the place for themselves. They also wanted to put up their first tags, and figured that in the former wireworks they'd feel less conspicuous than in the middle of Ghent. Each had nicked a couple of spraycans. They could have afforded to buy them, but, as any graf writer would tell you, stealing the cans was way cooler.

For two young wannabe graf writers, visiting Trefil Arbed was like art students making the trip to the Museum of Fine Arts. Part pilgrimage, part research. It was as much about paying dues as it was a recce.

Leaving their bikes chained together by the side of the road, Eddy and Wim scaled the wall by the railway and dropped down inside the grounds of the old factory. There was not just one building, but many. One large central warehouse-like space, dozens of smaller outbuildings and various irregular structures – workshops, hangars, toilet blocks, kitchens, a banqueting hall. Most of the exterior walls were covered in vibrant graffiti art: a full range from simple tags to cartoon figures and complete paintings with complex compositions. The two boys wandered around wide-eyed, slack-jawed. The crews and individuals who had been busy here were the Bruegels and Bosches, the Ensors and Delvauxs of their day. There was so much coverage Wim and Eddy couldn't find a single blank wall to put up their tags, so they decided to take a look inside. The small outbuildings were *so* small there didn't seem much point. The boys found an open window allowing access to one of the main factory buildings. Once inside they immediately became aware of the hush. Birdsong, the murmur of the distant road, the clanking of the railway – none of these could any longer be heard. A sudden whirring clatter gave them a fright, but it was only a pigeon disturbed by their progress. The boys took a few steps. It was like walking on a cloud. A carpet of feathers and droppings that stretched away in vanishing perspectives.

The graf writers had been at work, but there were more gaps inside than out.

'Here?' Wim suggested.

'Yeah.' But Eddy sounded uncertain. Something about the place had spooked him. He wasn't sure he wanted to stick around. He felt as if they were being watched.

Wim had found a spot and was getting down to it with his spraycans. Eddy, meanwhile, wandered off. A little passageway led out of the main part of the structure, through a set of double doors, which grated against rust as Eddy pushed his way through. He walked on.

He knew something was wrong even before he'd actually seen anything. The sensation of being watched suddenly intensified. He felt like a fly caught in a web. He stopped, obscurely convinced that to take another step would be to plunge through the sticks and leaves of a forest-floor booby trap. The hairs on the back of his neck prickling to attention, he stared into the shadows.

A pair of eyes stared back at him.

He recoiled instinctively. The eyes didn't blink, or look away. While their owner was shrouded in a vaguely sticky, cobwebby darkness, the eyes reflected a dull gleam of light admitted by a crack in the nearest wall. Eddy took another step back and, his heel catching on a loose board, lost his balance and tumbled backwards as something behind him gave way. He felt soft things crumbling as they came into contact with his skin. Hard edges digging into the back of his skull. Then, a split-second after he seemed to have come to a rest and was gingerly preparing to pick himself up, he fell again, crashing backwards, and it felt as though the entire building were coming down on top of him.

The dust still settling, he looked around, realising that although he'd had a bad fall, he was still alive and, as far as he could tell, unharmed.

He had fallen into some kind of den or hideaway, an inhabited – or formerly inhabited – space. It felt no less abandoned, however, than the rest of the wireworks. The smell was the same. Musty, bitter, damp.

Instead of one pair of eyes watching him, there were several. More than a dozen shop-window dummies, all female, were crammed into the once-confined space. Some had painted eye-sockets, some had eyes that looked blank, as if closed. Others – older models, he guessed, like the one he had thought was staring at him before the wall had given way – had glass eyes. The mannequins were covered in dust and wreathed in cobwebs, but they didn't have about them the same air of abandonment that pervaded the wireworks. They looked too recently cared for. For a start, they were arranged. This wasn't a storeroom full of old dummies that had somehow been part of the nail- and wire-making business. These life-size dolls had been arranged by someone with a sense of – what? Fun? The bizarre? They stood in a semi-circle. In fact, not all of them were standing. A couple of them were not able to, since their legs had been sawn off below the knee.

As well as the mannequins there were candles. Dozens of candle stubs affixed to different surfaces, mostly burnt right down. The walls of the former hide-out – those that were still standing – were plastered with clippings from *Le soir*, *Het Laaste Nieuws*, *De Standaard*, *La dernière heure*. Even some foreign papers – the *Herald Tribune*, the *Guardian*, *Libération*. Eddy scanned the clippings. They told of parental neglect, desertion, even child-killings. *La mère qui a tué*. *Walk-out mother abandons kids, 2, 5*. *Les enfants hors du paradis*. Mixed in among these were a handful of more mundane stories: mine closures, industries run down, workers thrown on the scrapheap. The arrangement of the clippings appeared haphazard. They were neither in date order nor grouped according to location. There wasn't even a strong bias in favour of French or Flemish.

Eddy suddenly stopped reading. He'd vaguely registered a noise but didn't know if it was Wim, or a trapped bird, or the inhabitant of the den. Holding his breath, all he could hear was the insistent beat of his own pulse. He looked out beyond the shattered wall through which he had fallen. Daylight sloped into the factory through glass panels in the roof, illuminating trapezoids of floating dust, which seemed undisturbed. He listened but couldn't hear anything apart from distant birdsong and the barely audible hum of traffic.

Eddy had wanted to come out here and put up some tags every bit as much as Wim, but he now felt his enthusiasm diminishing with each passing second he spent in the former wire-works. He felt an abrupt and overwhelming desire to go and find his friend and suggest they get the fuck out.

10

ASTRID PARK PLAZA

In 1991 you were twenty-eight. The Hubble Space Telescope was launched after a seven-year delay; Rajiv Gandhi was killed in an explosion while campaigning in India; and Harry Kümel's lavish nineteenth-century costume drama *Eline Vere* was released in Belgian cinemas. The film flopped, but a small-screen version, shown in three one-hour episodes on Dutch and Belgian TV, was a notable success.

You were staying in the south-eastern outskirts of Ghent in a former wireworks, Trefil Arbed, that had recently been shut down. The place was huge, like a small town. Warehouses, manufacturing units, dozens of small outbuildings. Kids came over the walls with spraycans, but the place was so big, so rambling, that it was possible to hide away. It became clear to you that others had had the same idea. Tramps sleeping rough. You saw signs.

You worked for a small business in Ekkergem on the west side of the city that manufactured mannequins for retail display. You learned how to make a mould and how to use one to create a complete dummy. You didn't drive a vehicle, but walked everywhere instead. A few minutes from the mannequin business was an old textiles factory, Halsberghe-Van-Oost. Closed for a number of years, it sat right on the N466, the Drongense Steenweg, the main road out to Drongen and Deinze. No attempt having been made to secure the premises, it had been completely overrun by graffiti writers. An artists' commune had lived there for a while. As a place to stay, it was too accessible, but you liked walking there. The main buildings appeared to be slowly giving in to the forces of nature, as buddleia thrust its way through weakened mortar and colonies of stinging nettles and rosebay willowherb advanced across the moist earth, keeping pace with the slow, graceful collapse of most of the roofs.

The grounds extended 500 metres back from the road to a series of ponds and small overgrown lakes where middle-aged men and young boys sat fishing for carp. Between the ponds and the factory buildings was a series of twenty-metre-square dipping pools that had been used for dyeing fabrics. Invaded by moss, algae and bullrushes, these were separated by low walls of red brick just wide enough to walk along by placing one foot carefully in front of the other. You would sit on a ledge overlooking the first of the pools with your back against the factory wall, watching the electric blue flashes of dragonflies as they danced over the green water like sparks.

The girl was there one day, in your spot, tugging with her teeth on an improvised tourniquet around her upper arm. You watched as she picked up a needle from the ledge and inserted it slowly, lovingly, into her vein. She pumped in the drugs, then withdrew the needle and loosened the tourniquet, letting it drop on to the ledge. You watched her for a minute. The pallid skin. Discolourations. The too-short denim skirt. Greasy hair. Stage make-up.

As soon as the head went back, you stepped up. Grabbed the tourniquet – a plastic belt, you noticed, that didn't belong with the clothes she was wearing. You slipped it round her neck. Knee in the back. Pressure. Resistance. Kicking.

Then she was still. Arms trembling, you eased her bottom over the lip of the ledge and allowed her to slip down into the pool, which received her without argument. The green waters, the lily pads, the film of algae closing seamlessly over her head.

Frank and Siân had moved into a new hotel. On his own, Frank might have made do with his tiny cabin on the boatel, but Siân expected a higher level of comfort, so Frank had booked a double room at the Astrid Park Plaza. A large, modern building festooned with ugly cladding, the hotel was pleasanter inside than out. It needed to be. As if to contrive maximum contrast, the Plaza was located directly opposite the majestic Centraal Station.

Frank was surprised to get back and find their room empty. He'd expected that Siân would be back before him, but he'd had a few beers with Harry Kümel (the director had stuck to claret) and so was feeling relaxed. Later he would regret not having called Siân's mobile immediately.

He went into the bathroom and started running a bath. While the tub was filling, he sat on the bed and leafed through a large-format Delvaux monograph. With prolonged exposure to the Belgian's world, he was beginning to fall under his spell. There was something undeniably hypnotic about the procession of dreamlike nudes, most of whom looked remarkably alike. Frank had read one writer on the subject who had argued that the oversize pink or red bows worn by some of them conferred a symbolic virginity. He paused over a colour plate of *The Pink Bows*. The women in the centre of the picture, standing on the red carpet and wearing large pink bows, were still virgins, accord-ing to the theory. Those to either side, who had cast off their bows and were fully naked (one was even running) were not. Frank flicked past a few more pages, stopping at another plate, *The Anxious City*, the work Vos had been intending to recreate with Katya Egorova among the extras. Painted in 1941, the pic-ture was believed to reflect Delvaux's feelings about Nazi Germany's occupation of Belgium. With its great crowds of figures locked in various kinds of embrace – fighting, making love or merely gazing into each other's eyes in search of answers to unknown questions – it reminded Frank of Bruegel. The fore-grounded skull and the three skeletons in the background served, presumably, as a potent reminder of the presence of death in the midst of life.

Frank put the book aside and, vaguely aware of the bath still filling up noisily behind him, looked out of the window across Koningin Astridplein at the station and, immediately to its left, the zoo. Much of the square in front of the station was a con-struction site. The tunnelling machinery sat, for the time being, idle, but it wouldn't be long before the enormous bore-screw was jabbed like a hypodermic beneath the city's skin to burrow ever deeper.

As clouds of steam escaped around the bathroom door, Frank stepped away from the window and slipped out of his clothes, leaving them on the floor. The bathroom was so full of steam he had to navigate by touch. He wiped a clear patch on the mirror, as if to check he was still there. He looked tired. Dark shadows under his eyes. Grime collected in his pores. When this business was over he would take it easy. Maybe he and Siân should go away somewhere. Somewhere that had nothing to do with film, so that he couldn't do any work even if he wanted to. He resolved to wrap up the Johnny Vos story as quickly as possible and, with any luck, no more prostitutes would be murdered and the press would lose interest.

The clear patch steamed up and Frank stepped into the bath, easing his body gradually into the hot, foamy water until he was prone, his head resting against the end of the tub, which didn't rise at too sharp an angle to make adopting such a position prohibitively uncomfortable. He, too, appreciated luxury and he silently gave thanks for Siân, without whom he might still have been floating on the nauseating waters of the Schelde. The boatel hadn't even had a bath, merely a shower. Showers were fine for getting clean and being efficient about it, but useless for a complete surrender of control. Frank ran his hands over his body, enjoying the sensation of the moisturising bath foam on his tired skin. He closed his eyes and dipped his head under the water. Sounds that he hadn't even been aware of were abruptly cut out and he heard instead the thump of his own pulse. He listened to it curiously. One day it too would cease. Hearing it reminded him of that. Reminded him of how Sarah's had ceased. One moment his wife's heart had been beating, the next it had stopped. The fact that death had been instantaneous had never been the comfort that TV scriptwriters always presumed it to be. She had been killed – simple as that. Tragic accident. Frank had moved on, although for a long time he found it impossible to form meaningful relationships of any kind. Then he met Siân and their relationship did mean something. But still there was never a day that went by without his missing Sarah.

He heard a low rumble, like thunder or the growl of a big cat
– the hotel's plumbing? Or possibly his own? Harry Kümel's face
appeared on the screen of his mind, eyes hidden behind dark
glasses. The director's lip twitched – whether with amusement,
intent or by involuntary spasm was not clear. His face turned
slowly into shadow and out of the darkness came the face of a
tiger escaped from the zoo into one of the new tunnels under
Koningin Astridplein. The beast stuck its whiskered head above
ground, sniffing the air. Pedestrians scattering. Car horns.
Motorbikes skidding. Shriek of a tram's brakes. The tiger is followed out of the hole in the ground by another, then another and
so on until all of the zoo's tigers are prowling the square in front
of Centraal Station. The only people indifferent to them are the
women now pouring into the square from Pelikaanstraat, De
Keyserlei and Gemeentestraat. Sleek, graceful and elegant, they
seem at home, yet out of time, their slow gesticulations bringing
to mind the movements of synchronised swimmers. The tigers
walk among them, weaving in and out of their long, bared legs,
pressing against their calf muscles like domestic felines. Tiger fur
brushing against the women's minutely rendered pubic hair.
Hallucinatory clarity, close-focus detail. The two broad pave-
ments on the west and east sides of the square have turned into
red carpets. Some of the women wear huge ribbons tied into
bows across their chests, others have discarded them and they lie
like dead roses in the middle of the square, sniffed at by the tigers
as they prowl around. The still, heavy air is slashed like a canvas
by the knife-edge screeches of tram wheels negotiating a curve.
Somewhere water is lapping. A dull, repetitive thump persists, like
a bass line. The water is grey, choppy – a humped shape breaks
the surface, disturbed by the wake of a passing freighter. A blank
face is forced up against the waterline porthole, consistency of
wax, lips blue not red. The woman in the river. Katya. The
Russian. One of Johnny Vos's extras. The one who never made it.
So, she got to take her clothes off, after all. Just not in front of the
camera.

Thump-thump . . . thump-thump . . . THUMP-THUMP.
FADE TO BLACK.

Part Five

THE PUBLIC WAY

11

DIAMANTCLUB

Penny's depression failed to lift. Nothing I said or did seemed to make the slightest difference. I wondered if she was homesick, but the suggestion of a trip back to England was met with silence. I advised she see the doctor, get Prozac, go shout at the swans in the park – whatever she thought she needed. No response.

In the end, I had to think about practical matters. Bills were mounting up and I was still waiting for the diamond money to come from London. In the meantime, I had to go to work. With my membership of the Diamond Bourse in Hatton Garden, I was in a good position to become a member of one of Antwerp's four such institutions. Plus, I had the contact I'd obtained in London. I called him and he suggested we meet in the Diamantclub.

'Pelikaanstraat,' he told me. 'Number 62.'

I walked past the grand, nineteenth-century building that housed the Diamond Bourse at 78 Pelikaanstraat and stopped outside the much newer, more discreet Diamantclub at number 62. I had to surrender my passport at security in return for a visitor's swipe card. The building was purpose-built: clean lines, neutral atmosphere, bland functionality. I bypassed the lift and took the stairs to the third floor. A long featureless corridor extended towards its own rectangular conclusion. The numbered doors on each side bore the names of companies or individuals. When I recognised that of my contact, I stopped and knocked three times. There was a brief pause before the door opened with a whispered click. It was only when I stepped into the coolness of the air-conditioned interior that I realised how humid it had been in the corridor. A large gentleman rose to greet me. Jewish possibly, though not Orthodox. Antwerp was a bigger market than London – the biggest in the world – and so its players were likely to be more suspicious. I had to stick to the rules. The man's handshake seemed to tell me this in the strength and duration of its grip. I held his stare, too. He dressed well, without being ostentatious, and wore a cologne that I didn't recognise.

'Please,' he said, gesturing towards a leather chair.

We sat down on opposite sides of a wide, black-lacquered desk. I noticed a daylight lamp, a blotter, a photograph of the man, smiling as he was with me now, posing with his arm around a young woman. To my right was a picture window. I looked down across a courtyard into a much older building, where I saw a long narrow room bedecked with flags from various nations. A number of Orthodox Jews sat across long tables from each other.

'The Diamantbeurs,' my host purred. 'Diamond Bourse. Over there they deal mainly in polished diamonds. Here – at the Diamantclub – we deal in both polished and rough stones. And, at the Diamantkring, unpolished stones. These are generalisations, of course, but just to give you an idea. You are new to Antwerp?'

'I've been here a few weeks. My family are originally from here.'

'Of course, of course.'

He seemed careful to appear friendly, yet remain impartial.

'You are dealing mainly in polished stones?' he asked.

'Mainly,' I said. 'I also have some unpolished stones. May I ask what you are looking for particularly?'

The man looked out of the window, then back at me.

'High-value single stones. Two, three carats.' He straightened his tie. 'Flawless.'

'Flawless?'

'Internally flawless.'

I felt the blood drain from my face.

'If you're cold,' he offered, 'I can adjust the air-conditioning.'

'I'm fine,' I said. 'Thank you.'

'I have a customer,' he went on, 'who is looking for large, flawless stones.'

I nodded.

'Maybe you can't help?' he said.

'I'll see what I can do.'

It wasn't until he looked away that I realised how tightly my buttocks had been clenched. There was also a band of pain across the back of my shoulders. It was strange: in London, I had experienced no nerves, yet here I was, still acting above-board, and I felt tense and anxious. I knew I didn't possess any large IF stones, however, so why had I implied to the man that I might? I couldn't afford to alienate myself in Antwerp.

'I need to speak to some people,' I said.

'Take this,' the man said, passing me a laminated business card. 'Call me.'

'I will.'

He rose as if to accompany me.

'I can manage,' I said, keen to regain the corridor on my own. The last thing I wanted was to be bundled politely into the lift.

On my way out of the building I contrived to trespass on to the trading floor. I stepped, unchallenged, through a set of double doors, then turned immediately right, not allowing my gaze to linger on the two gentlemen at the nearest table haggling over the price of a small mound of unpolished yellow fancies. I estimated there to be 150,000 dollars' worth of naturally coloured stones on the table between them.

I scanned the notice boards, on which were posted the names and photographs of members who had been suspended or permanently excluded for activities ranging from conducting unofficial business (tax avoidance, black marketeering) to actual theft of diamonds. Members were exhorted to be vigilant and to report any sightings of those pictured to security personnel. I let my eyes skim over the mugshots, half expecting my own image to be among them. As far as I could see, it was not.

It struck me as a somewhat primitive security system. Some of the pictures were poorly photocopied from low-quality originals. A lot of the names were Asian – Indian, mainly. Indians had taken over much of the global diamond business from the Jews.

Labour costs being much lower in India, the Indians had flooded the market with cheaper stones and Bombay was beginning to rival Antwerp as the world centre of the trade.

Moving away from the notice boards, I walked towards the far end of the room and turned left into the cafeteria, which was separated from the trading floor by a wall of windows. I waited while the woman behind the counter served the man in front of me.

'Thank you, Eva,' the man said as he pocketed his change and took his tray to one of the tables.

I ordered a coffee. While the woman worked the machine, I chatted with her, making sure to use her name once or twice. She was tall and slender, very striking, with long legs and a short body, her deep red-dyed hair cut in a severe, angular style – high fringe, sharp points that scythed across her face when she bent down to snap the ground coffee in the trash – like a colourised Louise Brooks. Her green eyes seemed full of an intelligence that overqualified her for the work she was doing. Her mouth was small and neat and she didn't talk much. I liked that. I sat down at a table facing the trading floor. I watched club members discuss deals on the other side of the glass, while behind me I listened to Eva clattering about behind the counter. My hands were clasped around my coffee cup to keep them from shaking.

When I got back to Sint-Jozefstraat, Penny was gone.

I was used to her absence, but when on entering the house I called her name and heard no reply, I sensed that something was wrong. This time, she wouldn't turn out to have been just sitting in the park or wandering along the wharves. I looked for signs to confirm my gut feeling. In our bedroom I looked through her stuff, but since I didn't know how many items of underwear she had, I couldn't say how many were missing. Her passport was in the top drawer, so she hadn't gone far. Not literally; but, laterally, she could be a world away already. Belgium was a small country, but it boasted the densest motorway network on the planet, and the most concentrated clash of cultures, too. A person might stumble across one of a number of numinous frontiers and pass into no-man's land. It was a country where going missing had become commonplace. Marc Dutroux might be behind bars, but the idea of him, the assumption of what he had done, was in the air, and it further discouraged a people already downcast and dispirited. Moral decay was spreading, with almost viral efficiency, throughout the whole country.

I didn't know where to go, in what kind of places to look, so I prowled the streets in the neighbourhood, my eyes boring into the backs of women's heads. Suddenly, Penny was no longer unique. Every woman was her double in one detail or another. I zoomed in on whatever features these strangers shared with her, my eyes leading my brain into a series of deceptions and disappointments.

I headed out of the city. Through Cogels-Osylei, then, passing under the railway line, into Berchem. She could be on her way to the coast, or deep in Wallonia. I walked in ever increasing circles, turning at random. I was reminded briefly of a time when I had dropped a diamond on a carpeted floor and had got down on all fours to search for it. Everything then had been focused on finding the stone, just as now I could think of nothing but Penny. I remembered the day she first came into my shop, a look of profound loneliness in her eyes. I remembered how I talked softly to her, how eventually she gave in and told me everything, trusting me. I remembered how she smelled, of the sea, of seaweed and driftwood mixed with the damp wool of her coat. But most of all I remembered how she appeared to me. Vulnerable yet independent. Solid and fragile at the same time.

I didn't know where I was, couldn't even work out what part of town I was in. The streets were unfamiliar, even the people seemed different. They passed me in close huddles, their faces brown and weather-beaten. I felt lost. Buildings drifted in and out of focus. The pavement swayed beneath my feet. Lights had come on. Red lights. Blue. Ultra-violet. Then I did realise where I was. Why did I always seem to end up here? It was uncanny.

I looked in at the windows as I went. The women darted towards the glass, pushing out their chests. My eyes trailed, like jellyfish stingers, over their exotic bodies. Did I really think Penny might have come here? That I might see her reflection as she came up behind me? Or that she might be sitting in one of the booths, her full figure punished by provocative lingerie, her face parodically smeared with paint?

Or did I just like looking?

Over the next few days I continued my search until simple exhaustion prevented me from leaving the house. I switched on my daylight lamp and spent an afternoon sorting diamonds, having always found it a relaxing antidote to stress.

Through the loupe I examined the largest stone I possessed, trying to work out if I should run the risk of offering it to my contact at the Diamantclub. It was barely one carat and strictly speaking it was not flawless, but it was a VVS1, at least. I kept moving it to allow the light to penetrate every corner. I angled the stone so that each facet in turn reflected the light like a tiny flat white screen. I imagined each one presenting me with a different moving image, a series of possible outcomes. At one end of the spectrum I saw Penny walking in through the front door and us picking up our lives not from where we had left off but from some earlier, happier point in time. Penny contacting me, assuring me that she was OK, but that she had to be some place else, away from me, on her own or with another, with her memories of Iain Burns perhaps. I saw myself accepting her departure for what it was, a vanishing, and moving on, taking the opportunity to do something different. I saw numerous other women passing in front of my eyes – on screen, behind glass, in the flesh – one in particular with swinging curtains of ruby-red hair, mannequin legs, eyes green as a Bruges canal.

Six months passed before I heard from Penny. I had become a little distracted from my business in the Diamond Quarter and had been back again and again to the red light district. Mostly I just walked around, looking; I also visited peep shows. I got to know a few of the girls by sight and I would nod to them as I passed. I spoke to no one, however. I just looked. Any dialogue on the soundtrack wasn't mine – just background stuff. Extras.

The house in Moriaanstraat, when I bought it, was a shell – and most of that needed to be dismantled before a largely new structure could be built in its place. All I was really buying was the plot of land and the permission to build on it. Given that I was more or less writing on a blank page, I took the opportunity to influence the design of the house, making sure, for example, that no room contained any concealed corners or alcoves. At what point did I acknowledge to myself what I was doing? When I bought the abandoned house? During its refurbishment? Or only when the job was complete and I installed the digital video cameras?

Although I'd lost a degree of impetus in the diamond business, Pelikaanstraat had not disappeared from my mental map. Partly this was because of Eva. I continued to show my face at the Diamantclub, ostensibly to keep in touch with my contact there and let him know I was still trying to find some large IF stones for him, but mainly I lingered in the coffee bar, chatting to Eva, slowly winning her trust. I learned that prior to joining the ancillary staff at the Diamantclub she had worked somewhere closer to the docks. I made an educated guess as to the whereabouts.

'Anywhere near Falconplein or Verversrui?' I asked, naming two locations in the red light district.

'Yes, very near there,' she replied.

The way she held my gaze while she said this was all the confirmation I needed. Eva was a tart. She didn't mind if I knew it, either.

'You probably know more about how this place is run than anybody?' I suggested.

'You mean the coffee bar or the Diamantclub?'

I think, at that point, I might have smiled. Eva certainly did. There was almost a grin on her face as she wiped a cloth over the counter.

I remembered that look, that half-smile or near-grin, when I began planning what I was going to do with the house on Moriaanstraat. It was the confidence about it that I liked, as well as the suggestion of complicity.

Eva recruited the girls and helped them settle in. Initially she was only going to be assisting me for a limited period, for a generous fee, but I managed to persuade her to fill the position on a permanent basis. It meant quitting her job at the Diamantclub, but we both figured it was worth it. She knew she'd easily find

other work if the Last House was a flop, and I was willing to
sacrifice having an insider in the Diamond Quarter if she could
help my new project generate enough cash to obviate the need
to get back into dealing stones.

Once the girls moved in, I didn't need to set foot in the house
again. I engaged a local new media operation to set up and maintain the networks and website. Users stumbling across the site on
the web were offered a free preview, little more than a selection
of stills, and promised live video feed if they became members.
All we needed was a credit card number. There was, in theory, the
technical guy told me, no limit to the number of members we
could support; in the first week we picked up a hundred, which
more than trebled by the end of the second week. One month
in, the project was paying for itself, all bar the capital outlay on
the house. Two months later even that was taken care of. I logged
on to the site from my computer at home in Sint-Jozefstraat and
idly watched the girls as they walked from room to room and sat
and talked, but in truth they held little interest for me. I soon
realised I was waiting for glimpses of Eva, who didn't parade herself before the cameras, but neither did she go out of her way to
avoid them. That would have been impossible, in any case.

And then Penny made contact. One morning, there was a
postcard in the mail. It was an art card. Paul Delvaux's *La voix
publique* – or *La voie publique*. The title translated as either *The
Public Voice* or *The Public Way*, the latter making more sense, since
the painting featured a tram approaching four of Delvaux's
trademark melancholy women. The painting was hanging in
the Museum of Modern Art in Brussels. I'd seen it there. They
sold the postcard in the museum shop. But no doubt elsewhere,
too.

The card was handwritten, stamped, postmarked 'Oostende'.

'Wim,' Penny had written, 'I'm fine. Please do not try to find
me. With affection, Penny.'

Do not try to find me.

I could be in Ostend within a couple of hours. You could be
anywhere in Belgium within a couple of hours. Was Penny playing a game? It was in a seaside town that I had found her in the
first place. Did she want me to find her all over again? Was it her

way of injecting new life into our relationship? Hadn't she waited
rather longer than necessary, if this was the case?

I didn't know what to do, although I had to admit to myself
that if it had arrived a week after she'd disappeared I would have
got my coat and halved the distance between myself and the coast
in the time it takes to walk from Sint-Jozefstraat to the red light
district. Was the only reason I didn't do exactly that simply
because she had asked me not to? Clearly not. Was it that I
doubted I would find her? I *did* doubt that I would find her, it's
true, but to what extent that doubt affected my motivation it
would have been hard to say. Perhaps the key lay in the length of
time she had been missing. One month, perhaps two, even three
months after her vanishing act I wouldn't have thought twice. So
I hadn't reported her disappearance to the police, but what would
have been the point? The police had questioned Marc Dutroux
in his home while two girls, who'd been missing for some weeks,
were locked up in his cellar. When screaming could be heard,
Dutroux explained it away as children at play in the street. Given
that the police bought that, I didn't hold out much hope of their
finding Penny. In any case, I didn't want to have anything to do
with the police if I could help it. I didn't want them asking awkward questions. And if she had gone away merely to slit her wrists
in a grim hotel bathroom in some tired industrial town in the
depths of Wallonia, what good would it do anyone for the police
to lead me to her cold prone body in the local morgue? Her
behaviour before her disappearance had been such that this was
a distinct possibility. If she was dead, then she was dead. If she had
wanted simply to be away from me, then who was I to deny her
that wish? And if she had wanted me to find her, she would have
needed to give me something to work on. Her abandoned passport had been a start, but not much of one. So, if she had *really*
wanted me to find her, sooner or later she would have to send a
clue.

The postcard could be that clue, yet she specifically requested
that I not try to find her.

I got as far as Bruges before turning back. It would have been
only another fifteen minutes to Ostend, but my mind was made
up. I returned home and went straight inside and logged on to

the Last House site. My records later showed that I didn't log off until six o'clock the following morning. I showered, slept for a couple of hours and logged back on. For two weeks I didn't leave Sint-Jozefstraat; nor did I log off from the site. I watched continuously, flicking from room to room in pursuit of Eva, but also watching the girls, the former prostitutes, as they chatted together, ate meals (Thai, Chinese, spaghetti), read books (Patrick Conrad's *Limousine*, Nicolas Freeling, Simenon; I had stocked the bookshelves myself), showered and slept. I approved of the relationship of trust that appeared to be developing between Danuta and Katya, despite the traditional enmity between their countries of origin. Over time, most of the girls had become more relaxed and relatively insouciant of the cameras, with the notable exception of Danuta, who remained overwhelmingly camera-aware. That this might be bad for business was not what concerned me; it was simply that it constantly reminded the viewer of the artificiality of the set-up. There was rarely a time, however, when one or two of the girls were not walking around in nothing more than a skinny top and underwear. I watched the way their legs moved below their T-shirts, as lithe and deceptively powerful as a cheetah's. It did not frustrate me that complete nakedness was still the exception rather than the rule. It seemed to me that most of them were settling into the kind of routine they would adopt in any normal house shared by a group of women.

Their legs reminded me of Penny's. She might have been older than these girls, but she still had athlete's legs with good muscle tone, more through good fortune than choice – I couldn't remember her taking any more exercise than her habitual walks up and down the Suffolk beaches, and later her aimless wanderings in Antwerp. I tried to picture them now and couldn't. I started wondering instead about Eva's legs. She wore trousers, always.

I had been meaning to call Eva to have a word with her about Danuta, when Eva called me with the news that Katya's body had just been fished out of the Schelde. She had only just started giving me the details when she said she had to go. I gave it five minutes and called her back, but the call went straight through to voicemail, so I ordered a cab and set off for Moriaanstraat.

★

Eva and I didn't meet up till the next day. There was still a police presence at Moriaanstraat, so we met at a bar in the red light district.

'How are you?' I asked her, once she had sat down, taken out a cigarette and reached for her matches.

'Hmm,' she said in the brief moment between lighting the cigarette and turning her head away to blow out the first lungful of smoke. 'OK. Considering.'

She sucked deeply on her cigarette. The smoke was blue against the brown decor of the bar. Finally she looked at me and gave a twisted half-smile.

Eva smoked extravagantly, blowing out smoke like she was trying to extinguish candles on a cake. I suspected the confident manner masked an inner insecurity. Perhaps she, too, was lonely. I didn't know for certain that she was even single. Our conversations had rarely strayed beyond the practical or other matters pertaining to our surroundings, which meant we had discussed either the Diamond Quarter or Moriaanstraat and, by extension, the red light district.

'What did you tell the police?' I asked her.

'Nothing, of course,' she replied without hesitation. 'There's nothing to tell.'

'What can you tell *me*?' I persisted.

'What do you want me to tell you? That I murdered Katya and dumped her body in the river?' she asked, eyes wide and nostrils flared. 'When would I have had the time?' she added sarcastically, blowing smoke directly at me.

'Look,' I said gently, placing my hand on her arm, 'I know it must have been difficult for you.'

She didn't shake my hand free, so I left it there. She did continue to smoke, but directed it out of the corner of her mouth.

'It's not difficult for me,' she said. 'It's difficult for Danuta. She knew both girls. Now the others are worried that one of them will be next.'

'Why? Why should one of them be next?'

'They're exposed. They feel vulnerable.'

'Did Katya have enemies? A former pimp, perhaps?'

'Not that I know of.' Eva destroyed the remains of her

cigarette in the ashtray and immediately lit another. 'There's this creepy guy, Jan, who emails Danuta obsessively.'

'But that's Danuta.'

'He's obsessed with her,' she went on.

'He's probably harmless,' I said, but my attempt to reassure her didn't seem to help. 'Has he emailed her since Katya's body was found?'

'No,' she admitted. 'Although he did email her after she got back from identifying Hannah's body in the water tower.'

'Who is he?' I asked, since I could see I would have to do something. 'Give me his details and I'll run a check.'

She nodded. 'I'll forward them to you when I get back.'

She seemed eager to be gone.

'Send me those details,' I advised her. 'Call me whenever you want. Day or night.'

She was already halfway out the door.

It had started to rain while we had been in the bar. The red and blue strip-lights in the neighbouring windows shivered in partial reflection on the wet cobbles. Tap, tap, tap on the glass. I kept walking. By the time I got back to Sint-Jozefstraat, Eva's email was waiting for me. I read it and reread it over and over again, looking for some hidden clue as to her feelings for me, or even just an opinion of me. I wasn't convinced it contained any.

Wim — the guy's name is Jan. His address: jan 7230@freeze.com. Later. E

I composed an email to technical support, asking them to track down this guy, Jan, and to see if they could get a full name and address, although I obviously knew how easy it was to hide behind a false identity, particularly since the arrival of the Internet. But I felt a compulsion to do something to please — or appease — Eva.

Part Six

STREET OF TRAMS

12

CARGO

Cargo was on the west side of Leopold De Waelplaats facing the Museum of Fine Arts. The initial impression was one of contrived elegance: acres of stainless steel and glass; slender, statuesque wait-staff; white tablecloths starched to the point where they would have stood on their own four legs if you'd whipped the tables out from under them.

Siân paid the driver and got out of the cab. She watched the vehicle as it moved off, its haste earning it a rebuke from the driver of an approaching tram. The tram stopped and a fash-ionably dressed couple stepped out, turning left and heading towards Café Hopper. She looked down at her own clothes, a new outfit that she had bought that day in Het Modepaleis. She hadn't dressed up for Vos. She had been trying on her new clothes when he rang. In the mirror in the hotel bedroom it had looked right. Now, here, she wasn't so sure. Maybe it wasn't her style. Too tarty, perhaps. Too low in the neckline, a bit tight in the bodice. There was nothing she could do about it.

Cargo resembled the kind of exclusive Modern European restaurant Siân liked to visit in London — when someone else was paying. She crossed the pavement and entered. Vos caught her eye immediately, standing up at her approach. As he offered his hand, she took in as much as she could of his appearance. He had changed into a fancy purple shirt with long pointed collars that

overlapped the narrow lapels of a rumpled black linen jacket, his
blue jeans having been replaced by a black pair.

'You look fantastic,' he said. 'Sit down. I'll get you a drink.
Beer?' He signalled to the waiter. 'Can we get two De Konincks
here?' The waiter nodded and left. 'It's local,' Vos said, turning his
attention back to Siân. 'Brewed in Antwerp. Very good. Light and
not too strong.'

'God save me from beer critics.'

'What's that?'

'Nothing.'

Vos drained his glass.

'I shot a big scene here,' he said. 'Out there in the square in
front of the museum.'

'One of Delvaux's paintings?'

'I had twenty-four, twenty-five naked girls walking across the
square,' he said with a half-crazy, lopsided grin.

The waiter arrived with two De Konincks in wide glasses like
ice-cream bowls.

'To beautiful women everywhere,' Vos announced, clinking
his glass against Siân's.

'That, presumably, is the attraction? With Delvaux, I mean.'

'You mean in the paintings or the girls I'm using on the film?'

'You tell me,' she said, unable to prevent a smile reaching her
lips, which shaved a little of the edge off the challenge. 'What is
it about Delvaux that gets to you? Surely it's not just the nudity?'

'I guess I want to know what made him tick.'

'Whoop, whoop – cliché alert!'

'I want to get inside his head.'

'Only his head?'

'Head, heart – whatever. I want to get inside him.'

'Well, how far are you away from doing that?'

'I'm getting warm,' he grinned.

'Really?' She smiled. 'So what is it with him and all these
women?'

Vos leaned back in his chair and shook a cigarette out of a
softpack. He lit it with a matchbook. Siân tried to read the name
on the cover of the matchbook as he transferred it to his jacket
pocket, but couldn't.

'He was close to his mother,' Johnny began, obviously enjoying the chance to talk on his favourite subject. 'But she was a
repressive influence on his sexuality. When he should have been
developing as a young man, as a sexual being, he was hanging out
with skeletons instead.'

'Supermodels? In the 1920s?'

'Nineteen-hundreds. No, skeletons. Study aids. He became
obsessed by a skeleton that stood in a glass case in his school class-
room. He used to sketch it.'

'He was an art student?'

The waiter dropped by, but Johnny waved him away.

'He studied architecture. His father, a lawyer, wanted him to
study law and did not approve of him studying art. Architecture
was a compromise. That's where he developed his obsession with
cities and buildings and perspective.'

'So the naked girls were his fantasies?'

Johnny picked up the pack of cigarettes and offered them to
Siân. She shook her head.

'It's kind of a refreshing change being in a country where no
one shoots you if you light up a cigarette,' said Johnny. This time
he left the matchbook on the table. Siân read the name on the
cover: The Blue Zone.

'Smoking is pretty much compulsory here,' she observed. 'It's
the same all over the Continent.'

'But not in England,' Johnny pointed out.

'No, we're way too uptight.'

'In which case you're not exactly a typical English girl,' Vos
remarked.

It was pretty unsophisticated stuff, but the delivery made Siân
smile. He was charming her in spite of her natural reservations,
and he was good at it.

'You asked if they were his fantasies,' Vos reminded her, taking another hit off his cigarette before crushing it in the ashtray.
'The girls in his paintings. I don't think so. Not in the sense you
meant it, anyway. I think they stalked his unconscious. He was
never free of them.'

'Did he always paint them, right from the beginning?'

'Like any artist, he took a while to find a style that suited him, and with the style came the subject. But that was a coincidence. His subject matter was influenced by a chance discovery he made at the Midi Fair in the 20s.'

Siân saw a change come over Vos. As he expounded further he became more animated. Boyish enthusiasm dislodged his macho charm and rendered him more likeable. His face shed its tough exterior and regained some of the innocence it might have had twenty years earlier. In his desire to find out what drove his artist hero, he also revealed something of his own motivation, which made him appear more wholesome. Plus, he had bedroom eyes.

'At the fair in Brussels,' he continued, 'he came across this cabinet of curiosities. Skeletons, anatomical models and a mechanical dummy made to look as if it was a woman breathing. The chest rose and fell. The young Delvaux kind of fell in love. In no time he was obsessed. For the rest of his career, more or less everything he would paint carried traces of the influence on him of this mechanical figure, this *Sleeping Venus*. Look.'

He reached into the inside pocket of his jacket and took out three postcards, two of which he placed on the table so that Siân could see them.

'This one,' he said, pointing to a reproduction of a painting in which a half-naked woman was approaching what appeared to be some kind of kiosk or booth, 'is *The Spitzner Museum*, which was where Delvaux found the Sleeping Venus of the title of this second picture, painted a year later. He did several versions of *The Sleeping Venus* – this one was not the first, but it has become one of his best-known paintings. It's owned by the Tate Gallery in London. Maybe you saw it there?'

Siân shook her head. 'It's *so* sensuous, *so* erotic, I'm *sure* I'd have remembered it.' Could it hurt to flirt, just a little? 'What about the third one?' she asked, pointing to the postcard that still lay face down.

'This is interesting.' Vos turned the card over. '*Street of Trams*, 19– what?' He turned it over again. '1938, 39.'

It was the first time Siân had known him have to check one of the dates. Usually he rattled them off. Was he a little bit rattled himself?

'You see this area here?' Vos pointed to a section of sky on the right of the picture.

'What am I supposed to be looking at?'

'This sky. If you look at it carefully you can see that he originally painted something else underneath.'

While Vos explained excitedly about the artist's change of mind regarding the form of the buildings where the topless women sat in the windows, Siân watched him and realised with a sudden sense of giddy panic that it was years since she had looked at Frank like this.

'I'm sorry,' she said abruptly. 'I have to go.'

'But look,' he was saying. 'Originally he painted two identical buildings with girls sitting in the windows. That's safe to assume, right? And then he took one of them away. He made that second house smaller, more homely. There's no one sitting at the windows. What was he trying to hide? That's what I want to know. Is it a real street or an imagined one?'

'Johnny, look—' Siân held her hands up to halt the flow of questions. 'I'm really sorry. I have to go. I shouldn't be here.'

She stood up in a hurry, catching her shin on the leg of the table and cursing. She darted between tables to the door, aware of faces turning in her direction like flowers towards the sun. Outside, it was the crescent moon that silvered the square with its sinister Delvaux light. She ran across the road without looking, thinking only of getting back to the hotel and Frank. She dived into a side street that was narrow enough to leap across from one pavement to the other, then out into a wide avenue, which she crossed in a daze, navigating by instinct. Something – the crescent moon? – made long grey shadows out of parked cars. A man emerging from a doorway startled her. She yelped and ran faster. She knew that somewhere over to her left was the river and that it flowed north to the sea. She also knew that she needed to head north-east and that Centraal Station was a surprisingly long walk from the old centre. As she ran, she looked in vain for taxis. She crossed over two more narrow streets and burst into a road that cut across on a diagonal. There were cars parked down either side. It was as she noticed the tramlines running down the middle of the street that she felt a sudden

powerful shove from behind and went flying towards the cobblestones.

Henk Van Rensbergen was pleased. Coming to Oostduinkerke
seemed to have been worth the detour: the Gauquié-Hôtel
looked extremely promising. As he shifted his weight from his left
buttock to his right and eased his centre of gravity over the window sill, he knew the hard work was done. He was in. Carefully,
he dropped down to the floor. The volume of dust raised suggested the building had been out of use at least six months,
perhaps longer.

As he straightened up and looked around, senses alert, Henk
felt the familiar rush of adrenalin begin to subside and give way
to the unique combination of childlike excitement and anxious
impatience that he always felt once he was inside an abandoned
building. Getting in was a game; being inside was serious. It
meant something. Henk might not be able to tell you what, but
he could *show* you. His photographs spoke for him. His camera
was checked and ready. Assuming the results were good enough,
he would upload the pictures when he got home and at some
point over the weekend his site, abandoned-places.com, was due
to be incorporated into the Urban Exploration webring, alongside sites dedicated to the Paris catacombs, Toronto subways, disused docks in Rotterdam and condemned mental hospitals in
upstate New York.

Henk had a headstart on many of his urban explorer peers
thanks to a loophole in the law, which meant that abandoned
buildings in Belgium were often relatively easy to get into. The
owner of a building who wanted to knock it down and redevelop
the land was obliged to wait until the building was practically
falling down. Doors, therefore, were often left unlocked so that
vandals, graffiti artists and architectural salvage freelancers could
come and go as they pleased.

The front door of the Gauquié-Hôtel *was* locked, but a window on the first floor gaped invitingly.

Henk stood dead still. What he wanted was proof that he was
alone in the building; he prided himself on being able normally
to gauge that within a minute of gaining admittance. He watched

and he listened and whether it went beyond that or not – into feelings and some kind of 'sixth sense' – he wouldn't have liked to say. For all his interest in abandoned spaces – his love for them, even – he was a rationalist. Scientific background. No nonsense. An airline pilot by day, he could hardly afford to have his head in the clouds.

The Gauquié was still and silent, yet for once Henk couldn't swear to it that the place was untenanted. There seemed to be some nagging persistence at the edge of his senses. Nothing he could see or hear, yet he couldn't confidently proclaim the building empty. Put it this way: if he were a fireman, he wouldn't feel comfortable leaving the premises. It disturbed him that he couldn't put his finger on what was wrong, yet there did seem to be something that didn't fit. Acoustical tricks were a commonplace in this kind of environment, but he hadn't heard a sound, despite the hotel's proximity to both the town and the North Sea. The eye was constantly deceived on these incursions, surrounded as it was by a forest of never-before-seen symbols and data, but the Gauquié was unusually short on distractions.

Unwilling to leave on the basis of a hunch, he began his tour, shutter finger ready. The structure was still in reasonable nick. The rooms, with their stripped mattresses and washbasins that had not yet been wrenched from the walls, could have been anything from ready-to-let accommodation in some out-of-season Black Sea resort to isolation rooms in a secure hospital on the northeast coast of England. As a pilot for the Belgian national carrier, before it went belly up, Henk flew all over Europe and took advantage of stopovers to explore the local semi-urban, post-industrial wastelands.

First he went down to check out the ground floor. Apart from the dust and a scattering of keys on the reception desk, it was clean. He fired off a few shots. In the cellar his flash revealed cobwebs in corners, a thicket of wine bottles, the outline of an imagined murder victim daubed blood-red on the white stone floor by some joker.

Two hotels were built in Oostduinkerke in 1900; one was the Grand Hôtel des Dunes. It went out of business. A local baker, Honoré Gauquié, bought the place in 1907 and a name change was in the offing. Henk sat in one of the windows on the third floor looking out at the road that led north out of the town. A hundred years ago, shrimp fishermen had travelled up and down that road on horseback to haul their nets along the shore.

Henk had a friend who, when visiting someone in their home, couldn't relax until he had been all over the house, a quick check in every room. Henk had asked him what was he looking for, the first time the guy did it to him. The friend just shrugged. Perhaps he'd done it once or twice and it had become a thing he always did. A habit. Superstition. Henk had started to do the same with abandoned buildings. He couldn't leave until he'd looked in every room. He had a few rooms yet to check in the Gauquié and something about the place was bothering him.

He was beginning to get the sense that it was time he was no longer there, but one corridor remained, half a dozen rooms. Simple twist on the doorknob, quick scan of the interior, on to the next. It was surprising in itself that so many of the doors were closed. More surprising, although with hindsight it shouldn't have been, was the fact that the last door in the line didn't yield. He'd encountered locked doors before – they came with the territory – but why this one? Why was he denied access to this particular room when the hotel had allowed him to step inside every other? What was special about it? He got down on his knees, but the keyhole was blocked on the other side. He tried inserting a key but the obstruction wouldn't be dislodged. He put his ear to the door, but heard nothing. He sniffed at the gap between door and floor, but could smell only dust and salt.

He stepped back, looked at the door. Room 438. It occurred to him, finally, to knock. Which he did. But there was no answer.

On the ground floor, he rummaged through the door keys lying on the counter – there were two dozen or so, not enough for all the rooms in the hotel – and failed to find one for room 438. He left the Gauqié, via the same window on the first floor, mystery unresolved.

13

ROOM 318

When the sun comes up above the line of trees to the east of the Lemaire Institute it strikes a series of broken windows along the corridor, shattering them afresh. Examining the door to Room 318 in the virgin light, you notice that the plate bearing the room number overlies another. Trying with your fingernails to prise it free, you tear the edge of a nail from its pad of flesh, and your curses dance a zigzag ricochet down the corridor towards the broken door and the fire escape beyond.

You go downstairs to the van and return with an oily canvas bag in which you keep a few basic tools. Wrenches, hacksaws, pliers. The rest of the plate comes off to reveal the original number of the room you've chosen to inhabit: 319. The next door along, also numbered 319, is revealed to have been the door to room 320. You work your way down the corridor, to be certain. Somewhere in the hospital, it would seem, a room has been hidden and a clumsy attempt made to cover up its existence.

You take a closer look at the playing card you had pinned to the door, the one you found on the floor of room 318, née 319 – the joker. That sneer on his face! That curl to his lip! You wonder if the joke's on you.

You rip the card off the door and tear it into halves, quarters, eighths, scattering the tiny pieces out of the nearest broken window (all the windows are broken). You watch the fragments float down three floors towards the overgrown hospital grounds, confetti for the already failed marriage between technology and nature.

You know you'll have to check all the room numbers on all the doors, but instead of getting straight to it you decide to save it for later. A chore in store. Something to look forward to. Your life has been all about waiting. But now there is pleasure in waiting, whereas once there was not. Long evenings spent waiting for your mother. Some nights it seemed you'd be waiting for ever.

It's 1970 and you are seven. Four unarmed student protesters have been killed by National Guardsmen at Kent State University, Ohio; Brazil have won the World Cup in Mexico, playing some of the best football ever seen; Harry Kümel's *Daughters of Darkness*, having had a slow start in Belgium, is soon a major hit (by Belgian standards) in seventy countries around the world. Your mother takes you to a fairground at Seraing, south of Liège. Drunk, she shoves you into a miniature carriage on a children's Ferris wheel. The door is bolted from the outside and the wheel judders. The moment it starts to revolve, you feel queasy. By the time it's reached the top, you want to be sick, and by the time it's arrived at the bottom again, you are. But the wheel doesn't stop. It goes round and round and you feel progressively more nauseous, motion sickness being no respecter of vomiting. Actually being sick counts for nothing. Icing on the cake. You look out of the wildly swinging car and see your mother down below apparently wrestling with an unknown teenager in a bomber jacket, their heads locked in a hideous mutual sucking vice. Her frizzy red hair aflame in the gaudy light, she breaks off to press another coin into the palm of the earringed man operating the Ferris wheel and you begin to grasp something. That this isn't strictly for your benefit. Something else is going on here. You want to catch your mother's eye and appeal to her, but to watch her with the man makes you feel even worse. To look out of the car and be aware of the lurching horizon makes you feel so unbearably dizzy you feel yourself sliding into panic. The only thing you can do to minimise the nausea is grab your ankles and jam your head between your legs and try to forget that the thing is going round. Just focus on the fact that it can't keep going for ever. Every time you sense the car has reached the

bottom, you think it's going to stop and the man with the earring will unbolt the gate and you will roll off and collapse on to
the grass, but it keeps going round, as if in a nightmare. You don't
want to look out, but you have to keep checking. More than anything you want to see your mother separating from the boy in the
bomber jacket and remonstrating with the earringed man until
he brings the wheel to a stuttering halt. But each time you do
sneak a look, the view is unchanged.

It's not as if you've never seen your mother with a strange
man. You see it every day on the street where she works. But
never someone as young as this, and kissing is not part of the deal,
as far as you understand what *is* part of the deal. You usually wait
further down the street. Kicking empty beer cans. Pretending
you're Belgium's Wilfried van Moer, or the Brazilian, Pele.
Rivelino. Carlos Alberto. Staring into shop windows when you
get bored of playing football. Expressionless mannequins staring
back at you. You learned all about blank stares, vacant looks, and
what desires seethed behind neutral exteriors, just as, in the case
of your mother and her co-workers at the business end of the
street, alienation was the hidden truth behind the mask of enthusiasm. The men trudging past, coal-ingrained hands hanging
motionless by their sides as they stopped to gaze in each window
– these were your father figures.

You remember trying to read by insufficient street lighting.
You read anything you could find – newspapers, industrial safety
pamphlets, an illustrated atlas of pulmonary diseases – in a bid to
better yourself. Vainly you tried to keep warm by scavenging cigarette butts from the gutter, cheap brands, and blowing on the
glowing embers. And draining the dregs of cans of Jupiler, bottles
of Maes. Even the beer was lousy. Why didn't they just bottle the
industrial froth off the nearby river and change the name on the
label from Maes to Meuse?

Your mother's face and the face of the boy in the bomber
jacket are still clamped to each other. The fairground lights spin
and blur. Hurdy-gurdy music grates and wails. You lurch forward
one final time, hit your head on the seat and black out.

You come to on the floor of the car, which is still revolving.
You get to your feet and look out. Your mother has gone. You

look again. It can't be true. It *is* true. Your mother has gone and the wheel is still going round.

When the Ferris wheel finally stopped going round and the man with the earring let you out, you stumbled around the emptying fairground looking for her, but she had gone. Home wasn't far away but it was dark now and there were shadows under every tree, dogs roaming freely. Whether out of sheer exhaustion or out of a desire to punish your mother, you curled up in a secluded hollow and somehow, despite the cold and the irregular susurrations of the night, fell asleep. Foxes sniffed at you as you slept, spiders spun their webs in your hair. A slug left its silvery trail across your bare legs. Anyone coming across you would have thought you dead. A part of you was. You woke to the sound of teeth chattering. You wrapped your arms around your body in an effort to get warm.

When you reached home, your mother was unconscious. Collapsed on the bed fully dressed, alcohol seeping from her pores, red hair rubbery with grease. On the wall above the bed was the strange picture of the nude women with the large pink bows that had been there, above your mother's bed, as long as you could remember. Beside her on the bed sat the blackened lobster that was the telephone, the receiver still gripped in your mother's right hand (her left, inexplicably, holds your dressing gown). The lead, which wouldn't have stretched from the phone point in the front room, had been ripped out of the wall. You realised how drunk she had been: drunk enough to unplug the phone and still try to use it, presumably intending to call the hospital or the police, to see if she could find her little boy. Maybe the dressing gown helped remind her who you were. But the drink had got the better of her. You recovered your dressing gown and put it on over your clothes, since you were still cold from sleeping rough. Then you extricated the phone, replacing the receiver and putting the device on the table in the front room where it normally sat, its bell untroubled for long periods at a time. Your mother knew a lot of people, but had few friends. You had only your mother – and the memory, increasingly dimmed, of your father.

You went into your own bedroom and sat on the edge of the

bed picking at the cord of your dressing gown with your ragged fingernails.

You take the tool bag back down to the van, then drive away from the institute down the rutted avenue to the main road, where you turn right and head for Brussels, then north towards Antwerp. You drive as fast as you can in the outside lane, like everybody else, but your van's a wreck, unable to shift like the BMWs and Audis nudging your exhaust pipe, full-beam headlights blinding you in the mirror. But you won't move across. No one moves across, unless to overtake. Let *them* move across. Let *them* drop to the middle lane. You used not to understand why they bothered building inside lanes on Belgian motorways – but now you do. They're for overtaking.

You slow down only on entering the city, where you get off the main boulevards and cruise the quieter avenues of the south side. You have an appointment, but you're early, so you drive around, changing direction at random. All the time you're driving, you're looking. Watching and looking. Looking at the road, watching the street.

Later, the drive back down the motorway. You take it more slowly. Carefully. Sitting in the middle lane. Last thing you want is a rear-end shunt. Anyone wants to overtake and the outside lane's full, they'll have to drop two and go inside. In the back of the van, all is quiet.

It was dark when you left Antwerp and darker still when you get back to Overijse. You roll the van up the track leading to the former sanatorium. Home again, home again.

It takes longer to unload the van than it had to load it. For the first night, a room in the basement, one already picked out, chosen for its security and seclusion. You barge through a swing door daubed 'Death Zone' by a previous visitor. The joke is lost on your precious cargo, the girl in the carpet over your shoulder. That might even have been her head hitting the door. Or her feet. You navigate by means of the torch strapped to your head. First door on the right. Push it open, using, once more, the rolled-up carpet. It makes no sound, apart from the bottom of the door scraping on the gritty floor. Broken tiles. Plaster. Dust. Beautiful, grainy dust. Sweet smell of decay. Mould, rot.

You drop the carpet, let it unroll. Make her secure. Soon you will begin the job of remaking her. Stripping away the imperfections. Making her into the ideal she once aspired to. Wish fulfilment. For you and her and the whole world, if it cares to witness.

14

LANGE NIEUWSTRAAT

The first thing Frank became aware of on waking was the pain in his head. It came and went with the rhythm of his pulse. He would have preferred it to be constant, then at least he wouldn't have been reminded every other second of what life could be like *without* the pain.

The second thing was that Siân's side of the bed was not only empty, but cold, unslept in. He sat up, listened, called her name. She was not in the room. He jumped out of bed, scanning every surface for a note, a clue. Nothing. Within two minutes he was dressed and checking through his pockets prior to leaving the room, aware of his heart beating alarmingly fast. The headache was getting worse.

One pocket yielded his mobile phone, which was dead. When would he learn? Until he had tried everything he wouldn't panic. Trying everything meant asking reception if a message had been left for him. Ignoring the lifts, he barged through the door to the stairs, then ran down five flights. Arriving in the lobby, he approached the desk and took several deep breaths while waiting for a member of staff to become free.

'Yes, sir?'

He asked if there was a message.

The clerk, a teenager, checked the pigeon-holes. As the boy ran his fingers along the dividing slats, Frank noticed a shaving cut on the side of the youngster's neck. Looking more closely, he also saw a small patch of bristles where, in his haste that morning, in his desire not to be late for work, he had missed a patch.

As the clerk turned back and Frank shifted his gaze from the shaving cut, he saw, in the boy's hand, a folded piece of paper. He saw his own hand reaching out to take it, then observed himself retreating from the desk to the shadows of the lobby before unfolding it.

Frank: Johnny V rang to invite us to dinner. (Must finally have realised you'd be a good person to get on his side.) Cargo, Leopold De Waelplaats. Opposite Museum of Fine Arts, apparently. Sorry for leaving note down here: couldn't find paper/pen in room and your mobile was not responding. Quelle surprise. Hope Kümel was good. See you later. Call, if you want. I'll have phone switched on (& charged up!).
Sxxx

Frank folded the note and placed it in his pocket. He pressed the call button for the lift. He wanted to be sure before he phoned either Siân or Vos or the police. Sure that she wasn't hiding somewhere in the room. That she hadn't passed out drunk in the wardrobe. So when he got back to the room it was to the wardrobe that he went first. Inside he found the bags of designer gear that Siân had hidden there on her return from shopping and before going out to meet Vos. He sat down on the edge of the bed and placed his head in his hands. She would have hidden them in the wardrobe so that he didn't see them and give her a hard time for wasting their hard-earned cash. He knew that she would have been planning to show him what she'd bought, but later and at her own speed and with the charm and humour that would ultimately win his approval for her purchases.

If she'd felt she could leave the bags in full view, he would have known, when he'd got back from seeing Kümel, that she'd been back also and had gone out again.

Frank dug out his charger and plugged in the mobile. He

dialled Siân's number. It rang, but she didn't answer. Eventually
the ringing tone stopped and an automated message told him
there was no answer. *Yeah, right. Thanks.* He tried it once more.
Same result.

He put the phone down with exaggerated care and looked
out of the window. He tried to run through the possibilities in
his mind, but the interference in his head was becoming more
severe. The gaps between the regular percussions of the blood in
his carotid artery were now filled by white noise.

There were two numbers he could think of to call. Vos or the
police. Calling Vos meant swallowing a certain amount of pride,
assuming Siân was with him. Assuming she'd spent the night with
him, and was safe. This was not a situation he wished for, but it
was preferable to most of the alternatives crowding his mind like
impatient passengers jostling on a platform, waiting for a train
that was never going to come.

He picked up the phone again and keyed in Vos's number. It
rang once and switched to his voicemail, requesting that the
caller leave a message. Frank hung up. He reached for the guide
book to find out what number to call for the police – 101.

Less than three hours later, Frank was standing on the good side
of a two-way mirror in police headquarters in Lange Nieuwstraat.
On the other side of the glass, Johnny Vos sat across a desk from
two detectives. One, a thickset, blond man in his mid-thirties with
a tired face but wearing a determined, don't-fuck-with-me
expression, folded his long, bejeaned legs under the chair beneath
him. He looked like Nick Nolte's lost Scandinavian son. The other
man was shorter, wirier, with a shaved head and a thick black
goatee; he wore a check shirt, untucked, and seemed full of sup-
pressed energy. Vos was looking pale and drawn. All three men
were smoking, each leaning towards the centre of the table from
time to time to flick ash. There was a sound feed from the interview room so that Frank could hear every word that was said. Vos,
virtually unrecognisable from Frank's interviewee in the Entrepôt
du Congo, was being polite and cooperative, which had surprised
Frank initially, but when he thought about it he realised it made
more sense.

He had admitted that he'd had a drink with Siân in Cargo the night before. He'd called Frank's hotel room, he said, to invite the couple to dinner, since neither of his two meetings with them had gone particularly well and he didn't want them to think ill of him since Frank was writing a piece for a newspaper and had gone to the trouble of coming over from England especially. Siân had answered the phone and had said that Frank was still out, and Vos had explained that he was at the restaurant and he'd got a table and since tables at Cargo were a relatively precious commodity he suggested she come over right away, leaving a message for Frank.

'Tell us again what happened next,' the fair-complexioned man instructed him, scratching his scalp through his disorderly brush of blond hair.

Johnny Vos breathed in through his mouth and out via his nose, then withdrew another cigarette from his softpack. The blond man offered him a light.

'I waited maybe a half-hour and then she showed up. On her own. She sat down. I got her a beer and we talked while waiting for Frank to arrive. Time passed – I don't know how long – and suddenly she got up, said she had to go. She left abruptly, on her own, as anyone who was in the place will tell you. That's it, that's all I know.'

'After she left, what did you do?'

'I smoked another cigarette, then I left too. It's kind of embarrassing sitting in a restaurant after someone walked out on you, you know?'

'So you were angry at her?'

'Not at all. Not a bit.'

'But you were embarrassed that she had, in your words, "walked out on you"?'

Vos took a drag on his cigarette before answering, and, when he did, he confined his response to a shrug.

'You were angry at her, weren't you?' asked the goateed man in the check shirt, breaking his tense silence.

'Did you want to teach her a lesson?' asked the other.

'Look, I didn't touch her. I didn't see her after she walked out of the restaurant. You said this would be just a couple of questions, very informal, and that I didn't need an attorney. It's beginning to feel kind of *not* like that. So either I call my attorney or we wrap this up.'

The two detectives looked at each other.

A third policeman, who was also observing the interview from behind the glass, leaned towards Frank.

'What do you think?' he asked Frank in a low voice. 'Is he telling the truth?'

'I don't know,' Frank admitted. 'Are there no other witnesses? What about the restaurant?'

'The manager's statement confirms what Vos is saying, that he had another cigarette and then left. It's what happened after that's unclear.'

Frank was starting to sweat. It was hot in the small, windowless office and Frank was aware of time passing. He and the police should be out there looking for Siân.

'Mr Vos,' the blond man said, 'you're not under arrest, but we could place you under arrest if necessary. It's just easier for everyone concerned if we run through these questions and then you can go.'

Vos looked irritated, but seemed to concede that the interview could continue.

'What did you do when you left the restaurant?'

'I went over to the river and just walked. I was thinking about my work, about the picture I'm shooting.'

'Yes, we know about that,' snapped the goateed man, his shaved skull shining under the fluorescent lights. He dropped his cigarette on the floor and squashed it with an expensive climbing shoe. 'What time did you get back to your hotel?'

'Bertin is pissed off,' remarked the third policeman to Frank. 'He was supposed to be going climbing in the Ardennes today. They cancelled his leave for this.'

Frank frowned and asked, 'What about the other guy? Does *he* want to be here? I mean, is *his* heart in it?'

'Dockx? He loves his job. He cares about it.'

Clearly, irony didn't translate.

'I don't know,' Vos was saying. 'Maybe an hour after leaving the restaurant. I didn't hurry. I was lost in thought. It's how I do my most productive work – taking a walk and thinking things over.'

'No one at the hotel remembers you returning,' the blond man, Dockx, pointed out.

'Why should they? It's a big hotel, anonymous. That's why I chose it. No one bothers you. You keep your room key when you go out. The place was perfect for me. I like to do my own thing.'

'We just want to know what that is, Mr Vos. Your thing.'

Dockx levelled his ice-blue eyes at Vos, who stared back, jaw muscles twitching.

Frank was close enough to Vos to see a bushy tuft of coarse hair protruding from his ear. Did he believe that this man had kidnapped Siân and had her hidden away somewhere? Wasn't it more likely that he'd caught up with her, they'd slept together and Siân was right now roaming the streets wondering how to undo what she'd done, how to come back to Frank and some-how make it all right? Then he remembered the unanswered mobile and his mind started picturing where it might be: tossed into a builders' skip, sinking into the mud at the bottom of the Schelde, or still tucked into the pocket of Siân's jacket, itself wrapped around her still, cold body.

'Two women murdered, both working on your film,' said Bertin, the angry climber, lighting another cigarette and offering one to his colleague but not to Vos. 'A third goes missing. What the fuck are we supposed to think?'

The third policeman shot Frank a glance and murmured, 'He is not happy.'

'Think what you like,' Vos retorted, losing his patience. 'Shouldn't you be questioning Harry Kümel instead of me? In any case, Ms Marchmont wasn't working on the movie.'

On top of everything else, it was weird for Frank hearing Siân described as Ms Marchmont. It was her name, but in these men's mouths it made her sound like someone else. He wished she was.

'A fine distinction,' Dockx said. 'Her boyfriend is publicising it.'

'It doesn't work like that,' Vos snapped.

'He's right,' Frank muttered.

'What?' the policeman asked him.

'Nothing. He's right, that's all,' Frank said. 'It doesn't work like that. I'm not working for him.'

'You don't think we should be questioning him?'

'I didn't say that.'

'You think we should be talking to this other guy, this Harry Kümel?'

'I can't believe Kümel's mixed up in this.'

'Why not?'

'I just saw him yesterday. He's a respected filmmaker, a public figure.'

'Then what's this guy Vos?' asked the detective.

'He's only made one film. He barely registers. No one really knows anything about him. He could be a freak. His first film was weird enough.'

Dockx's chair scraped against the floor. He made some kind of signal to his colleague and crossed to the door. He left the room and joined Frank and the third policeman, towering over both of them.

'We're going to let him go,' he said to Frank.

'You're what?' Frank spluttered.

'I think he's telling the truth. I don't think he saw her after she left. But we don't know, so we'll keep an eye on him. We've got officers searching his hotel room as we speak. If anything comes up, then we'll get him in again. I suggest you go back to your hotel, see if Ms Marchmont has turned up and check back with us later.'

Frank stared at the detective, incapable of a response.

'He could be more use to us out there, you see,' Dockx added before returning to the interview room.

'What does that mean?' Frank asked the third policeman.

'We can watch him,' the detective replied. 'See what he gets up to.'

Dockx reappeared beyond the two-way mirror.

'You're free to go, Mr Vos,' he announced. 'Thank you for coming in. If you remember anything, anything at all that might help us find Ms Marchmont, or anything that might help us with regard to the two murdered women, you'll call us.'

'Sure,' Vos agreed, getting to his feet.

Bertin didn't move, except to raise his head to make eye contact with Vos one last time, his bleak gaze betraying his evident suspicion. Vos and Dockx headed out of the room, their footsteps receding down the corridor. The third policeman led the way out of the small office, but Frank stayed put. Bertin was now facing the two-way mirror and staring in Frank's direction. Frank assumed he couldn't be seen, but the detective seemed to know exactly what he was looking at, his cold grey eyes drilling through the glass partition and into Frank's.

15

TRANS-EUROP-EXPRESS

As Johnny Vos left police HQ on Lange Nieuwstraat, he had a discreet look around for the car he knew would have been detailed to follow him. An unmarked blue Audi was parked across the street. Two occupants. Engine running. He started walking. Let them tail him at five miles an hour if they really wanted to.

He walked to his hotel on Groenplaats, making no effort to conceal his destination. Once in the foyer, however, he went straight up to his room where he grabbed a few things and left again inside two minutes, taking the service lift down to the first floor. Switching to the fire escape, he left the hotel by the side entrance, his Yankees baseball cap pulled down low over his eyes. He quickly blended into the crowds clogging up the Meir.

The city's main shopping street, the Meir was the main link between the old town and the fringes of the Diamond Quarter. Vos walked to Centraal Station and boarded the first train for Brussels. Picking up a discarded copy of *Le soir*, he tried to hide behind it while keeping an eye on who was boarding the train, and he found that it wasn't quite as straightforward as they made it look in the kind of movies other directors tended to make.

Satisfied he'd shaken his tail, he put the paper down as soon as the train started to move. He watched four- and five-storey buildings edge past on the right-hand side, among them the Diamantclub and the Diamantbeurs. He felt a subtle uplift inside his chest as the train snaked out of the city, although he was surprised at how easy it had been to give the police the slip and so cautioned himself to remain on his guard. As soon as they realised he'd left Antwerp he'd climb a couple of places on their list of suspects, possibly becoming a target nationwide, but that was too bad: he had to get out of the city, away from the heat, in order to think about the film. That had to be his top priority, even if he risked arrest.

Among the items he'd gathered from his hotel room was a Walkman. A contact in London, Gareth Sangster, when he'd heard Vos was making a film in Belgium, had recommended cult Belgian band 48 Cameras for the soundtrack. Sangster was a journalist who specialised in fringe magazines funded by arts organisations, the kind of publications that would be most likely to give space to someone like Vos, but the American was a realist and knew that he had to get into the broadsheets. You could be a cult figure all your life and never step out of the shadows. Not for the first time, however, Vos wished it had been Sangster who'd been sent over to interview him, and not Frank Warner, who seemed to have brought nothing but trouble.

He slipped the 48 Cameras tape into the machine and pressed play. Ethereal guitars, sombre drum beat, the occasional etiolated flourish in the higher registers. It wasn't a million miles away from what he had imagined might work for the film. He'd never intended to use the music of Delvaux's day, whether string quartets or early ragtime. On the tape a man's voice could now be heard, melancholy and pregnant with foreboding, reading strange texts. They weren't lyrics, exactly. Perhaps they were poems, yet they told stories, which verse, in Vos's experience, rarely did. Whatever they were, Vos found the combined effect of music and words hypnotic; he leaned back, eyes closed, and, as the train sped towards Brussels, he let the work conjure him far from the problems that had started to dog him in Antwerp.

As his thoughts wandered, however, he realised that, because he hadn't seen it when scanning the contents of his hotel room, he hadn't collected his notebook.

'Fuck,' he said, rather more loudly, because of the Walkman, than he might have intended.

★

Frank left Lange Nieuwstraat in a slow swirl of panic. Having relied on the police to interrogate Vos until he broke down and told them where they would be able to find Siân safe and well, he was now cast adrift. He looked this way and that, as if expecting to catch sight of the back of Siân's head, or the departing profile of Vos. Where would he be now? How far ahead? In which direction?

He pulled out his phone and tried both numbers again. If Vos answered, he would beg him to reveal what he knew. He would absolve him from all blame, they'd work out a deal. He didn't care, he just wanted Siân back. No one answered: neither Vos, nor Siân. Already, what he desired was for Siân to be with Vos and for the killer to be somebody else. Even if it meant she'd never come back to him, he wanted her to be alive. Alive and free. Alive and chained to a radiator was no good, not if death was all she had to look forward to. He'd withdrawn himself from the equation, despite the fact that without her he was nothing. His writing, what was it? A comfort blanket, something to do while she was at work. From being the most important thing in his life it had suddenly switched to being of no significance. He didn't care if he never saw another film again. He just wanted to know that Siân was OK. He'd trade it all for that.

At Groenplaats he looked around, wondering if the police might have followed him as well as Vos. There was a blue Audi fifty metres away. Vos's tail, perhaps? He entered the hotel and went immediately to the left, away from the desk, towards a row of house phones.

'Hi,' he said, having called the desk. 'I was just talking to Mr Vos and we got cut off. Could you just remind me of his room number, so I can call him back?'

His breezy confidence worked. The girl gave him the room number. Frank thanked her and hung up, then walked around to the lifts, taking the first one straight up to the fourth floor. He listened outside Vos's door for a moment, hearing only the thump of his own heart. He knocked on the door and stood back, then knocked again. He looked up and down the corridor, and, seeing that it was empty, shoulder-charged the door, which failed to give way, so he kicked it as hard as he could. Splintering, the door swung open. Frank moved inside quickly and closed the damaged door behind him.

He leaned back against the door to catch his breath, allowing his eyes to rove around the room. The bed, a desk, the bedside table and parts of the floor were covered with books, papers, maps, postcards, videotapes, notepads. On closer inspection, most of it related directly to Delvaux. Frank picked up a magazine open at an interview with the actress Asia Argento, daughter of Italian horror film director Dario. His eye was caught by a nude photograph of the actress in which she was showing off a tattoo on the lower part of her stomach. The tattooist had copied the female figure in Delvaux's painting *Chrysis*, adding a pair of angel's wings. Frank skimmed the text.

'When I was a little girl,' Argento was quoted as saying, 'my mother had a poster of a painting, I think it was called *The Public Voice* or something, with a naked woman lying on a sofa and three ladies behind her. It fascinated me. The armpit, the nudity, the light. It moved me in a very dark way.'

Frank put down the magazine and picked up instead a leaflet and a couple of postcards, slipping them into his inside pocket. He got down on his hands and knees and looked under the bed, where he found a small black notebook, which he also took. He left the room, closing the door behind him as best he could, and slipped like a shadow out of the hotel.

He walked directly to Koningin Astridplein and checked for messages – there weren't any – before going up to his and Siân's room. He put the mobile phone on to charge and sat on the edge of the bed. He called the police only to learn that there was no news and that, they somewhat hesitantly admitted, they weren't exactly sure where Vos was. Kümel had been into the station, they told him, and in their view he was telling the truth when he said he knew nothing about the murders and nor did he know anything about a missing girl.

'It's not him. I told you that,' Frank said before hanging up.

From his pocket he took out one of the items liberated from Vos's hotel room. It was a leaflet produced by the Paul Delvaux Museum in St-Idesbald. He remembered finding the museum's site while trawling for Delvaux references on the web. He stared out of the window at Centraal Station as he weighed the leaflet in his hand, tapping it against his thumb. Everything in Vos's room had pointed to a genuine, indeed obsessive, interest in Delvaux. Nothing that he had seen had suggested that the occupant was capable of the abduction and murder of women.

He flicked through the black notebook. Pages of scrawled notes on the Delvaux film, from Vos's insights into the meaning of the paintings to his plans for blocking out particular scenes. He put the notebook down.

What should he do? What *could* he do?

As he stared at the majestic dome of Centraal Station he recalled a film, Alain Robbe-Grillet's *Trans-Eurep-Express*, in which the lead character, Elias, played with characteristic cool by Jean-Louis Trintignant, had boarded a train in the Gare du Nord, Paris, bound for Amsterdam, but had disembarked at Antwerp's Centraal Station. In keeping with Robbe-Grillet's narrative concerns, Elias found himself shunted from one fictional track to another: one minute he was running drugs, the next he was a diamond-smuggler. Frank considered the options open to anyone leaving Centraal Station by train. Basically, south to Brussels or doubling back via Antwerpen-Oost, where the first body had been found, to go north to Antwerpen-Dam and then on past the docks towards Holland. He wished he could search in all directions at once: Holland, the Belgian coast, Brussels, Wallonia. Merely considering how close also were the borders with Germany and France made him feel suddenly nauseous. Spreading out the map of Europe in his mind, he had to admit that Siân could be anywhere. What point was there in moving even fifty metres in any one direction if it took him fifty metres further away from her actual location?

He looked at the station. The great dome seemed to float, as if untethered by its multifarious potential, and yet the backside of his trousers remained stuck to the bed, woven through the fabric, the soles of his shoes nailed to the floorboards. Indecision and a growing sense of powerlessness rooted him, and as he sat there the sky changed colour and the telephone did not ring. The ruins of the day collapsed into the embers of the evening, the ruby-red sky over the Diamond Quarter promising a fine day to follow.

But, first, the night.

It was a dark night. For Frank, the darkest. He stayed in the hotel room, sitting on the bed, until all the natural colour had been forced from the sky and only artificial light remained, caught in a canopy of nicotine-coloured cloud like cigarette smoke trapped by a pub ceiling.

'Now it's dark,' he thought, unclenching his hand and straightening his fingers. The tension flowed out of him, but the relief would be momentary. Five minutes later he was outside, wired as a caffeine freak, navigating by sixth sense. He crossed and recrossed the Ring, plunged into unnamed side streets, skittered over tramlines. He entered the red light district unexpectedly and wondered if he was merely proving that part of Freud's theory of the uncanny, that a man stranded without a map in an unknown city will eventually fetch up in the red light district, or if there was another logic to his arriving in the Schipperskwartier. It was, after all, where most lost girls in the city would end up. As he trailed past window after window, gazing at oriental adolescents squeezed into blue velvet and black leather, he began to worry that in addition to losing Siân he had also mislaid his mind. Siân couldn't be here, so why keep on looking? She could still be alive, so why waste time? The echo of his footfalls became faster, the appearance of his reflection in neon-lit windows more fleeting. His hair lifted from his forehead, sweat cooling on his scalp. Heads turned as casual punters, girls in windows, disinterested passers-by all watched the running man.

He left the red light district, heading south, and didn't stop until the street opened out into a little square. On his left was St Paulus' Church. A pointlessly remembered guide book fact leaped to the front of his mind: when the church had caught fire in 1968, prostitutes from the red light district had helped to save the paintings within, works by Rubens, Jordaens, Van Dyck.

This image, of sex workers divorced from their normal context, reminded him of the woman he and Siân had seen in the café near Moriaanstraat. The café could be no more than five minutes' walk away. He turned left. When he reached the bar, he discovered it was not only empty, but closed. Moriaanstraat looked quiet. No visible police presence. He stood outside the house he and Siân had seen the blonde woman enter. Blinds were drawn at the windows, but a few lights burned. Frank thought about knocking on the door, but left without taking action.

He found himself outside the jazz bar where he and Siân had downed a few beers on the evening of her arrival. Moments later he was inside. Then at the bar ordering a beer, the same beer he'd drunk that night. Westmalle Tripel. It didn't taste so good this time, but he drank it all the same. On the dais at the end of the bar a jazz trio were preparing to start their set. He ordered another beer. The piano player leaned closer to the microphone: 'We'd like to start with a number by the late, great Thelonious Monk: "Round Midnight".' Frank looked at his watch. It was five to twelve. His mouth twisted into a bitter smirk. By the time the trio had finished mauling Monk, it was ten past and Frank was on to his third beer. When he left the bar it was like stepping on to the open deck of a ship in heavy seas, the cobbled street swaying and plunging beneath his feet. With extraordinary difficulty he made his way the short distance around the side of the cathedral to the Grote Markt, where he staggered from one bar to the next, flinging open the doors one by one and sticking his head inside each smoky fug, blearily, uselessly hoping to spot Siân among the crowds, who barely glanced his way. From the Grote Markt to Groenplaats was no more than two minutes' walk, but Frank took considerably longer to cover the ground. He walked straight – or as straight as he could – to the blue Audi still parked, conspicuously, out front and, since its occupants were both looking the other way, rapped on the window with his knuckles.

The two men swapped looks of concern, which evaporated when they buzzed the window down and Frank's beery breath drifted inside the car.

'Why don't you stick a f-fucking blue light on top, you f-fucks? I mean, you might as well. What is this – undercover? Christing fuck! *I* could do better than this.'

Frank pushed himself away from the car and negotiated his way out of the empty square as if it were a packed restaurant.

Behind him the only noise from the blue Audi was of the window being wound back up. Not that he'd have cared if the officers, whom he hadn't recognised from his visit to the police station, had tumbled out of the car and pinned him up against the hotel. In fact, he might have preferred it, since it would have demonstrated a level of commitment that seemed to be lacking. Did they think Vos was still in the hotel or – even more pointlessly – were they waiting for him to come back?

As soon as Frank got back to Astridplein, despite extreme weariness and disorientation, he packed his and Siân's stuff and checked out of the Plaza. He left no note. There was no need. If Siân could get to a phone, she would call his mobile. The police had his number. On the adjacent side of the square, but at the opposite end of the accommodation scale from the Plaza, was the Hotel Miro. With its single door still open and a harsh, fluorescent light burning at three o'clock in the morning, it looked ideal. Frank didn't know how long he'd need the room, but the guy at the desk didn't care. Frank could stay there a week for the cost of one night at the Plaza, whose luxury now seemed neither appropriate nor affordable. He crashed out for three hours.

By eleven o'clock the next morning he was on a train to Brussels, trying to convince himself it didn't matter that he'd lost an entire day. Constantly he folded and unfolded the leaflet for the Paul Delvaux Museum that he'd picked up in Johnny Vos's hotel room. Instead of reading it, for what would have been the sixth or seventh time, he stared blankly out of the window. He was trying to get into Vos's head, trying to work out if he was wasting his time following him. Did he really believe Vos had Siân or knew where she was? The answer was he didn't know. But what other leads did he have?

As he leafed through the black notebook, his mobile kept ringing. The number that came up each time was that of the newspaper's switchboard. On each occasion, he broke the connection. He didn't know what to say to them, couldn't handle that particular problem on top of everything else. He switched the phone from ring to vibrate and stowed it in his jacket pocket.

At the Gare Centrale in Brussels, Frank checked the timetables. There was a train to Ostend in eight minutes. Waiting, he paced like a prisoner. The platforms at the Gare Centrale were underground, where scant effort had been made to match the art deco charms of the station's upper levels. There was a fetid air of desperation, of people anxious to get away. It was less like the peaceful crossroads of Europe in the third millennium than the shattered capital of some totalitarian state stuck in the middle of the previous century, its defeated people fleeing underground as gunfire tore apart the streets above. The low platforms meant that when the train rumbled in, it towered over those waiting to get on.

The train was already three-quarters full and those boarding more than filled it. He found a seat, but was hemmed in by mothers and children standing in the aisle. The women sought to make eye contact with anyone who had a seat and looked as if they might be soft enough to give it up. This train thing wasn't going to work. Frank got to his feet and forged a path through the crowd, reaching the doors as they started to close. He squeezed through as the rubber flanges snapped together behind him.

On the station concourse, two flights up, he stood in line at a car hire desk.

The Belgians might drive like the world was about to end, but at least it meant they got places quickly. It took Frank less than an hour to reach the coast. Under any other circumstances he would have wanted to have a closer look at Ostend. Maybe later. For now, he kept driving, the North Sea glimpsed on his right between one parade of shops and the next, then hiding behind high-rise apartment buildings. Every two or three kilometres he would pass an old building, invariably on the side of the road furthest from the sea, its owners presumably having resisted ever increasing offers to sell up and see their home bulldozed. Each one was surrounded by vacant land, where the old had already been cleared away to make way for the new; in Brussels and Antwerp, developers sat on their arses, chewing bitter cigars to leafy mulch as they waited for people to die.

Middelkerke, Middelkerke-Bad, Westende-Bad, Westende. The small towns and their attendant resorts passed the car on either side. At Lombardsijde-Bad, Frank was forced to turn ninety degrees inland in order to cross the River Ijzer, then, via Nieuwpoort, ninety degrees back towards the sea again. Oostduinkerke, Oostduinkerke-Bad, then signs to Veurne, where Delvaux had spent the last twenty-five years of his life. Finally, after driving through Koksijde-Bad, Frank came to St-Idesbald. He nearly missed the sign to the museum, but swung off the main road just in time.

He slowed to a crawl as the car entered a maze of narrow lanes within which low houses crouched behind high hedges. The houses were all painted white with red roof tiles. The sky was blue and very clear. The car made almost no noise. Frank had the strange feeling that he had taken a side road out of the real world. He half-expected one of Delvaux's ghostly nudes to come sleep-walking around the next corner. Instead, he spotted a tiny, empty car park.

The museum was a short walk away down another narrow lane identical in all but name, for this was Paul Delvauxlaan. Frank pushed open the little gate and walked down the path to the museum building, which was low and whitewashed exactly like its neighbours. A woman at a window registered his presence, pressing a button to release the door.

One woman stood behind a desk. Another, opposite, stood in the doorway leading to the gallery. Both wore neutral expressions. Had they been naked, it would have been a perfect Delvaux tableau. Frank abandoned his plan to come straight out and ask if they had recently had a visitor fitting Vos's description. Instead he bought a ticket from the woman behind the desk and turned to enter the gallery, the other woman standing aside to let him pass. The aloofness of their attitude was perhaps inevitable in a world that, in general, valued Delvaux little despite the fact that in his homeland he was revered as a great artist. They perhaps had a right to be suspicious.

The gallery was cool, low-ceilinged, quiet as a church. Spectral images hovered in the dimness picked out by clever lighting. The woman hung back but Frank was aware of her eyes on him as he moved slowly from one painting to the next. There was no comparison between flicking through a Delvaux monograph and being in the presence of the work itself. The mood of Delvaux's world was infectious. Frank remained aware of the woman hiding in the shadows, but she no longer distracted him. The paintings were full of detail that should have been disturbing – surreal juxtapositions, anguished expressions, teasing subtexts related to sexuality, neurosis, psychopathy – but there was no threat, no sense of menace. Instead the effect was to offer solace, to enchant. It was like being in a dream, yet with the awareness of being there. Frank felt himself relaxing for the first time in days, lulled by the languor in the women's reclining bodies.

In addition to dozens of paintings, the museum contained items from the artist's studio, even model trains from his personal collection. A ramp led down to a basement level where there were drawings, watercolours and more paintings. The woman continued to shadow Frank.

He stood in front of a mock-up of an artist's studio.

'His studio,' Frank said, without looking round.

'An exact reproduction.'

He turned round. Unexpectedly, the woman smiled.

Back in the lobby, where one wall was dominated by postcards of Delvaux's work, Frank asked the woman if they had been visited, in the last twenty-four hours, or at some point prior to that, by an American.

'Guy with long hair, going grey,' he added. 'Baseball cap with a New York Yankees logo.'

One woman looked at the other; both shook their heads.

'It's very important,' he said. 'My girlfriend is missing. I think he may know where she is.'

'I'm sorry,' the woman behind the desk said quietly.

'Look,' Frank said, 'I'll write down my number. If he comes in, please, *please*, call me.'

He handed a card to the woman behind the desk, who took it without making any promises, but Frank didn't press it any further. He thanked the women and left.

Frank returned to Ostend, parked the car in a side street and walked down to the seafront. A semi-circular viewing point, with benches and a telescope, protruded from the promenade over the

beach. Frank gripped the iron rail with both hands and received
the fresh breeze on to his face, allowing it to brush away tears of
frustration and helplessness. He lowered his head and opened his
eyes. The beach was a twenty-foot drop, the sand soft and hillocky.
He shook his head, looked up. The beach was practically deserted
in both directions. Over to the right, near the casino, where Frank
recalled that Delvaux had painted a mural, he saw a tall man carrying a young child on his shoulders. The child wore a red coat.
Directly ahead of him there was no one at all. The tide was out,
the sea distant. Over to the left, level with the colonnade in front
of the Hotel Thermae, where Kümel had filmed the exteriors for
Daughters of Darkness, stood a solitary figure close to the water's
edge. From this distance it was impossible to tell if it was male or
female.

Frank took a handful of change from his jeans pocket. He
looked at the slot. It requested 20 Belgian francs. The new cur-
rency in his hand was useless.

He looked again at the figure on the waterline. He decided it
was female, but the size was wrong. Siân was both shorter and
slighter.

He waited ten minutes, but she didn't move. He looked at her
one last time before turning away from the sea and walking back
to the car. He half-turned the key in the ignition and the radio
came on. He didn't speak much Flemish, but he heard the name
'Harry Kümel', then 'Orson Welles'. Welles had starred in
Kümel's third film, *Malpertuis*. Frank looked at his watch. It was a
minute past the hour. He was listening to the top item on the
news. In among the unknown gutturals, he recognised enough to
realise, with a sudden painful squirt of saliva into his mouth and
an unpleasant weightless sensation in his gut, that a third body
had been found, accompanied by the next video in the series.

He reached into his jacket pocket for his phone, which was
still on vibrate. The readout on the screen indicated a missed call
and gave an Antwerp number. Checking his call records, he saw
that the police had rung four times, presumably trying to reach
him before they released the news to the media.

Still holding the phone, he looked up and stared at the windscreen. He studied the pattern left by the wipers, the semi-circles

of dirt that the wipers couldn't reach. He looked closely at the rubber strip around the edge of the windscreen. He stared until his eyes started to hurt.

He opened the car door and got out. He closed the door carefully, then, without locking the car, walked in the direction of the seafront. He walked down the steps on to the sand. He was conscious of the wind on his face, first drying the tears on his cheeks and then producing more. The tall man and his child had disappeared. The only other person on the beach was the woman he had seen before. She was still standing very close to the water's edge. The beach was broad and flat. A few patches of corrugated furrows glittered with captured seawater. There were scattered shells. Frank kept going, splashing through puddles as he walked towards the distant figure. He got to within twenty metres of the woman before she turned around.

Part Seven

THE MAN IN THE STREET

16

TIMECODE

The first thing she was aware of was the darkness. Total darkness. She waved her hand in front of her face and there was nothing to see. She touched her fingers to her eyes to ascertain if she had been blindfolded. She had not.

She remembered being struck and hitting the surface of the road. After that, nothing. She had been running from the restaurant where she had met Johnny Vos. Running back to the hotel, back to Frank, but she hadn't made it.

The darkness was disorienting, alarming, threatening. It wasn't just that it was night: it was darker than that. Where was she? In a windowless room? In the countryside? Why couldn't she move her left arm? Using her right hand, she investigated. Her left wrist was attached to some kind of pipe or rod. Her head also ached and she had a sore throat.

She must have slept or lost consciousness, because she had no memory of being brought into whatever place this was. Had she been conscious at all during the ride here? Was she even correct in assuming she'd been moved in a vehicle? Could she have been dragged, instead, into a cellar next to where she had fallen? Perhaps her arm had become stuck accidentally and she was only that simple realisation away from freedom, from Frank. She tugged at the left arm, but whatever was holding it held it fast. Should she call out? No, because if she was someone's prisoner, she didn't want to see him until she was ready.

Maybe there was no gaoler. Could she have lost her sight in an accident? No. As she stared into inky space and her eyes slowly became accustomed to the conditions, she realised that the darkness was not uniform. Some patches were darker than others. But she lacked perspective and focus. The areas of relative brightness were unstable, unreliable: if she stared directly at them, they disappeared. Only by looking away could she make them come back. She felt the ground around her with her free hand. It was gritty, damp. Her fingers ghosted across a small stone and latched on to it. It had a sharp edge. She kept it in the palm of her hand, a talisman. Breathing in through her nose, all she could smell was her own sweat, her fear. She strained to listen but couldn't hear anything beyond an occasional drip. There was no hum of traffic, no chittering of insects, nor any birdsong. If there was a gaoler, he was keeping quiet, or staying far away. If it was the dead of night he could be asleep. The sweat running down her back made her shiver. It was cold. She thought of Marc Dutroux, which was about as bad as it could get, and she admitted to herself: yes, it could easily be that bad. Dutroux himself might be locked up, but the fact that his case didn't come to trial more quickly demonstrated Belgium's inability to come to terms with its dark side. There could be many more out there like Dutroux.

Siân found herself suddenly beset by unwanted images of the dungeons Dutroux had constructed in his cellar. Images seen briefly in the papers, on the news, but which had obviously made an impression. Unremembered until now. The rough-hewn walls, the yellow bars. She pictured his greasy hair, his sparse moustache and straggly beard. She imagined someone like him bending over her. His breath would be stale, sour. No one to tell him to rinse. A loner. She knew the profile; she watched the shows, saw the movies. No job, no routine. Or a routine of his own devising, one based on paranoid fantasies. Watching women, masturbating until friction drew blood. Self-disgust, expiation. Action, target, achievement. As much a job of work as an existentialist act. Suffering? Suffering all round. Part of the process.

Suddenly a thought struck her that she found immensely comforting, despite all of the above. Also out there somewhere was Frank and he would be looking for her. He could be an obstinate bastard when he put his mind to it. Getting the BFI to agree to his doing a BFI Modern Classic on Harry Foxx's film *Nine South Street* had been by no means straightforward. Nor had it been easy to make the switch from staff writer to freelancer, but he had stuck at it and made it pay in the end. Rescuing his girl-friend from a locked cell in the middle of fuck knows where might not be the logical next career step, but, if it was a question of character, she had a chance at least because Frank was not a quitter.

Then she thought about the early days and the other women. Indeed, for a long time she'd been one of them. Frank's wife Sarah might have been dead, but he was still married to her ghost. Then she remembered Yasmin, one of Frank's exes. Frank had been a little reluctant to put Yasmin fully in the picture regarding Siân, and it had taken an ultimatum to make it happen. But still, Frank had finally acted and since that time Siân had never had any cause to doubt his commitment. She knew he'd be looking for her, not settling for whatever efforts the police might be making.

She thought about her parents and, for once, was glad that her mother was not around to be going through this. Her father would receive scant comfort from his miserable neighbours in Clacton-on-Sea. She pictured his white stubble, his pinprick pupils, irises the colour of washed-out denim. The tip of his tongue moistening his lips. She hadn't liked to be kissed by him, not on the mouth. She felt a sudden hot shudder of guilt at that and then another for the infrequency of her visits to Clacton. She would put that right, she made herself promise, if she got out of this mess. She swallowed dryly, her throat still painful.

Now she wanted the man to come. Whoever he was, however terrible, she wanted to see his face. She needed to know where she was being held and by whom, and until she did, she was help-less. Maybe it was some kid who'd flipped and might just as easily flip back. She needed to know how bad it was. She needed to know before she could begin to think her way out. And until she could begin to think her way out, she felt as if she might be stuck there for ever. It was at this point that she put a name to the increasingly sharp pain at the back of her throat: raging thirst.

With difficulty she turned to face the wall and, using the stone she'd found on the floor, started to scratch her name on to the brickwork.

It's 1971 and you are eight. Idi Amin seizes power in Uganda, initiating a reign of terror that will last eight years; East Pakistan becomes Bangladesh, starting a war of independence in which millions will die; Harry Kümel's third full-length feature, *Malpertuis*, a big-budget international co-production starring Orson Welles and Susan Hampshire, bombs. Your mother is out every night. If she's working the street, she may take you with her; if she's calling at different addresses, you're left at home. Either way, she's back by the time you wake up in the morning.

At school you read and listen, but trust no one. You take everything in but give nothing back. Weekends, increasingly, you're left to your own devices. Either your mother's out with men or she's in her bedroom, on her own, but lost to you. You sit and stare at the jagged glass that still hasn't been removed from the fanlight above her door that was broken three years ago. You know your mother puts something in her arm, but you don't know what it is. You understand enough to know that when she's got some she's OK, and when she hasn't she's in a bad way. You're just beginning to make the connection between the long hours she works and the acquisition of whatever it is she puts in her arm. It seems to be taking the place of food, since she eats little and rarely. Weight is falling off her, but when she's got the stuff to put in her arm, she doesn't mind. At other times, you can't even get her to talk to you. You prepare your own meals (she keeps the cupboards stocked, usually by giving you a 100 franc note and sending you out to the shop).

Then one morning she's not there when you wake. It's a Saturday, no school, so you sit in your dressing gown picking at the cord and reading a book while you wait for her to show up. She doesn't. By evening, when there's still no sign of her, you go out. The red light district is a ten-minute walk. She's not there. No one's seen her since the night before and nor can anyone remember who she went off with, if indeed she went off with anybody. They look concerned, but they've a living to earn as well. You feel fairly certain that if you lay down in the street one or two among them might take you in and make you their responsibility, but you're not there yet.

You go back home and wait. Still she doesn't show. Night follows day and day follows night and the food is running out. There's no one to call or if there is you don't know the number. You consider going to the police or the hospitals, but you have some idea of how much sympathy you might get as the child of someone who does what your mother does. You have heard about foster parents and children's homes and they don't sound like the answer.

On the Monday you leave the house in time to go to school, but instead keep walking until you hit the river, which you walk beside, crossing and recrossing it until you no longer know which side you are on. Looking back, you wonder if this was deliberate. Did you want to lose yourself? Could an eight-year-old have such a sophisticated desire? You left the river and became aware that the ground was sloping upwards. You climbed until Liège and its river were beneath you. Ahead of you was a strange-looking building, something like a castle in one of the fairy tales your mother hadn't read you when you were younger. It loomed up from the wooded hillside, its windows black holes, some of them broken. The ground levelled out. Trees closed in. You weren't sure which way was back, but had a sense you wanted to return. You heard a twig snap, spun round. And round again. You started running, heart pounding. You tripped and fell. Rolling, somersaults, hitting a fallen tree. You'd found the slope again, or it found you, and then you were no longer rolling but falling, through a clatter of dead branches and fallen leaves and cut by thorns and over and over you went until you finally came to a sudden, violent stop by a hole in the ground into which you could easily have fallen. Hurting, you pick yourself up and walk around the hole. Twenty metres away is a much bigger hole, one you can walk inside, like a cave. The walls are lined with crossed wooden beams, making you think of the skeleton of a whale. Props support the roof. The light reaches right into the back of the cave, although the cave doesn't actually seem to have a back, and so you keep on walking. You trail your hand against the wall and it comes away black, as black as your father's coal-ingrained fingers as they reached down to touch your cheek.

When the light goes, it does so suddenly. Looking back, you see the tunnel has turned a corner and you make out a sliver of daylight like a crescent moon. Tired, thirsty and hungry, you lie down. Sleep overtakes you. When you wake up, you are aware that something has changed. It's darker and there's a new smell, sharper than the coal and damp earth you had become used to. A form detaches itself from the darkness, a figure in rags and abandoned miner's boots. Bends over you. His face is black, hair long and matted, eyes white and bloodshot. He opens his mouth to speak and you get a blast of dragon's breath. He tells you he doesn't want to hurt you, he'll look after you. Your screams bounce off the tunnel walls, hurting your ears. Eventually you stop whimpering and follow him.

Deeper inside the mountain, the man has made a lair inside a twisted metal cage – the miners' lift, he tells you, for getting down to the coal face. He gives you a plastic cup filled with spring water, a choice of spoilt fruit, stale crackers. A feast. Because he's been kind to you and because you sense you might need his help to get out of here and find your mother, you don't object when he puts his hand on your leg and gently strokes it like your father might once have done. Nor do you wriggle out of reach when his hand slips up under your T-shirt and uncurls in the small of your back.

I stuck Penny's postcard, *La voie publique*, to the wall above the computer. On the rare occasions that I raised my head from the screen, the train appeared to be coming out of the wall towards me, but Delvaux was subtler than his compatriot Magritte.

I was logged on to the Last House site permanently, attracted not by the occasional flash of flesh, but by the chance to see Eva. She was relatively relaxed in front of the cameras, but I knew that she knew they were there, whether she showed it or not. I wanted more. I wanted something more erotic than rehearsed nonchalance, something more arousing than practised indifference. I wanted the visceral thrill of total unselfconsciousness.

I could have arranged to see her, either at the Last House or elsewhere, but I liked the intercession of a screen. I finally admitted to myself that I found it easier to see her and not be seen *by* her, than to spend time with her one to one. It wasn't only easier: covert surveillance gave me more pleasure. But still I was frustrated. I needed more. Thoughts of Penny came, too, but they did not distract me. Penny had gone, I realised. Whether she ever came back was no longer an issue. I had moved on.

I stood on the corner of Moriaanstraat and Oude Waag, a mobile phone held to my ear in case anyone was paying any attention. I wasn't talking; there was nobody on the line. A short block away from the Last House, I was watching the door. I loitered for half an hour before I saw Eva leave the house and turn immediately to her left. I waited until she turned right into Korte Koepoortstraat, then stowed the phone in my pocket and walked down Moriaanstraat. Because of the nature of the business in which I employed Eva, I had never kept the kind of records that a normal employer might keep, so I had no idea where she lived. Possibly if I asked her, she might tell me. She might even invite me over. But I wasn't after an invitation.

As I turned into Korte Koepoortstraat, she was thirty metres ahead of me. Tall, her red hair bouncing in time to her long-legged stride, she was easy to keep in view. She was heading in a northerly direction, but every so often would cut down a cross street, with the result that we were drifting west. Between Moriaanstraat and the red light district it's possible to find some little streets that have been smartened up in recent years. There are some very well-off people tucked away there quietly enjoying lives of relative luxury. So I was astonished when I saw Eva stop in a doorway and enter too swiftly for me to see how she had gained admittance, whether she had used a key or been buzzed in by a third party.

Anyone who has not known obsession, particularly a man's slavish attachment to a woman, might think that an hour is a long time to wait in a doorway. An hour, to me, seemed a reasonable length of time to give her, even if most of those sixty minutes were spent constructing scenarios in my head to account for Eva's calling at the building. None of them pleased me, and although one hour was the limit I set myself, the last thing I actually wanted was to see her step back out into the street after that exact amount of time. It would seem to suggest she was working to a schedule and being paid for it.

Fifty-five minutes later, Eva appeared. I stepped back into the shadows. She started walking west and I followed. Close to the river she waited at a bus stop. Half a dozen people were also waiting. I stood far enough away to remain out of sight, but close enough to be able to board the bus when it came. Eva sat near the front. I pulled my hat down low and raised my hand to my brow, passing so close to her that I was able to recognise the perfume she wore mingled with soap and cigarettes.

Danuta was in a lonely place. She needed some support. She had talked to Eva about the emails from Jan. Eva told her she had asked the owner to take care of it.

'I'm still getting them,' Danuta had said, 'and it's freaking me out.'

Whereas the punters who emailed the girls in the house all seemed more or less seedy, there was something different about Jan. Something infinitely creepier. It wasn't so much what he said, as what he left unsaid. Whether he knew stuff about what was going on, he gave the impression that he did. Danuta felt trapped and she sensed that he knew it and that he was getting off on watching her squirm, like bait on a hook.

Whichever way she turned in the Last House, there was a camera watching her. She felt their glossy black lenses crawling over her skin. Not only could she not relax, but her muscles became rigid with tension. There was a band of pain strung out across the back of her shoulders. She started moving so oddly that one of the other girls asked her if she had slept badly and hurt her back. In response, Danuta fled to the toilet, only to remember, once she was hunched over the seat, that there was a camera in that room, the smallest room, as well. Hundreds, maybe thousands of men could be watching her. She thought about just one of them.

She raised her head and looked straight at the camera.

'Fuck you, you fucking freak.'

This outburst would bring as many emails of complaint as

requests that more of the girls in the house should follow Danuta's example and start talking dirty.

Danuta assessed her situation. Two of her friends had been murdered. Was she the link or was it the Last House? She'd been trying to get Hannah into the house; Katya, of course, had been there almost as long as she had. Either way she felt personally responsible for what had happened and anxious that the same fate might yet befall her, and if not her, then one of the other girls. Or someone else she knew. Jan had developed an unhealthily exclusive interest in her. She had to get away from him. She had to get out of the Last House.

The first thing you hear on waking are the planes. You sit up, senses suddenly sharp as the broken glass beneath the window, but there's nothing else to hear. The only birds within earshot are mechanical ones and their song is a subsonic drone that comes and goes with the wind.

You picture the basement, the Death Zone, as one graffiti writer tagged it. It will be dark down there, dark and silent. Unless she's woken up. Is it perhaps too quiet? Could she have escaped? Impossible.

You tip back a plastic bottle of Spa spring water, firstly in order to take a drink, then allowing the cool liquid to splash on to your face, reviving you. Done, you shake your head. Briefly you are reflected in the glass, but you look away. You step through one of the glazed doors on to the balcony and lean on the hand rail. Directly opposite are the RTBF TV and radio masts. A light aircraft buzzes overhead. You wonder where it's going and how long it will take to get there.

Dawn chills the bones. The trees and long grasses are soft-focused by dew fall. You lean over the rail, consider the drop. It would probably kill you, but there's no guarantee. Last thing you want is to end up paralysed, helpless. The world may be a shallow grave lined with seven kinds of shit, but at least you're not lying down in it. Not yet.

You turn away from the balcony and step back into room 319, as you now think of it, your right knee swollen and tender. Broken glass explodes under your feet as you limp across the floor and leave the room, turning left towards the main stairs. You step across empty door frames, splash through puddles of rainwater. Halfway down, you pause, hold your breath, listening. Had you heard something? Is there someone else in here with you? Your acute hearing picks up a steady drip from a broken length of guttering, as well as the mingled drones of flying insects and a jet just taken off from Zaventem. You refocus and continue your descent through the cracked and crumbling body of the building.

The bus travelled north with the Schelde on our left, Bonaparte Dock on our right. The skyline was soon dominated by the silhouette of the huge disused grain silo at the top of Kattendijkdok, then the bus looped around Siberiastraat on to the flyover that carried the road over the stretch of water that separated the compact, southern end of the docks from the massive industrial sprawl of the port to the north. We crossed the main road between the docks and the city, churning with tanker trucks and container lorries, and when the bus pulled in to a stop adjacent to three giant blocks of flats on Groenendaallaan, Eva stood up. I allowed several other passengers to follow her before doing so myself.

I was only twenty metres behind her as she walked towards the third block. If she were to turn around now, it would be all over. I slowed down while she crossed the open space, waited until she was close to the colonnade at the base of the building before making up lost ground. Thirty metres separated us again as I followed Eva north along the colonnade. On our left were columns supporting the floors above, to our right a series of lobbies behind security doors. Eva entered one and within moments a pair of elevator doors closed behind her.

I stepped out from under the colonnade and watched for a light coming on in any of the windows above. Most of the windows of the flats served by the entrance Eva had used were already glowing pink and yellow and orange in the twilight. I waited two minutes and was rewarded by a glow appearing at a window on the top floor. I waited a further minute or two, but nothing else happened, so I turned away and started walking back to the main road.

I waited twenty minutes for a bus. Several people joined me at the stop, but Eva was not among them.

When I got home, I did something I hadn't done for some weeks. I took out a wrap of stones, found my loupe and switched on the daylight lamp.

The house had changed little in 100 years. A double-fronted two-storey detached house set back from the road, it was easily recog-nised from Delvaux's 1967 painting *The House Where I Was Born*. The cobbles had gone from the pavement between the forecourt and the road, and the gate had been widened, allowing the current owner to park his car. The key difference was a dis-creet plaque bearing the name and dates of the artist.

To get a better view, Johnny Vos stepped back into the road. A horn blared and Johnny felt the turbulence of a passing vehicle. A close one, but he didn't particularly care. To get the perspective Delvaux had enjoyed, you had to stand in the middle of the road. Johnny positioned himself along the white line and watched the house. Cars passed on either side, the sound of their horns flung out in front and then strung out behind them.

The village of Antheit was a short distance north of Huy, a town on the River Meuse. Johnny was travelling without any major schedule, but he had a list and Antheit was on it, for its being the birthplace of Paul Delvaux.

He raised the camera and shot ten seconds.

A man came out of the house and walked to his car. He opened the passenger door, looking for something. Straightening up, he looked across at Johnny Vos and Johnny thought about introducing himself and explaining his mission. It would be good to get a look at the kitchen and see how much it had changed from that painted in *The Kitchen at Antheit* in 1960, but the man didn't look especially approachable and Vos was conscious that he shouldn't leave a trail. Plus, he had other calls to make. He retreated to the far side of the road. It was only a matter of luck that nothing was coming.

He walked the four kilometres back into Huy and waited for the next train out.

★

When she heard someone coming, she felt both terror and relief. She knew it would be him, whoever he was. She didn't imagine it would be Frank, or whoever else might come to her aid. It would be her gaoler, she was sure of that. The waiting was over. She might see his face. Maybe he would release her. Or do whatever he was planning to do with her. Was she about to die? The thing she hoped for above all was water. If he was concerned with keeping her alive, for whatever purpose, he would bring water.

A door opened and a shadow appeared. She hated herself for acknowledging it, but, in a short space of time, this man had become the most powerful figure in her life. She would have preferred to pretend he didn't exist, but knew she couldn't if she was to have a chance of surviving. Instinctively her mouth opened, lips chapped, throat dry.

'Water,' she whispered. 'Water.'

He came closer. He bent down and his knee joint popped.

At the age of five, on a Clacton beach, Siân had been patting a friendly Labrador when it knocked her over and jumped on her, licking her face and batting her with its paws. She had never forgotten the rank, meaty stench of the beast's breath. She was reminded of it now as the man bent over her. She heard a faint metallic rasp.

'Water,' she said again.

The next time I followed Eva, I stayed closer, so that when she entered the building between Moriaanstraat and the red light district, I was able to catch the door behind her and slip unnoticed into the hallway. I watched Eva's long legs as she climbed the stairs. Unusually, she was wearing a skirt, which allowed me to see her calf muscles flexing. I was confident she was running in order to be on time rather than to escape a pursuer. Had she known she was being followed, she would have turned and confronted me. I waited till she was one flight up.

As I rounded the first corner, I saw her ankle disappearing through a doorway. The door closed before I could reach it, although I knew that to have caught it and attempted to maintain pursuit would have put me at an unacceptable level of risk. But, in truth, I was acting first and thinking later.

Danuta didn't get very far. Trains departing from Centraal Station routinely stop five minutes down the line at Berchem. Hers was no exception. As the express sat motionless at the platform, she fought a fierce internal battle, its only outward sign a muscle twitching in her jaw.

When the doors snapped shut and the train pulled out, Danuta was standing on the platform. She watched the train leave, then turned and headed for the exit. Leaving the station, she headed towards Cogels-Osylei. There was a bar on the corner of the street. She sat down at one of the tables outside and waited for someone to come and take her order. It took a surprisingly long time.

One hundred kilometres south of Brussels, Liège is unloved and knows it, but doesn't seem unduly concerned. The city may not be beautiful, but nor is it ingratiating. It doesn't paper over the cracks. Georges Simenon lived here: the author of 400 crime novels, he claimed to have slept with thousands of women, many of them hookers.

Vos was barely out of the station before he stumbled into the red light district around rue Varin.

The Musée de l'Art Wallon was half an hour's walk away in the east end of the city.

In the basement, your eye lingers: 'DEATH ZONE'. You might almost have scrawled it yourself, but didn't. Surprised that you still can't hear any sound coming from the room on the left, you advance into the corridor. It gets darker with each step. The door is still closed. How could it not be? You lean against it and it doesn't move. You listen. Nothing, so you push again. The edge of the door scrapes on the floor. It's dark inside, even darker.

The building was old and the door to the apartment Eva had entered was fitted with two locks: Yale and mortise. I knelt and put my eye to the keyhole. At first I couldn't see anything and imagined a coat hanging on the back of the door. But then light flooded the darkness on either side of my field of vision and I realised I was looking at Eva's back as she walked up a narrow hallway towards an open doorway.

As he paid to get into the museum, Vos asked about Delvaux. The clerk shrugged, blew out a lungful of smoke, handed over a little blue ticket.

'There may be one or two,' he said when Vos bristled. 'I don't know. They could be out on loan. I could try to find out . . .'

'You know what? Don't bother,' Vos said dismissively as he walked towards the elevator.

There was one. *L'homme de la rue*, 1940. *The Man in the Street*.

Your eyes adjust and make out a shadow slumped against the wall. You step inside, noticing the smell. You cross the room and bend down, knee joint creaking. You grope the dark mass in front of you until it makes sense, at which point you snap the switch on the miner's lamp strapped to your head.

The brightness blinds you. You blink, giving the cones and rods time to react, then squint at the face in front of you.

In the room beyond, smiling as Eva approached, was a man in a wheelchair. With cropped iron-grey hair and steel spectacles, he could have been anywhere between 50 and 70. When Eva drew level, she bent at the hips like a dancer. The man strained forward to be kissed. Behind him was a Gérard Musy print, monochrome photograph of a dominatrix, head out of frame, breasts partially exposed, fingers tugging at the long laces of her calf-length boots.

Siân could no longer swallow. She had to have water. If he didn't give her water, she would die. She began to believe that death was inevitable – and imminent. She couldn't even bring herself to be that bothered. She was too tired.

A further wave of drowsiness washed over her, causing her eyes to flicker, then close. She tried to listen, half-aware that hearing was the last sense to go, but someone had turned down the volume.

★

Johnny Vos studied the bowler-hatted man approaching the viewer on the left of the picture. His head buried in a newspaper, he's oblivious to two ivy-clad nudes in the foreground who are equally unaware of him. Johnny imagined what a critic might read into the picture: the man would be the artist, his paper representing his efforts to keep in touch with the real world, in which, in 1940, the Germans would just have invaded Belgium.

Outside the bar, Danuta watched people go by. She was thinking, but the twitch in her jaw had ceased. Her glass empty, she sat there a further ten minutes, then paid the waitress. Crossing the street, she turned left into Cogels-Osylei. When the disused water towers came into view, she walked faster. Within half an hour she was back in Moriaanstraat. She entered the house and, aware of the cameras, ran up to her room.

Eva and the grey-haired man were talking. I could hear enough to recognise that they were speaking Flemish, but not enough to make out the words. After a moment, Eva turned and walked out of frame to the right. The man sat and watched. I could only imagine what she was doing. The man's hands lay in his lap, one folded over the other. I could see his eyes moving behind his spectacle lenses.

You snap the miner's lamp on and off a few times, watching how quickly the pupils react. Not so quickly that you can't see the change take place. You like that, find it stimulating; it's like seeing in the dark. But the pupils remain surprisingly dilated even under the harsh light.

The lips are moving. The girl is trying to speak. Uninterested, you switch the lamp off once more and leave the room.

Just as she was going under, she heard something, something different, something that might be a clue to where she was being held prisoner, if only she could make sense of it. But she couldn't. She knew what it was, but couldn't give it a name. It was like waking from a dream and having a clear feeling about the dream, but being unable to find the words to describe it.

★

I pictured Eva, out of shot, dangling her bag on a chair, letting go of the strap. She would move her shoulders back, shrug off her jacket, dropping it on the varnished floorboards behind her. She would rest her hands on her slender hips before easing down the waistband of her skirt, letting it fall to her shoes. She would step out of it and kick it across the floor.

The nudes, since the Man in the Street was unconscious of them, were his fantasy, the object of his subconscious desire, but the fact that both were covered with creeping ivy suggested that they had been there like that, ignored, for some time. It was well known that Delvaux, as a young man, had been sexually repressed, even the slightest interest in women frowned on by his domineering mother.

Still the man's hands were folded in his lap. He didn't move as he watched Eva. Reflected light flickered on his glasses. I became aware of a pain in my leg. As I straightened, my knee audibly crackled and I fell against the door. Recovering my balance, I sought the keyhole. The man was looking towards the door to the apartment. His hands moved to the wheel rims.

You return a short time later labouring behind an old trolley with two wayward wheels that you salvaged from the hospital kitchens. The trolley is laden with silicone, petroleum jelly, pre-coated plaster bandages, a hacksaw, water and a plastic straw.

'Get up,' you say to the girl.

She croaks something in response, probably asking for water.

'Get up and I'll give you water.'

You help lift her.

This, however, was the other way around: Siân wasn't awaking from anything. Nor would she again, it increasingly seemed to her. Consciousness instead was retreating, like land from the stern of a boat, her mind having slipped its moorings. The sound was evocative, melancholy, almost within her grasp, but the ship was drifting away from shore now, heading into deep waters. She fought to cling on.

★

She gets up, asks for water again. You release her, gambling on her enfeeblement that she won't try to escape. It seems a safe bet, since she can barely stand up on her own.

'This way,' you say, helping her to cross the room. 'Stand over here. This will not take long. If you can just stand still I will give you water. I promise.'

Johnny didn't know *what* the newspaper symbolised, or the creeping ivy, or the fact that none of the figures in the painting was meeting the gaze of any of the others. All he did know was that this painting, like Delvaux's entire output, made him *feel* something. It put him back in a certain place at a particular time. It made him feel alive.

It's 1986; you're twenty-three. A nuclear reactor cracks open at Chernobyl; US Space Shuttle *Challenger* explodes after seventy-three seconds; Harry Kümel's *The Secrets of Love*, period erotica, cleans up in Belgium and France. You rig up a noose from your dressing gown cord, looping it through the busted fanlight above the door to your mother's bedroom. You pull tight and kick the chair away.

I got to my feet as quickly and quietly as possible and, without checking the keyhole again, fled. I reached the door to the street before I heard the apartment door open one flight up and a man's voice ask, in Flemish, 'Who's there?' I stepped out into the street.

Her clothes tear easily. She whimpers and you promise water if she can stay on her feet.

'It will not take long,' you repeat.

Faintly, she heard the noise again, one last time, before shutdown. It was deep, sonorous, lasting two seconds or more, but fading . . . fading . . .

The dressing-gown cord snaps under your weight and you damage your knee in the fall. You will always limp in damp weather.

Part Eight

THE PINK BOWS

17

SPLIT SCREEN

In a café overlooking the beach at Ostend, Frank sat by the window. On the table in front of him was a glass of beer. He didn't know what brand.

Across the table from Frank sat the woman from the beach. The woman he'd seen from behind and thought might be Siân. She wasn't. She was ten years older, perhaps more. If she'd told Frank her name, he'd forgotten it. He thought she had a familiar face, but couldn't place her. Perhaps it was just that she looked English.

She fiddled constantly with a key ring. Single old-fashioned key. Plastic fob, bronze-look. Split ring.

His phone, from which he had not yet made a call since hearing the news on the radio and noting that the police had been trying to reach him, had turned to molten lead in his pocket. He knew he should call someone – but whom? The police? The paper? Siân's next of kin? For the time being, it was easier to do nothing and let this unknown woman look after him. If that was what she was doing.

'My husband is a diamond dealer,' she said suddenly.

Frank turned from the window to look at her.

'I haven't seen him for six months,' she added in a curiously flat voice.

'He's missing?' he heard himself say, neutrally.

'No. *I'm* missing.'

Frank frowned. Staring at the woman, he experienced an abrupt buzzing sensation on the left side of his chest and wondered disinterestedly if he was having a heart attack. It was his phone, on vibrate. Before he could stop himself, he reached into his pocket and took it out and answered it. He listened for a few moments, then got up and left the café. He looked in the direction of the sea as he spoke to the police. He stayed on the phone for two minutes. They did most of the talking, but he asked a couple of key questions. 'I'll be there,' he said finally, then closed the phone and put it away, but didn't move from where he was. He just stared at the sea that he wished he and Siân had never crossed. Eventually, the woman appeared by his side. The salty breeze lifted her hair from her head. He noticed it was streaked with grey. The harsh light revealed deep lines in her face. She was still an attractive woman, if evidently an unhappy one. He wondered vaguely if this level of appraisal made him no better than Johnny Vos. Siân would condemn it, he knew.

'I have to go,' he said.

'Where to?'

'Antwerp.'

'I don't suppose there's room in your car for ...' she trailed off uncertainly.

'Running away again?' he asked.

'Not exactly,' she said.

He couldn't think of a good reason to refuse and so led the way to his hire car.

Once Frank got the car on the road, his insides began to revolt, and he soon wished he'd used the facilities at the café. His stomach felt as if it had been filled with water and then frozen. His head ached and his mouth was dry. His driving was nervy and erratic, but his passenger didn't seem upset by it. She sat staring out of the window on her side, her head angled away from him so that he couldn't see her face. He shouldn't have been bothered by her presence – he had a serious enough problem of his own – but he found himself becoming faintly irritated. Who was this woman and how had she inveigled her way into his car? He really needed to be alone so that he could scream profanities at the windscreen or lower the windows and howl his despair at the passing fields. Still her fingers played with the key ring. Momentarily taking his eyes from the road, he glanced down. Impressed on the plastic fob were the words 'Gauquié-Hôtel'.

'Shouldn't you have returned that,' he said, indicating the key, 'if you're leaving town?'

'This? I found it washed up on the beach.'

He looked again. Beneath the name of the hotel in smaller print was the name of a coastal town: Oostduinkerke. There was also a room number: 438.

Frank returned his attention to the road and drove on. The woman looked out of the window on her side and continued to play with the key ring. After a while, Frank took his foot off the gas and indicated right, rolling into the side of the road. When they had stopped, the woman turned and looked at him and he looked at her and he could see nothing in her eyes but a hollow sadness that was close to grief, and he opened his mouth to speak, but nothing came out. Instead, he shouldered the driver's door and a warm breeze gusted in. He stepped out on to the grass verge and raised his arms: ran his hands through his hair, rubbed his scalp. He faced the road and watched the passing traffic for a few moments, then turned and got back into the car.

'Have you ever seen a film called *Malpertuis*?' he asked the woman once they were moving again.

She turned to look at him.

'No.'

'It's a very strange film,' he said. 'A masterpiece of Belgian cinema. It's set almost entirely in this weird place called Malpertuis, a house full of endless corridors and hidden rooms. Orson Welles plays a dying man, Uncle Cassavius, who, despite being bedridden, seems to know everything about everybody who lives in the house. He appears to be in control of their destinies.'

'I've never even heard of it,' she said neutrally.

'A body's been found,' he said, conscious of hearing the words as he spoke them, 'with a copy of *Malpertuis* on video. They say that you feel a kind of relief when the worst thing that could happen does actually happen. I don't feel any sense of relief.'

The woman shrugged, understanding nothing.

'Maybe it's not her,' Frank half-whispered, scared that even to voice the thought would jinx it. 'Maybe he's got her and she's still alive, or maybe this isn't him.'

The road unrolled beneath the wheels and Antwerp drew closer.

The woman asked to be dropped by Centraal Station, after which Frank drove on to the red light district. It wasn't difficult to find where he was going. The end of Verversrui was taped off and several squad cars were parked at various angles across the street. A protective awning had been erected around one of the windows. Frank saw the blond cop, Dockx, talking on a mobile phone. The policeman ended the call when he saw Frank approaching.

'We don't know if it's her,' were Dockx's first words.

Frank looked away from Dockx, but was aware of the detective's head bobbing and swivelling as he sought to maintain eye contact.

'The body hasn't been moved yet,' he said. 'Forensics.'

Dockx seemed ill at ease. Frank felt a degree of pressure to help him out. Just then, a flap parted in the white tent as a guy in a white boiler suit walked out, allowing Frank a brief glimpse inside. All he got was an impression, but it was more Van Gogh than Monet.

'Normally, identification would happen later, once the body is in the morgue,' Dockx said, 'but that could take a long time and I figured you'd want to know sooner rather than later. Plus, we really need to know, as soon as possible, what we're dealing with.' The detective paused, rubbed his nose. 'Are you ready?' he asked.

Frank looked at him and couldn't speak. Dockx motioned towards the white flap. Frank's legs wouldn't move.

'I'm sorry,' Dockx said, moving his body between Frank and the tent. 'Ideally the crime scene would have been cleaned up by now. It's taking longer than usual.'

'Let's get it over with,' Frank said, voice breaking.

Dockx pulled aside the flap and Frank ducked under. The white tent covered the window and the adjoining doorway providing access to that particular cabin. The window was intact. Which only meant he had a better view. Frank turned away, bending double as he retched. He pushed his way back through the tent into the street.

'That tape . . .' he said to Dockx, referring to the videotape wrapped all around the woman's torso like the latest fashion to come out of Het Modepaleis.

'We haven't checked it, but it came from a video cassette with a hand-written label.'

'*Malpertuis?*'

Dockx whipped out a notebook.

'*Malpertuis,*' he read slowly, syllable by syllable.

'It's Kümel's third film,' Frank interrupted.

'Yes.'

'So does this mean he's still got Siân, or she simply hasn't been found yet?'

'Are you saying this isn't Siân?'

Frank shook his head distractedly.

'It *is* Siân?' the cop asked.

Frank looked at him, as if seeing him for the first time since coming out of the tent.

'It's *not* Siân,' Frank said.

'Are you certain?'

'Of course I'm fucking certain.'

'Right. Right.'

Bertin, the short, wiry cop with the intense grey stare and the jet-black goatee, had joined them.

'If it's not Ms Marchmont,' Bertin said, 'who is it?'

Frank shrugged. 'I don't know,' he said, puzzled, thinking: *Like I fucking care.* 'I don't understand why this isn't Siân. It should be Siân. No one else is missing, are they? Are they? You thought it was probably Siân, otherwise you wouldn't have called me. Has he still got her or what?'

'You're jumping to conclusions,' Dockx said. 'We don't know he's got Siân. We don't even know that this isn't the work of a copycat killer.'

Dockx's remark earned him a glare from Bertin, which Frank just caught.

'Copycat killer?'

Dockx, realising his mistake, looked at Bertin. Bertin scowled and looked away, then looked at Frank.

'The legs,' Bertin said.

'You knew this was a copycat killer?'

'It looks that way.'

'And you still got me to come here, thinking it was going to be Siân?'

'That possibility had to be ruled out. You had to be prepared for the worst.'

'What about the legs?' Frank asked.

The two policemen exchanged a glance.

'He cuts them off,' Bertin said.

Frank felt as if he'd gone over a hump-backed bridge.

Bertin: 'Just above the ankle.'

Frank: 'Jesus. Why?'

'We don't know.'

'This girl,' Frank said, indicating the white tent. He could picture her propped up like a sack of potatoes behind the window. Unnatural pose. Redhead, like Siân. Glass-eyed gaze. Skin-tight videotape mini-dress. The legs were a detail he hadn't retained.

Bertin shook his head.

'The first two girls had been suffocated,' he said. 'This girl doesn't appear to have been. It's difficult to say until we get her back and examine her. But the initial signs are this is a different guy.'

'Siân is still missing,' Frank said.

Bertin nodded.

'She might still be alive,' Frank said, trying hard to control his emotions. 'What do we do now?'

'We assume this killing is a one-off,' Dockx put in. 'Copycat killings invariably are. We're looking for the guy who did it, but we don't believe he's about to do it again. The other guy, meanwhile, the first guy . . .'

'Yeah, I know. The first guy has not finished.'

'What are you going to do?' Dockx asked him.

'I don't know. Try and get some sleep.'

The cops nodded.

'Don't leave town,' one of them said, but Frank had already turned away. His legs felt like tripe.

'Yeah, right,' he said as he staggered away.

He called the hire company on his mobile and asked what

kind of penalty would be imposed if he failed to return the car, leaving it to be picked up instead. The woman on the other end said they didn't pick up cars.

'I'm walking away from it right now,' he told her. 'If you want it, you'll have to come and get it.'

He gave her the address. As he lowered the phone from his ear he could hear her tinny voice droning on about fines and the threat of prosecution, but he was no more bothered than he would have been about a wasp in a sealed box. He folded the phone and walked away.

The people at the Film Museum on the Meir were very helpful. When Frank explained the situation and outlined what he wanted, they set it up for him in less time than it can take to stand in line at Blockbuster.

A back room at the museum. Two TV/VCRs. Tapes of *Daughters of Darkness* and *Malpertuis*. A copy of *Monsieur Hawarden*, Kümel's first film, had proved beyond the resources of the museum.

'We could call Harry,' they suggested, 'see if he's got one.'

'I'll call him,' Frank said.

Frank called Kümel and explained where he was and what he was doing, making it clear that he wasn't seeking to implicate Kümel in the murders, but that he was desperate for anything that might help him track down Siân. Kümel couldn't help with a tape of his first feature, but he offered to come and sit through the films Frank had got hold of, in case he had any questions.

'I think I'd feel a little awkward,' Frank said. 'I'm going to have to whip through them, both films at once. It's not exactly the way a director would like to see his films being watched.'

'I've known worse,' Kümel responded. 'It's the least I can do. I'll be there in ten minutes.'

While he was waiting, Frank checked out the titles sequences of both films. *Daughters of Darkness* went for a simple, stark Euro-design, lower-case text against a single changing colour, while *Malpertuis* signalled its mood of high fantasy by referencing *Alice Through the Looking Glass*.

As good as his word, Kümel arrived at the Film Museum ten

minutes later. Frank asked him if he could think of anyone at all who might have a grudge against him.

'Impossible to say,' Kümel responded. 'You don't work in this business for forty years without putting one or two noses out of joint, but it would be a big step from that kind of thing to this, wouldn't it?'

'You can't think of anyone you might have offended so badly they'd want to pay you back like this?'

'Look, I've thought about this, obviously. I have a season coming up at the National Film Theatre in London. I asked myself if this could be someone trying to ensure that the season does not take place. It's ridiculous. Who would do such a thing? I find it impossible to believe this is someone with a grudge against me. It's more likely to be a fan, but even that seems improbable.'

Although Kümel had not made a film for ten years, he had a track record and a following. There was a ton of stuff on the Net, mainly relating to *Daughters of Darkness*, but the other films were not ignored. That the killer was a Kümel freak was a possibility that had struck Frank early on and he'd started to think it too obvious, but now he reminded himself that a serial abductor and murderer would not be concerned with degrees of obviousness. Like many psychopaths, he probably sought capture, while at the same time trying to stay one step ahead of those seeking to achieve it. *Daughters of Darkness* was about a string of murders. Bloodless bodies in Bruges. Maybe the killer intended his own sequence of murders to be read as a homage to Kümel and his best-known film. A way of marking its thirtieth anniversary.

As he continued to glance from one monitor to the other, he tried to keep track of everyone who appeared on screen. Maybe the killer was someone who had been associated, however tenuously, with Kümel since the early days. An extra, perhaps. Even as this idea occurred to him, Frank noticed how empty most of the shots tended to be. No unnecessary details, and that included figures. Street scenes, such as the sequence at the beginning of *Malpertuis*, seemed to have been filmed just after dawn. Yann chases a woman who he thinks is his sister Nancy but turns out to be a cabaret singer. Glimpsing the hem of her dress disappearing at the end of an alleyway, he gives chase, only to lose her around the next corner. It reminded Frank of a similar chase scene in *Don't Look Now*, which came out two years later.

'Don't mention Nic Roeg to me,' said Kümel. 'He should have remained a director of photography.'

The exaggerated reactions of the bystanders in the scene in *Daughters of Darkness* where Stefan and Valerie witness the recovery of a girl's body from the building in which she has been murdered reminded Frank of a similar shot in Polanski's *The Tenant*. He held his tongue, imagining Kümel's displeasure at the comparison. Frank looked hard at the face of the retired policeman – credited simply as 'The Man' – who looked like a slightly sinister Monsieur Hulot in his pork pie hat and pale raincoat, wondering if this apparently harmless character actor might have been somehow snubbed by Kümel and gone on to follow his career with the kind of close interest that only resentment can encourage. It might not be enough to turn someone into a killer, but you had to assume there were other forces at play.

'This guy?' Frank said, indicating the Hulot lookalike.

'Georges Jamin. This was his last film. He died the year it was released. Nice guy, but the part was added at the insistence of the financiers.'

Frank watched the screens.

'The extras idea is a red herring, isn't it?' he said. 'You hardly used any. I was thinking maybe of someone not engaged on the films, but who knew they were happening and managed to get in on some shots. Crowd scenes, street scenes – it would be easy in a certain kind of film. But here—' Frank indicated *Malpertuis* '—everyone's in period dress. You've got to ensure there's no one in the shot who shouldn't be. You have control over the set.'

Kümel nodded.

'What about a set designer? A sound man? Someone you fired or offended?'

'I'm sure I've offended many people, but probably other filmmakers rather than crew members. I had a good relationship with a lot of people and worked with them again on film after film.'

'Cinematographers, screenwriters, assistant directors?'

'No major quarrels. Eduard van der Enden lit four films for

me. Jean Ferry and Jan Blokker both worked on scripts for me three times. I like working with people I know because the most important thing is the film and I know they're going to do a good job.'

Frank nodded as his gaze flicked between the two screens. Watching two films at once made it seem as if time was unspooling at an even more rapid rate than normal and Frank was acutely aware that time was limited.

'Maybe it's something to do with locations?'

'But these films were shot all over the place,' Kümel pointed out. 'Ostend, Bruges, Ghent, Brussels. Where were the murders committed? Antwerp.'

'Well, we don't know that.'

'I hardly need remind you the women were abducted in Antwerp and the bodies found here, too.'

Frank winced as if he'd been slapped.

'Have you filmed in Antwerp?' he asked.

Kümel shrugged again. '*Joachim Stiller*,' he said. 'But not in the red light district.'

'What about the water towers? They're near you. Near where you live.'

'Everything is nearby in Antwerp. It is a small city. The water towers are by the railway line. I filmed a scene on that line, but further north, Antwerpen Dam.'

On the left-hand screen Orson Welles was a ragged Uncle Cassavius sitting up in bed under a red counterpane, issuing regal imprecations in a guttural whisper. The screen on the right showed Danièle Ouimet's Valerie looking out of her hotel bedroom window as a ferry sails by, cutting through the sun's reflection on the sea.

'Clever shot,' Frank said.

'It's pretty simple,' Kümel said. 'The interior is a hotel in Brussels—'

'The Astoria.'

'—and the exterior is Ostend. Focusing through the net curtain, we dissolve to the shot of the boat.'

Frank found the constant intercutting between Brussels and Ostend disorienting, despite the fact that, because the man sitting next to him had cheated so artfully, you genuinely couldn't see the join. Being in one place and thinking you were in another. Frank could relate to that. Like Valerie, Frank found himself looking away from the screen and out of the window. He gazed past the wheelie bins, old bicycles and piles of empty cardboard boxes and thought: 'Why the legs? Why the *legs*? Why does he cut the fucking legs off?'

18

LIFE CAST

You've got an old work lamp, battery-operated, bulb-in-a-cage job. You switch it on, hang it from a nail sticking out of the wall. Now you can see what you're doing. From your pocket you take out a postcard of *The Pink Bows* and nail that to the wall above the girl. Then you reach for the tub of Vaseline off the trolley. She flinches as you slap the first dollop of petroleum jelly on to her shoulder and begin spreading it over her upper torso.

'Keep still. I'm not going to hurt you.'

She knows it's a lie, but it's what she wants to hear.

You keep working at her flesh with your hands. She sways, moans, like a tree in the wind. You reach for the silicone. In the mannequin business, a reaction test would have been run on the model's wrist three days before the moulding session, ensuring there would be no adverse reaction when applying the silicone to the entire body. In this case, the reaction test is unnecessary.

You mix the silicone with ultra-fast catalyst for a shorter cure time, essential when working with a reluctant model, then begin to apply the silicone in a smooth, even layer. It doesn't take long. The girl remains quiet. You replace the silicone pot, accidentally knocking a thirty-centimetre hacksaw to the floor with a clatter. You stoop to pick it up and notice the girl's eyes shining in a deflected arrow of light.

'Not long now,' you say as you take a strip of pre-coated plaster bandage and dip it in the bowl of water, then place it around the girl's upper arm. Her lips move but no sound comes out and you continue the wrapping with small pre-cut strips of different sizes. Down each arm, covering the hands, around the thumb, each finger individually. The shoulders, torso, stomach and back. Not until she's covered elsewhere do you start on the face. You take the straw from the trolley and insert it between her teeth. Her lips close around it as she hopes for water. You lift a strip of bandage from the pile, dip it and lay it across the bridge of the nose. Her tongue darts out to catch the drips. You lay more strips across the back of the neck, forehead, chin. As she's desperately sucking at the moisture on her lower lip, producing a grating nails-on-blackboard squeal, the straw falls out of her mouth. You pick it up, stuff it back in.

'You need this,' you whisper through your teeth. 'It won't take long. Keep still and you'll be all right.'

You're losing patience. Doesn't the girl know what's good for her? Can't she manage the simplest task? You feel a prickling sensation as sweat begins to trickle down from your hairline. As you wield your forearm to wipe away the perspiration, you knock the miner's lamp to one side and for a brief moment see the girl backlit by the work lamp while the beam from the miner's lamp falls like a spotlight on the postcard of *The Pink Bows*.

It is 1968 and you are five. The US has sent troops into Vietnam; in Paris, students tear up paving stones to use as missiles; Harry Kümel's debut feature, *Monsieur Hawarden*, a period adaptation and monochrome homage to Josef Von Sternberg that could not be more at odds with the Zeitgeist, does poorly in the Netherlands, faring little better in Flanders. It receives recognition in London, however, and its reputation will grow over time, but across the depressed post-industrial wastelands of southern Belgium it has zero impact. Of more immediate concern to the working-class communities of Charleroi and Liège is the gradual shutdown of the coalmining industry.

Your father's mine is not among those first to close and he still goes off to work every morning or evening wearing his dark blue miner's jacket and trousers all sparkly and shiny with coal dust. The loose end of his black leather belt curls out between the jacket flaps, and your mother, as she does every day, playfully pushes it back inside, patting the bulge it makes with her hand.

Invariably, by the time he walks out the front door, the end of the belt has popped back out again.

Your father smiles at you less than he used to, but, being only five, you take what comes. He talks less to your mother. If he does open his mouth it's to snap at one or both of you. Sometimes the reprimand is accompanied by a slap that leaves a soft grey smear on the side of your face. When he's not looking, your mother spits on to a hankie and wipes your cheek. You don't like the taste of her spit and try to twist out of reach, but her grip is still firm.

You forget what laughter sounds like, become used to the sound of brooding silence. Soon all you see of your father, when he is at home, is a lumpy shape in your parents' bed under the big picture of the naked women with the pink bows.

One day you and your mother return to the house after shopping for groceries. She opens the front door and you see it straight away, only you don't know what you're looking at. You'd say your father has somehow hung his miner's jacket from the door frame leading to your parents' bedroom (nineteenth-century miners' cottages in Liège were humble affairs; bedrooms were improvised wherever there was space, often downstairs). Sticking out the bottom of the jacket is a pair of false legs. But when you draw level, you see your father's head twisted traumatically to one side, his black leather belt cutting into the swollen red flesh of his broken neck. His face is turned away from you. The belt is tied around the top of the doorframe, where the glass fanlight has been punched out. Shards of glass are scattered across the carpet. A chair lies on its side. The legs are not false, after all. Crumpled around the ankles are your father's dark blue work trousers, fallen down through want of a belt. Only his bulky boots have prevented the trousers sliding off his legs altogether.

You feel obscurely embarrassed on your father's behalf.

Your mother drops the shopping bags on to the floor and slumps on a chair.

'What are we going to do?' she asks. 'What are we going to do? Look at all this food!'

You fix the orientation of the miner's lamp. The girl's face is washed out in the direct light. A face on a slab. Death mask. The merest flicker of the tiniest hair at her nostril betrays the life that persists. You get another strip of plaster bandage, moisten it, lay it across her nose, smoothing the ends down. The water runs. Her tongue quests. A cracked wheeze escapes her dry lips. She won't remain on her feet much longer. You whisper reassurances, promise her that the job is almost done.

'Use the straw to breathe,' you remind her as the final strips go on and the whimpers escalate in pitch.

By the time the face is done, the legs are ready to come off. You pick up the hacksaw, move around to the side. The serrated blade engages with the plaster like the wheel of a car biting into a clay soil. You can feel the girl trying to struggle inside the cast, but she's too weak now. The blade rasps across the plaster as you cut along an imaginary line. The mould parts from the skin. A thicker coating of Vaseline would have offered greater protection to the hairs on her legs. You work your way upwards with the hacksaw, being careful not to damage the mould. Once the legs are free, you encourage her to kneel while you work on the upper body.

Finally, she lies, exhausted, on the floor, the various parts of the mould safe on the trolley. Distractedly, you run your fingers through her hair, which is dotted with tiny fragments of scurf-like plaster.

Later, upstairs, room 319. Light cascading through the window. Released from the assembled mould, like a butterfly from its chrysalis, the perfect, idealised version of the girl in the Death Zone. This one's going nowhere. She won't let you down. Won't disappoint you. You move the sections of discarded mould to the other side of the room and carry the mannequin over to the corner behind the door. Standing in front of the figure, you place your hands gently on her hips. The surface is still tacky, but you run your hands up the sides of her abdomen and torso until they are caught under her arms. You cup your hands to her breasts. You feel nothing, which is what you want to feel. Neither one thing, nor the other. Neither elation, nor despair. Just a temporary sense of equilibrium.

At the back of your mind, the girl in the cellar. The Death

Zone. It will soon be time. For now you move your hands over the synthetic curves of the facsimile. Her legs seem unnaturally long as you linger almost regretfully over the delicate turn of the ankle. Poignantly you stroke the lower calves.

Later still, back in the cellar. You pluck the *Pink Bows* postcard from the wall and examine it by the light of the miner's lamp. Nights when your mother didn't come home, you slept in her bed, a print of this picture on the wall above your head. The enigmatic gaze of the woman in the foreground. The giant pink bow around her torso. The legs cut off by the frame just above the ankle.

The edge of the postcard is furred and worn with use and beginning to curl up, but as you squint in the weak light, you see that the artist actually severed the legs just below the ankle, rather than above. Your mother's picture must itself have been poorly framed.

It makes no difference.

The girl is sprawled on the floor, breathing slowly. You turn to look at the trolley and see the hacksaw glinting there. You look back at the girl, then lean towards her to hook a fallen curtain of hair behind her ear, so that you can see her face one last time before you do it. Her eyes are closed, her lips dry. A slight movement of your head causes the beam of the lamp to fall on her leg, just above the ankle. It's time.

You get to your feet, cursing your creaking knees, and as you pick up the hacksaw from the trolley you think you can hear another noise. You stop, tensing every muscle. It seemed to come from above. Outside, or one of the upper floors. A pigeon. They come in through the open windows. A draught. A door blowing shut. A plane overhead. Acoustical trick.

You hear it again. Neither a door nor a window. But movement of some kind. Someone – or something – is in the building with you.

Still carrying the saw, you pick your way carefully to the door. It grates unavoidably against the floor as you push it open and step out into the corridor. Your foot lands in a puddle and the sole of your shoe slides towards the far wall. The single beam from the miner's lamp draws an instant ECG line on the ceiling before you regain your balance and hold your breath, straining to listen for any reaction above. Hearing nothing, you straighten up, move on. You reach the bay just beyond the end of the corridor. Dark, empty passage to the right. Steps up towards daylight, shoes scrunching on gritty concrete. Turn through 180 degrees. Having reached the ground floor, you stop, listen. Look all around. Down the main corridor, carpeted with shattered glass. Nothing, no one. Through the mangled doorway leading to the round room, its windows all broken. No sign of life. Slowly, deliberately, placing each step with great care, you climb the stairs to the first floor. There's nothing to see there, so you keep climbing to the third floor. Room 319. The door is closed. Had you left it closed? You can't remember. The draughts play house here.

You lean against the door. The room is empty.

You walk inside. Step through the broken windows on to the balcony. The grassy area in front of the sanatorium is clear. You come back into the room. The mannequin is still standing in the corner. You pick her up and lay her on the floor, then kneel down behind the door, the back of your hand gently pressed for a moment against the side of her face, then you turn and position the edge of the hacksaw blade at right angles to the mannequin's leg, just above the ankle. You start to saw. After half a minute, you stop for a rest. In the sudden silence you detect a new, foreign quality. You twist around to look through the crack between the door and the jamb.

Standing in the doorway is a man. Dark hair, leather jacket. Carrying a camera. Your sawing must have covered the sound of his approach. You judge that your shoes are all he can see of you. What happens next depends on who makes the first move. He can also see most of the dummy.

'What are you doing here?' you ask, thinking about the girl in the basement. You begin to get to your feet.

He says nothing. Turns and runs.

You are round the door in an instant; he's already at the end of the corridor, barging through the fire door and heading for the stairs down. You let him go, your mind working on a dozen different scenarios for how this might play out. Almost as if carried along by his momentum, you follow him on to the stairs and start walking down. You can hear him in the distance. He must be at the ground floor by now. You're still working out the best thing to do, but your gut feeling is that you need to be on the ground floor, too − or lower. You're walking slowly as you turn over the options in your head.

★

The motorway. Heading north. Brussels. Ring road. Keep going. Antwerp thirty-seven km.

You looked all round the outside of the institute and didn't see the intruder again, but it was a chance not worth taking. You recall he had a camera. You couldn't stay there a minute longer. The game had to move on.

Antwerp twenty-three km.

You glance down at the passenger seat. The tape's still there. Unmarked three-hour video cassette. Blank label.

Antwerp six km.

19

ABANDONED-PLACES.COM

Frank got a text message from the librarian on the paper.

frank: prbly nothing, but check email. paul/library.

It was the 'prbly nothing' that made Frank decide to follow up the message, having ignored several from the news editor leading with the word 'urgent'.

He'd finished speeding through *Daughters of Darkness* and *Malpertuis* with Kümel riding pillion and had no more than half-baked ideas about what to do next. The Film Museum was not far from the hotel, so in desperation he headed back there and connected up to the Net. Among his emails was one from Paul alerting him to a brief news item taken off the wires about a discovery made by two young graffiti writers who had broken into a former wire factory near Ghent. They had stumbled into an old den or hideaway plastered with press cuttings and containing a number of shop-window mannequins.

'Then check this out,' Paul's email advised, and he gave an URL that was highlighted in blue.

```
http://abandoned-places.com
```

Frank clicked on it. In a couple of seconds there appeared a grey background like an architectural blueprint with a few odd words in Flemish, then, in the foreground, green text in some unknown sans serif font offering a choice of photo galleries (1 and 2), 'impossible projects', 'why who', links and updates. He clicked on photo galleries 1 and a photo-wheel started to load with buttons around it for various shoots. He clicked on one. A disused coal mine at Cheratte close to Liège. Atmospheric colour and black and white shots of abandoned colliery workings, entrances to mine shafts, locker rooms, showers. He tried another and found himself in a former TB clinic outside Brussels, the Institut Joseph Lemaire, all flooded corridors, broken glass and vivid graffiti. He went into updates, where the top item was the one Paul had intended him to see. The items were dated with the month and year; the top one was current.

Colour photos of the Institut Joseph Lemaire and two paragraphs of text:

Return visit to Lemaire Institute cut short by weird encounter with threatening individual. I wander round the grounds and lower floors taking photographs. As on previous incursions, the only signs of life are the many colourful examples of graffiti art. Signs of death, also as before, are widespread: x-rays of diseased lungs, letters to deceased patients.

On the third floor I discover a man kneeling behind the door of one of the rooms. He appears to be in the middle of sawing the legs off a shop window mannequin, and stops when he hears me. He doesn't seem very pleased to have a visitor. I don't hang about to see what his problem is. Suffice to say the Joseph Lemaire Institute is off my list for the time being.

Frank called Paul direct.
    The librarian picked up: 'Paul Fairclough.'
    'Paul. Frank. How d'you know about the legs thing?'
    'Frank. Hi. Er, what legs thing?'

Frank paused, then: 'Nothing,' he said. 'Thanks for the messages.'

Frank sat very still, thinking hard. After a moment, he reconnected to the Net and checked the 'why who' page on abandoned-places.com, then emailed the site's host, Henk Van Rensbergen, photographer, urban explorer and, bizarrely, aviation pilot, according to his biog. Clicking back on to Explorer, he went to Favourites and selected the first of the Delvaux pages he'd looked at previously. An image of *The Spitzner Museum* started filling in a picture box, like a cinema curtain slowly descending. The painting reminded him of two things. Firstly, Delvaux's interest in mannequins – the Sleeping Venus from the Midi Fair; the dressmaker's dummies that appeared in a handful of paintings; and the female nudes themselves, which bore a striking resemblance to shop-window dummies – the long slender legs, emotionless faces, blank stares. Frank clicked in the address window and typed in www.spitznermuseum.org. There was a pause and Frank thought he was going to get an error message and the page wasn't going to load. But then it started to. It was slow because it was so picture-heavy.

There were three photographs on the main page. They took a while to finish loading. Frank could see what they were before they'd finished, but he waited all the same, grimly, to be absolutely certain. He sat and looked at them for a minute, thinking, trying to keep a lid on a growing sense of panic.

He checked his email again but there was nothing from Henk Van Rensbergen.

He clicked back on to Explorer and rummaged through the Spitzner Museum site until he found a contact email and then fired off a quick message. Before logging off, he went back to Entourage to check his inbox one last time and there were three new messages. One made him an offer on Viagra, the second was flogging pictures of animals, and the third was from Henk Van Rensbergen. Frank opened it and read it. Van Rensbergen had included his mobile number, which Frank keyed into his phone, committing it to the SIM card memory. He then called the number.

It rang, and rang and rang, finally transferring to voicemail. Frank left a message and cut the connection.

In desperation he logged back on to the Net and checked his email again. One new message. It was from Jan Spitzner, host of www.spitznermuseum.org. He opened the message. It was short. He read it, closed the message window and logged off the Net, then got to his feet.

He looked out of the window. The mechanical diggers were still scratching away at the earth behind the high screens in front of Centraal Station. He felt as if it was only a matter of time before the ground gave way beneath his feet. As he moved quickly towards the door he was seized by a sudden fit of giddiness. His knees felt momentarily weak and he reached out to hold on to the wall. Tiredness, he thought. Perhaps. Head down, he stared at the floor, where one of the postcards he'd taken from Johnny Vos's hotel room had fallen from the pocket of his jacket, which was lying on the bed. He bent down to pick it up. He recognised the painting. *Street of Trams*. He turned the card over. In small, untidy handwriting, which he recognised from Vos's notebook, he read: 'Rue de la Régence? Rue Royale? Astoria???'

Frank had a map of Brussels in his bag. Rue de la Régence ran north from the Palais de Justice, eventually turning into rue Royale. The Astoria, on rue Royale, was where Harry Kümel had filmed the interiors for *Daughters of Darkness*. Was Vos planning to film there? Was there some kind of link with Delvaux?

Frank felt the energy drain out of him. He sat down on the bed and allowed his head to sink into his hands. Siân was missing and he didn't know what to do. He had some leads, but he didn't know which one to follow first, and if he admitted to himself what he was starting to believe deep down − that he was never going to find Siân alive − then there was no point in doing anything. Actually, he didn't really know what he did believe, and he worried that if he did give up hope, it would somehow affect the outcome. Not that it would make him any less determined to find her, but that merely believing she was dead would itself kill her off. It would somehow *make her be dead*. Tattered threads of superstition, which was almost all he had left to cling to, insinuated that he had to have faith that she was still alive if he wanted to find her before it was too late.

But it was difficult. Overwhelming. He slumped down on to the floor, losing it. He started shaking. Tears rolled off the end of his nose. He curled up into a comma on the carpet. His grip on the passage of time loosened. When the phone rang, he almost didn't answer it.

'Hello,' said a voice. 'This is Henk Van Rensbergen.'

As the train from Antwerp approached Brussels Nord, Frank was waiting by the doors so that he could disembark without delay. Rue d'Aerschot, below and adjacent to the railway, was a sorry series of snapshots of girls sitting in windows lit by strip-lights – red, pink, ultra-violet. Compared to the red light district in the city Frank had just left it was decidedly second-rate.

Van Rensbergen met Frank on the platform. A tall man of medium build, chestnut hair cut short and neat, neutral hazel eyes and high, prominent cheekbones, his stance seemed to suggest a relaxed confidence in himself combined with a reasonable wariness of Frank. A quick handshake and they descended to street level.

'Let's get out of here,' the photographer said. 'It's not what you'd call a nice part of town.'

They reached Van Rensbergen's car and a minute later were edging forward in a queue of traffic. A bulky camera bag sat on the back seat. As soon as they got through the lights, it didn't take them long to hit the ring road.

'The Lemaire Institute,' Frank said, breaking the silence. 'When were you there last?'

'Three days ago.'

'So before the latest body was found in Antwerp? The one in the red light district. The third one.'

'When was that?'

'Day before yesterday.'

'Then, yes. Do the police think there's a connection?'

'The police don't think.'

They were moving fast in the outside lane, but still vehicles would cut inside them to overtake. Trees bunched on either side of the motorway.

'How long will it take to get there?' Frank asked.

'Not long. Ten minutes. Are you hoping to find your girl-friend at the institute?' Van Rensbergen's approach was matter-of-fact, unsentimental.

'No. Well, I don't know. Not really. If there's the slightest chance that the man you saw is the man who's got her, then I have to follow it up.'

'What makes you think he might be?'

'A detail the police haven't released to the media.'

'But they have to you?'

'Yeah. Doesn't that make you feel safe? Protected by the most incompetent police force in Europe.'

'It's different in Belgium. For years we had three different police forces. Who knows if they shared information? In any case, the system has changed now. Since Dutroux.' Van Rensbergen didn't seem to be leaping to the defence of the Belgian public services so much as merely stating the facts. After a moment he asked: 'What if he's still there?'

'I'll ask him where Siân is.' Frank looked at the dark ranks of trees sliding past the car. 'I don't think he'll be there. I think you'll have scared him off.'

'I'm not in any hurry to renew our acquaintance.'

'I don't want to drag you into anything. Just show me where to go and you can wait in the car.' Frank turned to look at Van Rensbergen. 'I don't know if I said, I'm very grateful to you for taking me there.'

'Don't worry about it.'

They drove in silence for a few minutes, exiting from the motorway, turning left and right, then getting on to a main road that took them through a straggle of ribbon development and into a brief stretch of open land.

'What about the police?' Van Rensbergen asked as he turned off the highway and drove under a square archway on to the right-hand lane of an overgrown avenue.

'I'll call them once I've had a look around. I didn't want them getting here first to screw it up before I had chance to check it out.' Frank looked appealingly at Van Rensbergen. 'They had a suspect, their first real suspect – they let him leave town. Despite

having a tail on him. No one knows where he is now. If any les-
sons *have* been learned, these guys soon forgot them.'

Van Rensbergen stopped the car and they both got out. The
photographer opened the boot and rummaged around for a
moment, finally producing a head-torch.

'I should have replaced the batteries in this,' he said, shutting
the boot. 'Maybe we won't need it anyway.'

'If you want to stay here . . .' Frank began.

'I'll show you where to go,' said the other man, leading the
way through the trees. 'It's always so still here. Completely quiet,
apart from the odd plane. You never hear any birds singing or
anything.'

'"What kind of garden is this?"' Frank quoted. '"No air. No
flowers. Not even the sound of birds."'

'What's that?'

'A line from a film,' Frank said. '*Malpertuis*. Directed by Harry
Kümel.'

Frank watched Van Rensbergen for any reaction. The photographer's face remained impassive, his eyes giving nothing away.

'Isn't he the guy . . .?' he began, trailing off.

Frank watched him, saying nothing.

'The girls' bodies were found with videotapes of his films?'
Van Rensbergen continued uncertainly.

'That's him,' said Frank.

Van Rensbergen turned away, directing his gaze at the exterior of the institute.

'I don't think I ever saw any of his films,' he said. 'Come on,
I'll take you inside.'

'Are you sure?'

'I don't think he's here.'

Van Rensbergen picked his way through the weeds that surrounded the institute like a moat.

'I meant are you sure you've never seen any of Kümel's films?'
Frank insisted.

'As sure as I can be,' said Henk, stepping through the frame of
a shattered plate-glass window. 'Should I have?'

'He's one of the most important Belgian directors, possibly *the*
most important.'

Van Rensbergen changed the subject: 'Mind the water.' He indicated the small lakes of greenish runoff.

Frank followed as Henk made for the stairs. The floor was carpeted with broken glass, slime, moss.

'Did it not occur to you,' Frank asked Henk's back, 'to call the police?'

'I didn't think there was any need,' came the response, 'until you called me. I didn't connect the man I saw with the murders in Antwerp. Why would I? You get a lot of crazy people entering buildings like this. As you can see. Plus, I didn't get a good look at him. I didn't see his face.'

They had reached one of the landings and Van Rensbergen indicated the graffiti with a sweep of his arm. 'Flatline'. 'Today is a nice day to die'. Eyes purple as peacock feathers. Blue cocks spurting green come.

They stopped outside the door to room 319. 'PARANOIA' sprayed across it in red.

'Was it closed when you left it?' Frank asked.

'No, but then he was still inside. He got up and followed me pretty fast, but the wind closes doors here all the time.'

'Only as long as there's someone around to open them.'

Frank took hold of the handle, twisted it and pushed the door. It remained shut, so he leaned his shoulder against it until, with a grating squeal, it opened.

'Something behind the door,' Frank muttered.

As the door edged open, he glimpsed displaced floor tiles, a green radiator, smashed windows, a hole in the wall. A French window leading to the balcony stood wide open. Still the weight behind the door offered resistance to Frank's pressure. Aware of his heart beating faster and with saliva draining from his mouth, Frank stepped over the threshold and thrust his head around the door.

'This must be what you saw,' said Frank, pushing the door open wider so that Henk could enter.

There was a mannequin lying full length behind the door, its legs roughly sawn off between ankle and knee. Frank knelt down to have a closer look, aware of Van Rensbergen standing behind him.

'It doesn't look like it's come out of a shop window,' said Frank. 'Look. Here and here–' he pointed – 'it looks kind of *rough*. Not finished, if you know what I mean. They're always perfect, aren't they, shop ones? That's the point of them. And look at the hair.'

'What about it?'

'They don't normally have any, do they? They stick wigs on them.'

'What are you suggesting?'

'I don't know. I just wonder if the mannequins are not quite as random as they might appear.'

'Not quite as random?'

'It doesn't exactly look mass-produced, does it? Maybe he makes them. What do you think?' Frank asked, turning round. 'Do you think he makes them?'

Van Rensbergen shrugged.

'And if he makes them,' Frank went on, feeling suddenly nauseous with narrowly focused terror as he examined the figure, 'who does he use as models?'

Frank got up and walked to the window. He glanced over the woods that occupied the hospital grounds, examined the clearing where only the grass grew long. The hill opposite prickled with radio and television masts. The mannequin did not look like Siân, but maybe another one, somewhere else, did. Perhaps Siân's facsimile was elsewhere in the building.

'You were here three days ago?' Frank asked without turning round.

'Yes.'

'And you didn't see any other sign of this man?'

'No.'

Frank examined the mannequin's face. It seemed familiar, but that could be his imagination seeking to make a connection. The cheekbones were high and sharp, like those of the girl in the red light district. Was it her? He'd only seen her for two or three seconds. What he remembered about the face was how lifeless it looked, how glassy the eyes. There was no more life in this face, but did they look alike? He tried to picture the dead girl, but couldn't recall her face in any detail.

'Was there any part of the institute you didn't check?' he asked the man behind him.

Van Rensbergen paused before answering: 'The basement.'

'Let's go.'

Frank led the way down the stairs, stopping to allow his guide to overtake when they reached the ground floor.

'This way,' said the other man, crossing the hall in the direction of a narrow flight of stairs that led down into darkness. Stopping to strap his torch to his head and switch it on, he said, 'We'll need this. I hope the battery holds out.'

With every step, they were more reliant on the torch. When they reached a landing and turned through 180 degrees, it became impossible to see where they were putting their feet.

'Mind your step,' Henk advised. 'It could be slippery.'

When they reached the bottom, all that could be seen was captured in the increasingly dim spotlight of Van Rensbergen's head-torch. This included a graffito sprayed on the door to the corridor ahead of them: 'DEATH ZONE'. Van Rensbergen turned to look at Frank, who could just make out the other's expression. Half-quizzical, half-amused, it struck Frank as some kind of challenge to which he wasn't sure how to respond. He nodded to indicate that they should proceed.

As they entered the first room off the corridor, the torch's feeble beam picking out pipes running down the wall, the battery died.

'Fuck.'

Frank heard something that could have been Henk removing the torch from his head and giving it a shake.

'It's finished,' he said.

Frank took the statement at face value, but when Henk said nothing more, and with not even the slightest trace of light illuminating the darkness, he became nervous. What if he had been too trusting of the photographer? What if, in his arrogant belief that he knew better than the police how to handle the hunt for Siân, he had been fatally naïve? In the darkness, Frank was helpless. At the mercy of the other man. Could *he* be the killer?

Frank instinctively backed away from the centre of the room, his hands groping behind his back for the wall, which he found, cold and moist. He could hear Van Rensbergen moving, but it was impossible to tell if he was stalking him, or if he too was merely trying to feel his way out of the darkness. Then he spoke.

'Do you have a match? Cigarette lighter?'

'I don't smoke,' Frank replied, wondering if he'd been tricked into betraying his position.

If Frank had been hoping that the passage of time and his eyes' growing accustomed to the conditions would have led to the restoration of visual perception, he was frustrated. The blackness before his eyes remained uniform. He was alert to the gritty scrunch of the other man's feet. Did something pass just below his nose? Some kind of movement had displaced the air. Henk's hand, seeking to grab him round the neck? Or his own, as he sought to regain his balance after his foot slipped in a wet patch? He couldn't tell. The disturbance brought a smell to his attention. Sharp, musky, like human sweat. Again, it could have been Henk's or his own, but equally it could have belonged to a third party.

'Siân! Siân!' he called into the dark.

'There's no one down here,' Henk said.

'Siân!' he shouted, panicking. 'How can you tell?' Was Van Rensbergen advising him to save his voice or warning him he wouldn't be heard if he put up a struggle?

'This way,' Henk said. 'I've found the way out.'

Frank heard the door scrape on the floor, Van Rensbergen's footsteps as he re-entered the corridor. He waited, allowing his breathing to settle. His head had started to ache, blood pulsing at his temple. After a moment, he moved towards the sound of Henk's voice.

'Come on,' the photographer was saying. 'I should have changed the fucking batteries.'

In the corridor, Frank could make out a ghost of light coming from beyond the door marked 'DEATH ZONE'.

'All right?' Henk checked.

Frank nodded. 'Just about,' he said.

When they were back on the ground floor, light flooding into the old hospital on all sides, Frank's nerves began to settle. If there was a question mark hanging over the photographer, he'd had ample opportunity to take action in the basement.

'There's nobody down there,' Henk said. 'There's no one in the building at all. I must have scared him off.'

'I guess so.'

'I'll drive you back to Brussels.'

Sitting in the car, Frank opened up his mobile and looked for the number for Bertin and Dockx in Antwerp.

'Calling the police?' Henk asked as he turned the key in the ignition.

'You realise they'll want to talk to you?' Frank said.

'No problem.'

'What about breaking into the institute?'

'The door was open.'

'Detective Bertin? It's Frank Warner.'

20

STREET FURNITURE

You're aware, eating up the outside lane as you narrow the distance between yourself and Antwerp, that it's all beginning to come apart. The tape is the wrong tape. The girl is the wrong girl. Or the girl is the right girl, but the tape is wrong. Or vice versa. Or neither.

Things that don't normally get to you are getting to you. People whose existence you wouldn't normally acknowledge are winding you up. Other drivers. Innocent bystanders. Forcing a reaction from you. Once you wouldn't even have registered. Now you're turning heads, in the quiet moments between the orchestrated crescendos, when you actually want people to take notice.

The appearance of the man in the Institut Lemaire has sent you into a spin. Not that you haven't previously encountered intruders in your chosen retreats. But this wasn't a fourteen-year-old truant with a stolen spraycan. This man was older, more engaged, greater sense of civic duty. Doubtful he would have kept his discovery to himself. It wasn't as if you wanted to stay there for ever, or even for another forty-eight hours, but you weren't finished. In the case of the Gauquié-Hôtel, you were ready to leave. Locked up and left. Key thrown in the sea. Trefil Arbed likewise, although you had stayed longer. Other disued spaces, more recently, closer to Antwerp. Short stays. Holiday lets in the last resort. Always move on, at your own pace. You needed a little longer at the institute. The job wasn't quite done. Nor can you do it now in the back of the van. Too messy. Undignified. Not your style, you joke. Like you have one.

You're going to take her back where she came from. Red light district. Do the legs in situ. If she'll let you. Is she even still alive? You don't know. Does it matter?

The other one was going to be next. Now she'll have to wait.

You slow down, drop to the inside lane. Wipe a patina of dust off the *Pink Bows* postcard propped up on the dash. Consider the question of the tapes. Let down by your supplier, who has sent you *De Komst Van Joachim Stiller*, when he should have sent a copy of *Malpertuis* (Is he stupid? Does he think you don't watch the tapes? You watched it with the girl), you face a choice. Wait for the right tape to arrive, break the chronological sequence or, on this occasion, leave no tape? Given that the tapes mean nothing to you, in terms of their actual content, does it matter if the wrong tape gets left with the wrong girl? If you break the sequence? As long as you make it *look* as if the sequence *is* intact. Label the cassette incorrectly. According to the sequence. Label it *Malpertuis*. See if the police spot the deliberate mistake. In a way it's quite appropriate. Labels, like names, are as unreliable as the things to which – and people to whom – they are assigned. Viz your supplier. You ask yourself in what other ways might he fail you?

When you come off the motorway and wait in a queue to get under the Schelde, you scribble a title on the blank label. *Malpertuis*. Let them demonstrate otherwise.

As Johnny Vos sat in a train travelling west from Liège, listening to 48 Cameras on his Walkman ('Some photos still existed/Torn from outside the cinema'), he looked out at the railway sidings, overhead wires and telegraph poles, the powerful locomotives, brick archways and dazed pedestrians ('Not the departure of bruises/That moans imprison/But the arrival of wax/That blood gives to affection'). The difference between Magritte and Delvaux, he realised, was that one's vision was entirely inward, while the other projected his personal obsessions on to his sur-roundings. Delvaux's work was tied to a time and a place, Belgium in the twentieth century, while Magritte's floated free and would evoke the same responses anywhere, at any time. Delvaux might travel less successfully (although his classical exteriors would always maintain a certain level of universal appeal), but here in Belgium his work would always have more emotional impact than that of his compatriot. Everywhere you looked in this small, fraught, misunderstood country, its psyche tormented by social fracture and frustrated dreams, you saw reminders of Delvaux, as if the fabric of the landscape had been woven into his canvases.

As a boy, Delvaux used to put his ear to telegraph poles. He'd been told that the vibrations he could feel were voices passing along the wires. For hours he used to sit and watch the trams that trundled up and down rue de la Régence. He regarded them as street furniture. At school he was taunted by other boys for having his head in the clouds, for retreating into a dream world. But his retreat paid off. The dream world represented in his paintings was a series of eerie scenes played out on sets meticulously reproduced from reality – whether based on the bricks and mortar of Belgium or the 'ridiculous numbers' of palazzi he was required to draw for his architecture teacher, Joseph Van Neck.

Vos had booked all the way through to the coast with a change at the Gare du Midi in Brussels. He had ten minutes to wait for his connection. Finding a cheap pair of scissors in one of the shops on the station concourse, he locked himself into a toilet cubicle and, not without some difficulty, gave himself a haircut. Flushing the grey-brown hanks out of sight, he left the cubicle and inspected his work in the mirror. Inevitably it was uneven, but under the unbranded woollen beanie he had picked up to replace his too-distinctive baseball cap it didn't look too bad. He dropped the scissors in the trash on his way out.

Vos reached the platform as the train was pulling in, and boarded swiftly. Missing his notebook, he fingered some postcards he had brought with him, studying them one after another. As ever, he became so entranced by the Belgian's silent theatre of erotic melancholy he hardly noticed when the carriage started moving. The journey passed without incident. Vos kept his mobile phone turned off, only switching it on if he needed to make a call. He didn't bother checking his messages, having a fairly good idea what they'd be about.

He took a cab from Veurne – the pretty Flemish town where Delvaux had spent the last years of his life – to St-Idesbald. As he ventured down the little path to the museum, he was aware that he might be walking into a trap. It was well known that his sole reason for being in Belgium was to shoot a film about Delvaux. Now here he was about to turn up at the Paul Delvaux Foundation, a museum devoted to the artist's work. It was possible that he might be expected. Hence the haircut and new hat. Somewhat half-hearted precautions, perhaps, but Vos wasn't especially worried. Belgium's was a police service without a reputation for efficiency. If they did catch up with him and took him into custody, so be it. They would have a hard time proving anything.

To be on the safe side, Vos decided not to speak, since he didn't have the voice skills to disguise his American accent. As he stood at the counter, however, proffering his entrance fee, he soon realised that by remaining silent, an approach that would have been entirely suitable for the taciturn gatekeepers of the Musée de l'Art Wallon in Liège, he was rather drawing attention to himself in this tiny, provincial setting. He felt the woman behind the counter shoot him in the back with her laser eyes as he turned and entered the exhibition space, where, to his dismay, another woman stood sentinel. They might have possessed the same quality of silence as Delvaux's painted women, but these individuals were more critical, less forgiving.

As soon as he found himself in the low-lit interior of the gallery, however, surrounded on all sides by oils and watercolours, sketches, studies and silkscreens, he forgot about the attendants and the police and the journalists and whoever else seemed to want to give him a hard time, and allowed himself to fall under the spell of Delvaux's portraits and landscapes of thwarted desire.

The train back to Brussels was busy and made numerous stops at little stations along the way. Vos looked out of the window, but all he could see were the paintings he'd seen in the museum, a seemingly endless procession of nudes and railway carriages, brick archways, tunnels and bridges. He had not spoken to the women and they had not bothered him. Leaving after half an hour, he had

walked into St-Idesbald and picked up a taxi to the railway station
in Veurne.

In Brussels, Vos caught a tram to Bourse. Delvaux's mural, a
realistic but nevertheless characteristic work painted in 1978 and
featuring early twentieth-century trams, appears on a long narrow panel running across the tracks. At first sight a simple piece,
it needs a little time before you begin to appreciate its subtleties.
Vos leaned against the hand rail, keeping one eye on the mural
and the other on the arriving and departing trams. You became
aware of three time-streams coursing alongside each other like
steel rails: the days of the early trams, which had so fascinated
Delvaux in his youth; the elastic moments of his executing the
painting at the age of eighty-one; and the restless present, with
Delvaux dead but today's trams passing endlessly to and fro
beneath the painting.

Vos went back down to the platform and boarded the next
tram going south. At the Gare du Midi he exited on the east side
of the station. If this was where Delvaux was supposed to have
encountered the Spitzner Museum a lifetime ago, there was no
trace of it today. Unwelcoming bars, Moroccan convenience
stores and the snarl of Belgian motorists dominated the *quartier*.
Vos walked east, skirting the Inner Ring. On rue d'Ecosse, he
approached number fifteen and allowed his fingertips to graze
the wall. Both hands now flat against the brick, he leaned closer
and turned his head so that his cheek rested softly against the
oven-fired clay. Then he pressed against the wall and recoiled,
stepping backwards into the road as he had done in Antheit. No
cars were coming. Again it was only a matter of luck. From the
other side of the street he gazed at the upper storeys, wondering
where the artist's studio had been. Delvaux's family had lived here
in 1924, when the young painter was still producing landscapes
in the Impressionist manner, only a year or so before his
Expressionist flirtation with outsize nudes and posed groups.

As Vos's eye wandered, he noticed an unmistakable form in
the window of the next house along, on the first floor. Rib cage
like a half-closed Venetian blind, the skull a cubist configuration
of shadows and light, the merest hint of texture, alternately
alabaster and abrasive: a human skeleton. Alongside girls whose

cheekbones were revealed by hair swept behind ears. The end of a pencil caught between teeth. Medical students.

Dwarfed by the dome of the Palais de Justice, Vos finally entered rue de la Régence. He was just two minutes' walk from the Museum of Modern Art.

Part Nine

THE SPITZNER MUSEUM

21

'MONSTRUM! MONSTRUM!'

Two floors down in the Museum of Modern Art, the calm is enveloping, womb-like. Vos sat on an upholstered bench in the middle of the room, the wide-eyed sleepwalkers of the museum's Delvaux collection gazing down at him from the walls. *L'incendie* (1935), displaying the influence of Magritte in the colours and in the stance of the sole figure; *Pygmalion* (1939), in which, despite the glimpsed appearance of a bowler-hatted gentleman, it's clear that the visual influence of Magritte is being superseded by a unique atmosphere of uncanny melancholy; *La voix publique* or *La voie publique* (1948), with its juxtaposed nude and widows (black dresses, purple bows), the tramline or 'public way', and the casually unfolded newspaper, *La voix publique*, providing the alternative titles; and *Train du soir* (1957), its slender crescent moon bathing white-walled station buildings, steel rails and platforms in an impossibly radiant glow, while hundreds of ceramic insulators on Delvaux's familiar telegraph poles burn with the brightness of as many candles.

But Vos was captivated by one particular canvas, *The Spitzner Museum* of 1943. He stared at it, unblinking, trying to unlock its secrets.

Fourteen years before losing his virginity to a prostitute twice his age on a cold autumn night in Liège, Johannes Spitz was born, with webbed feet, to fairground folk in Eupen, the centre of

Belgium's relatively small German-speaking community. His parents, sensing a goldmine, waited until he was four or five then took him on the road as a sideshow attraction. The goldmine never quite materialised, since the heyday of the freakshow was long gone, even in eastern Belgium in the 1960s, but the webbed feet of Johannes earned them a trickle of income and a certain notoriety on the fairground circuit.

Johannes's infancy, in a loveless household, was wretched. His birth had been an accident and his parents merely sought – and failed – to make it a fortunate one (for them).

From inside his glass case, he learned that by displaying his deformity to best advantage, he could arouse pleasure in others. But sneers, surprised faces and expressions of disgust were never far from the smiles he managed to elicit. 'Monstrum! Monstrum!' screamed visiting children in German.

At fourteen he ran away to Liège, but since fairs were all he had known, he continued to inhabit the same world and so was constantly looking over his shoulder. He had only been in the city a week when he met a woman at a fair held in Seraing, a steel town in the shadow of Liège. He wandered from one concession-holder to the next, seeking employment. The man running the shooting range told him to go home; the woman in charge of the lucky dip shook her head sadly. An earringed Romany operating the fair's miniature Ferris wheel told him there was no money to spare. A woman bundling her son on to the Ferris wheel overheard and smiled at Johannes. When she didn't follow it up with a laugh or grimace, he smiled back. Maybe he looked old for his age, or maybe the woman liked going with kids, but for whatever reason she seemed attracted to him. As the wheel started to turn, taking her boy away up into the sky, she smiled at Johannes again and drew alongside. She said that he looked lonely and asked if he was looking for company. She quickly added that she wasn't made of money, and she had her little boy to look after. When Johannes said nothing, she remarked that money wasn't everything and if he couldn't pay, he couldn't pay. It was no big deal. Johannes didn't understand, but he liked her smile and liked it even more when it was pressed against his lips. Nor did he mind the smell of alcohol on her breath. She put her arms around him and he responded with awkward enthusiasm as the wheel continued to revolve beside them and although he had his feet on the ground he began to feel giddy.

'Let's get lost,' she murmured.

'What about your son?'

'Let his father look after him for a change,' she said bitterly.

She handed the ride operator more money and asked him to keep the boy on for another turn, then, somewhat unsteadily, led Johannes away from the lights of the fair.

After the time with the woman at the fair (she never told him her name, although she did tell him what she did for a living and she took him back to her place and let him have it on the house, so to speak, three times before saying he should go, which he did, in a state of dazed euphoria), Johannes continued to haunt the region's fairs looking for work. He wound up running the waltzers in a small operation based in Tongeren, north of Liège. The money was lousy but the music was good (he got to choose and the jukebox was filled with Beatles tunes) and he learned a trick or two by watching the youths who came down on Saturday nights. He gave it a couple of seasons and then, armed with functional Flemish, hit the coast and broadened his experience in the leisure industry. He dealt blackjack under Paul Delvaux's vast mural in the casino at Ostend. He spun the roulette wheel at Knokke and every time he looked up from the table caught the eye of one of Delvaux's painted ladies there too. The casino manager, however, drummed into him the importance of watching the punters. Just as they entered the establishment strictly in order to gamble, so did many of them risk that little bit extra by placing a bet after bets had been closed, or attempting to switch from red to black or odd to even once the ball had settled. The manager told him to watch their hands, but he found the eyes gave them away before they'd even raised a finger.

He watched people carefully, but formed no relationships. In Antwerp he went to peep shows in the red light district, but stopped short of paying for sex. Talking to sailors in the Schipperskwartier, he began to think about the world beyond Belgium and decided he needed to see somewhere new. He hung around the docks for a few weeks, checking out the possibilities, and booked passage on a container ship registered in Panama, bound for New York.

In Manhattan, Johannes gravitated towards sleaze, which meant he hung around Broadway and 42nd Street. Just as Hollywood movies tended to cast Europeans as the bad guys, so too did real life. He found the transition from punter to player swift and easy: within a few months he was managing a string of strip clubs and sex shops, and renting a neat little apartment on East 10th Street under the assumed name Jan Spitzner. No one came back there and if he went out for a beer he didn't need anyone coming along to hold his hand. Overexposed as a child, Johannes had learned to be invisible. As far as the authorities were concerned, he didn't exist. He created no wake. When he returned to Antwerp in the 1980s, no one noticed, either there or in the city he'd left behind. He rented a flat, under another false name, on the nineteenth floor of a tower block on the Linkeroever.

He liked the view.

When the Internet came along, it was perfect for Johannes, especially once he'd figured out how to send and receive email via anonymity servers in Finland. He could now post stuff on the Net, or communicate with people, if he wished, from behind as many false layers of assumed identity as he liked. Although he'd more or less turned isolationism into an art, the Net was an unexpected liberation, as if he'd been sprung from a prison he hadn't known was holding him. He trawled the web for images and ideas. The bad-taste site rotten.com was an inspiration and Johannes started building up his own archive of tiffs, gifs and jpegs. He organised the material into different rooms, called it The Spitzner Museum and posted it on the web in such a place and in such a way that no one could trace it back.

Having mastered the technology, Johannes set himself up as a web designer and before long his agency, Monster Monster Design, had more business than it could handle, mainly but not exclusively Internet porn. Starting in the morning with a bunch of photos and some generic text, he could have a site up and running by tea time and charge his weekly rent for it. Since he wasn't interested in money per se, he only did as much design as he needed to, picking and choosing the more interesting jobs. As the technology developed and clients wanted to try new things, he was one of the people who facilitated that, so when diamond dealer Wim De Blieck approached the agency with his idea for an Internet voyeur house, Johannes was all over it. He continued to add to The Spitzner Museum while working on the site for De Blieck, which ended up keeping its working title, The Last House on the Left, when it was ready to go live.

Soon his entire existence was bound up in the two sites. He fixated on Danuta, one of the women in De Blieck's Last House in Moriaanstraat, but when emailing her was careful to keep his punter identity separate from his webmaster identity. His dealings with De Blieck had been conducted online without the two of them ever having to meet, and that was the way he liked it.

The figures on the right of the painting, Vos had read, were friends of the artist. The names were unimportant now, he thought to himself, but then he was instantly stung by the realisation of how upset he would be if, sixty years hence, some art historian were to say, *There was this American director made a film about Delvaux. His name is unimportant now.* Vos wasn't the first person to do Delvaux on film. He knew who his predecessors were – Henri Storck, Paul Haesaerts, Gustave Carels, Joseph Benedek, Paul Danblon and Alain Denis, Jean Antoine, Stéphane Dykman, Adrien Maben – and he would pay them due respect, but Vos's film would be the first full-length feature. The first true biopic of the artist and the man.

Or it would be, if he ever got it made.

Vos's head sank into his cupped hands and he registered the tremor of his facial muscles against his palms. Who the fuck was he trying to kid? This film was never going to get made. With one scene in the can, he was a long way behind any of the Delvaux-inspired filmmakers on his mental list, and he was nowhere near the achievements of feature film directors Alain Resnais, Alain Robbe-Grillet, Harry Kümel and André Delvaux, some of whose work had arguably been inspired, directly or indirectly, by Delvaux.

Vos was not disposed to introspection, and self-pity had always struck him as a category error. His emotional storm blew itself out as swiftly as it had struck. Looking up again at *The Spitzner Museum*, he imagined himself walking down that wide, empty boulevard, his face bathed in the unseen moon, his shadow flung down on the paved surface like a cloak. He pictured himself coming upon the entrance to the museum and climbing the red-carpeted steps. Paying the cashier and ducking beneath the velvet drape, watched by the skeleton on one side and the wax anatomical model on the other.

He remembered another red carpet, a dark, narrow hallway. The apartment two blocks from Broadway and 42nd Street. He recalled standing outside the building, leaning on the buzzer. A man exiting into the street, Vos's catching the door and entering. Climbing the stairs. The door to number six being ajar. The narrow hallway. The regular *thump-thump thump-thump*. The Frieda Kahlo print, heart shockingly exposed. The room at the end. The soft lighting. The honey-coloured body of the desired woman, Amber, still warm. The record sleeve. *Venus Asleep*.

It was why he was here. It was what had led him to this.

22

CROSSED LINES

Moriaanstraat. Morning.

Frank knocked on the door of the Last House. He wasn't expecting an answer and he didn't get one, but he wanted to speak to the blonde woman he and Siân had seen in the bar across the street and he didn't know how else to find her. He knocked again and still there was no response.

Frank had taken two calls on his mobile that morning. The first had woken him up just before nine (it had been a late night). The call was from one of the women at the Delvaux Museum in St-Idesbald. A man had been, she said, but he didn't fit the description. His hair was short and he was wearing a woollen hat, not a baseball cap.

'Was he American?' Frank asked her. 'Did he have an American accent?'

'That's what was strange,' the woman said. 'He didn't speak at all. Normally someone says hello or thank you, but he said nothing.'

'Like he had something to hide?'

'Perhaps, but I wasn't sure. That's why I didn't call you straight away.'

She told him when he'd been, how long he'd stayed.

'What did he make of the paintings?' Frank asked.

'Oh, he liked the paintings. His face changed when he looked at the paintings. He looked . . . alive.'

Frank's second call was from Detective Dockx telling him that they had identified the third girl.

'She was on some video we found in Vos's hotel room.'

'What video?' Frank asked.

'Tape inside a DV camera. We played it. It's basically lots of naked girls in Leopold De Waelplaats, by the Museum of Fine Arts. Some kind of soft porn.'

'It's not soft porn,' Frank said, not bothering to keep the disdain out of his voice. 'It's Vos's film. It's a recreation of a painting by Paul Delvaux. That's his thing. That's Vos's thing.'

'Whatever. She's one of the naked girls.'

'Are you sure?'

'Of course, we're sure.'

'And do you know where Vos is now?'

There was a pause.

'We're working on that,' Dockx said.

Frank remained silent.

'You know,' Dockx continued, 'Bertin wasn't very pleased about you going into the Lemaire Institute on your own.'

'I wasn't on my own.'

'I mean without us. Without even telling us. This investigation is being handled by the police.'

It was Frank's turn to say 'whatever'.

'If you get a lead, you should call us immediately and let us handle it. It's what we do. It's our . . . *thing*.'

'Yeah, right.'

'You know what Bertin says?'

'What?'

'He says *we* don't write film reviews. You know what he means.'

Frank decided he'd humoured the police long enough. 'I haven't got a fucking clue what he means,' he said.

'He means that you should concentrate on writing film reviews,' Dockx went on, ignoring the profanity, 'and let us get on with the police work.'

'OK, look,' said Frank, trying to keep a leash on his anger. 'My girlfriend is missing and there's some mad fucker out there abducting and murdering young women. Any time I spend talking to you is time wasted when I could be out there doing something. And you know what? I don't write "film reviews". I'm a journalist and critic. Call me if anything actually happens, like Johnny Vos walks into police headquarters and handcuffs himself to Detective Bertin – because it seems to me that's the only way you're going to find him.'

With that, Frank severed the connection.

The moment he turned away from the Last House and started to walk off, Frank heard the door open behind him. He turned around. The blonde woman appeared, stepping into the street. Frank tried to catch her eye but she had a distracted air and seemed intent on reaching Korte Koepoortstraat without delay.

'Excuse me,' he said, as she drew level.

'I'm sorry. I'm busy,' she said.

'I just want to ask you about Johnny Vos. Please.'

Mention of Vos's name brought her to an abrupt halt, but she said nothing. Some kind of interior struggle expressed itself in her face.

'If you remember,' Frank continued, 'you heard us talking about Johnny Vos in that bar over there. I was with my girlfriend, Siân. Do you remember? Very striking. Long red hair. She's gone missing. She's been missing for days and I'm desperate. I really need your help.'

'I've got to be somewhere. I promised a friend,' the woman said, the uncertainty in her expression replaced by resolve. 'You'd better come with me and we can talk on the way, though I can't tell you anything I haven't already told the police.'

'Where are we going?' Frank asked when they were sitting in the back of a cab heading north out of the old town.

'My friend Eva has been kicked out of her apartment and I said I would help her move. She's been kind to me.'

'Why's she been kicked out?' Frank asked.

'Someone told her landlord where she works. She works in Moriaanstraat with me. She looks after the girls.'

While they had been looking for a taxi, Danuta had told Frank her name and what the Last House on the Left was all about.

'Who runs the operation?' Frank asked, intrigued by the name of the voyeur house. He assumed it was a deliberate reference to Wes Craven's film, since the house was not actually the last one on the left, whichever way you walked along Moriaanstraat.

'I don't know the owner's name,' Danuta said. 'He doesn't come around much. But he's OK. He's offered to help Eva by letting her stay in the apartment at the top of the house.'

'What about Johnny Vos? How well do you know him?'

'Not well. I did a scene for his film.'

'The dead girls worked on the same scene, didn't they?'

Danuta looked down at her feet. 'Hannah and Katya were friends of mine. I feel responsible,' she said. 'I was trying to get Hannah into the house. She wanted to get out of the red light district. She said she could handle it, but she was so young. It was damaging her. I told her I would look after her.'

'What about Katya?'

'Katya was already in the house, but I put her in touch with Vos. I don't know who the third girl was.'

'I don't know her name, but the police told me she was in that same scene. They've seen the tape and IDed her.' Frank chewed at the inside of his lip. 'From what you know of Vos, do you think he could have done it?'

Danuta shrugged. 'Small dick,' she said, 'so maybe.'

He looked at her. 'You *didn't*, did you?'

She shook her head. 'He was naked in the scene, like the rest of us.'

'Except for the artist presumably? Was there somebody playing Delvaux? I've seen the painting,' Frank said.

'There was someone. We weren't introduced and he didn't hang around afterwards.'

They had reached Groenendaallaan. Danuta asked the driver to wait while she and Frank walked up the steps to meet Eva and help her with her bags. Five minutes later, the taxi was heading back to Moriaanstraat, Frank having moved into the front passenger seat to let the two women sit together in the back. They spoke quietly in a mixture of Flemish and English and although Frank tried to keep up with their conversation, it was difficult because of bursts of static from the driver's radio. But Frank recognised a name that kept cropping up – Jan. He twisted round in his seat.

'Not Jan Spitzner?'

Both women looked at him, at each other, then back at him.

'I don't know,' Danuta said. 'He just signs off "Jan".'

'His email address,' Frank said, trying to remember, 'is it jan@f—f-something? Free-something?'

'It's jan7230@freeze.com. I see it often enough.'

'Tell me about him,' Frank said.

'He's a member of the Last House website,' Danuta said. 'He emails me.'

'All the time,' added Eva. 'Who is he to you?'

'He runs a site of his own,' Frank said, then, turning to Danuta, asked, 'Do you answer his emails?'

'I don't say much,' she responded with a shrug. 'I just thank him for his messages. We're supposed to reply, but keep it brief.'

'What does he write?'

'Weird stuff. I mean, not that weird, but it's like he's obsessed with me.'

Eva was shaking her head. 'I don't like it,' she said.

'He says he misses me when I'm not in the house,' Danuta continued. 'Stuff like that.'

'Take my advice,' Frank said, 'don't write anything personal. Don't encourage him.'

'I haven't.'

'Has he tried to get closer to you, suggested you meet him or anything?'

'No.'

'Well, if he does, don't.'

'What is his website about?' asked Eva.

'You don't want to know,' Frank said. 'Believe me, you do not want to know.'

As the taxi approached the old town, Frank asked Eva about her predicament: 'Who told your landlord about your work?'

'I don't know, but if I ever find out . . .'

'Why would anyone do that?'

She shook her head. 'That's Belgium for you. A country of fuck-ups and hypocrites.'

'Where are you from, Eva?'

'I was born in Antwerp.'

'Right. So, now you're going to live above the shop?'

'The owner offered. He's a nice guy in a dirty business.'

'I'll take your word for it.'

Frank's phone vibrated. No number appeared.

'Excuse me,' he said as he took the call.

'You sent me an email,' said a nasal voice.

'I send a lot of emails,' said Frank.

'My name is Jan Spitzner.'

'One second.' Frank turned round again. 'I have to take this. I'll catch up with you later. Write your number down for me and I'll be in touch.'

Danuta passed her number across and Frank asked the driver to stop and let him out.

'Good luck,' Frank said as he leaned back in.

Watching the taxi resume the short journey to Moriaanstraat, Frank lifted the phone to his ear.

'Spitzner?'

'Still here. Lucky for you.'

Spitzner sounded Flemish. He spoke good idiomatic English with a slight American accent.

'I want to talk about some pictures on your website.'

'I don't do prints.'

'The three photos on your opening page.'

'Like I said, it's not an online store.'

'So what is it then? A freakshow? Porn for the morbidly obsessed?'

'It's a resource. It's a way of life. It's whatever you want it to be. It's—'

'Who do you know in the police?' Frank interrupted.

'What?'

'The police. Who's bent? How bad is it?'

'What are you talking about?'

'You've got to have someone on the inside to be getting hold of those pictures.'

It wasn't just the three pictures on the opening page: the Spitzner Museum was full of morgue shots, crime scene pictures, autopsy video frame grabs. You couldn't get that stuff without a helping hand from the point of source. Dockx's patronising attitude, peddling second-hand judgements from his bad-cop partner, had angered Frank, who wanted to know which one of the two of them was taking backhanders from the gross-out merchant.

'You think I'm in with the police?' Spitzner laughed.

'Just give me a name.' Frank paused, but Spitzner's rasping breath was all he could hear. 'Meet me, if you're worried about them listening in, though I doubt they know how. *If* you've got the balls.'

Silence. Then: 'Come to the Left Bank. King Baudouin Monument. You've got ten minutes.' And he rang off.

Ten minutes. Ten minutes to get there, or ten minutes' audience once he was there? Frank didn't know. *Come to the Left Bank.* Frank started to shift. He ran through the medieval equivalent of a wind tunnel created by the narrow gap between the cathedral and the various inns and bars on Lijnwaadmarkt, then across the cobbled square in front of the cathedral, where his was the only face not upturned to gawp at the magnificent, prickly spire sweeping 404 dizzying feet into the sky. Was Spitzner already on the Left Bank? Was that where he worked, where he lived? Was his choice of words a slip or merely a function of using a foreign language? Would Frank even be able to get there in ten minutes? It could take almost that long to walk through the St Anna Foot Tunnel.

Gasping, Frank staggered towards the tunnel entrance. He rested briefly on the down escalator, but when he checked his watch and saw he had only two minutes left he started walking again, taking the steps two at a time. The tunnel itself was busy – pedestrians, joggers, cyclists. As Frank ran, weaving in and out of the traffic, he noticed an anomaly he'd failed to spot when he'd taken the tunnel with Siân: the floor was asymmetrical. The long line of panels running down the middle of the tunnel floor was not dead centre, but, from his point of view, slightly favoured the left. There was room for five lines of stone flags on the right of the central panels, but only three on the left. Why not four on each side? What possible reason could there be not to make it symmetrical? Something specific to this tunnel, perhaps, or a necessary design feature of all tunnels of this type? Or maybe it was just a Belgian thing?

He emerged into bright daylight and ran out of the tunnel building to the right. He was two minutes late and praying Spitzner would still be there. The tendons in his neck jarred as he jerked his head in all directions. Apart from the other people who had exited the tunnel with him and headed off towards the bus stops and tower blocks, there was only one other single figure and a couple between himself and the King Baudouin Monument. As he got closer he saw that the individual was clearly a woman and that the couple – middle-aged tourists, sensible shoes, backpacks – were just beginning an inspection of the photographs of the former king slotted behind a Perspex screen attached to the monument. He walked towards the river, muttering to himself as his eyes were stung by an abrupt flurry of tears. He was blowing his nose when his mobile started to ring and so he didn't hear it at first. As soon as he did, he fumbled the device out of his pocket and flipped it open.

'Spitzner?'

Two beats, then Spitzner spoke. 'Look across the river,' he said. 'See the terrace?'

Frank could see a new-looking raised terrace-style walkway directly opposite on the right bank.

'Yes.'

'Do you see someone leaning on the rail?'

Frank's eyes pored over the tiny figures populating the terrace. Only one was stationary at that moment.

'Yes.'

'Good. Now raise your arm.'

Frank did as instructed.

'Now I see you,' Spitzner said. 'Move on to the jetty.'

Nervously Frank stepped forward on to the wooden jetty. The tide was rising, the clay-coloured waters of the Schelde splashing against the slimy piles that supported the ageing structure.

'We could have saved ourselves five minutes,' Frank said, 'and a lot of effort on my part.'

'This is close enough,' the man retorted.

Although Frank had a figure to focus on, the voice still seemed disembodied. The width of the river was far too great to be able to see anything of Spitzner other than a vague outline.

'You were going to tell me who your contact is inside the police,' Frank reminded him. 'I got the impression you didn't want to say *over the phone.*'

'You have no idea,' Spitzner sneered.

'So tell me.'

Frank heard only the harsh sound of the other man's breathing and the noisily vigorous advance of the tide.

'You think those pictures on the site are police photos?' Spitzner said at length. He didn't give Frank time to respond, continuing: 'I do use a lot of police pictures, from the US and Eastern Europe, but the three pictures you are asking about were not from the police.'

'So where are they from?'

'I took them.'

Tiny hairs on the back of Frank's neck prickled as they became erect.

'What?'

Spitzner remained silent.

Frank stared across the river at the man leaning on the rail. Everything beyond him – the old town, the centre of Antwerp, the dominating presence of the cathedral's sixteenth-century spire – seemed suddenly to get further away as Frank's vision rapid-zoomed on the man on the other end of the phone. The *Vertigo* effect was an illusion and didn't help him to see the man any more clearly.

'You took them?'

'Yes.'

'You killed those girls?' he said, hearing the question as if it had been asked by somebody else.

'No. But I took the photographs.'

'How?'

'I got there before the police. Before the bodies were found. You might even say I found them. All three.'

Frank felt as if he were under water, succumbing to pressure that seemed to be increasing as he sank deeper and deeper. He wanted to keep Spitzner talking in order to find out everything he knew, because Siân's life might depend on it, but also because he was trying, simultaneously, to work out a way in which he might be able to get hold of the man and either beat the truth out of him or deliver him to the police. This must be why they said you should never work a case in which you were personally involved. He was finding it almost impossible to think straight and achieve his objectives when faced with the man who, by his own admission, had photographed the three dead girls and who, presumably, therefore, knew something about the abduction of Siân.

'Can't we talk face to face?'

'We *are* talking face to face.'

'Without the river being in the way.'

'I'm not as stupid as you seem to think.'

'How did you get to take those photographs?'

As Frank waited for a response, he suddenly started to doubt that the man he was looking at, the man on the other side of the river, was in fact Spitzner. He didn't question that the man whose voice he could hear in the tiny handset was him, but he only had his word for it that the man leaning on the railing was actually Spitzner and neither some paid stooge, nor an innocent tourist admiring the view of the Schelde.

'I get a message,' the man said quietly, and as he did so, the man Frank was watching turned and started to walk along the distant terrace.

'What do you mean, you get a message?'

'I get a message when it's time, telling me where to go.'

The man stopped walking and leaned on the railing again looking out across the river.

'Who sends you the message?'

'A man I work for.'

'*A man you work for?* You mean the girls' abductor, their killer?'

There was silence for a moment. The man across the river walked back the way he had come and regained his original position leaning against the rail.

Then, quietly, he said: 'Their killer, yes.'

A wooden board creaked on the jetty behind Frank, whose adrenal glands got busy in the time it took him to swivel round.

The newcomer was a woman, the woman Frank had seen before. She was speaking on a mobile phone, or rather listening, a smile on her face as she gazed upriver.

Frank pressed his thumb over the mouthpiece of his own phone and hissed: 'I need your help. *I need your help.*'

The woman looked at him in surprise. With his free hand, Frank slid a card out of his pocket and dropped it on to the jetty.

'Please ring that number,' he whispered frantically, 'and tell whoever answers that the man they are looking for is on the right bank of the river directly opposite the Baudouin Monument. Talking on a mobile phone.'

The woman looked unsure. Frank could hear Spitzner's voice buzzing in the phone. He raised it to his ear.

'What is it?' Spitzner was asking.

'I lost you,' Frank lied. 'I lost the signal. My battery's low. It can't hold the signal.'

He lowered the phone again and covered the mouthpiece, addressing the woman. 'Please! You could be saving someone's life. Take the card. Call the police.'

When he could see that she had made the decision to help, Frank raised his phone to his ear once more and turned to look at the river.

'Who's that with you?' Spitzner wanted to know.

'No one. A tourist. I got rid of her.'

The man across the river had not moved.

'Fuck with me,' the voice said flatly, 'and you'll never find her alive.'

Frank held the phone tighter. 'What?' he said. 'Where is she? Tell me.'

'So now I have your attention.'

'Yes, you have my fucking attention. Now where is she?'

'Don't yell at me, asshole. I'm trying to help you.'

'Where is she?'

'I don't know.'

'You don't know.' Frank looked around. The woman had moved away and appeared still to be on the phone, though whether she was speaking to the police or to the previous party, Frank did not know. 'So who killed the girls?'

'A guy. I don't know his name.'

'A guy. You don't know his name. Fucking hell. You want to give me his phone number?' Frank's sarcasm had a bitter edge to it.

'He got in touch one day. Asked me to help him. A job offer. He wanted me to get things for him.'

'Things. What things? Not the *girls*?' Frank said, as the possibility dawned on him.

'The girls. The tapes.'

Frank heard movement behind him. It was the woman with the mobile giving him the thumbs up. He waved his thanks and indicated she should make herself scarce.

'You abducted the girls?'

'Yes, but not your girlfriend.'

'Why should I believe you?'

'You think I care? He took her.'

'So where is she? Is she still alive?'

'I already told you. I don't know.'

'How do I know you're telling me the truth?'

'You don't.' He fell silent.

Frank listened, but put his finger over the mouthpiece.

'The last tape,' Spitzner started. 'They said it was *Malpertuis*, because that was Harry Kümel's third film, but the tape I supplied wasn't *Malpertuis*. It was *De Komst Van Joachim Stiller*. They got it wrong. They just assumed it was *Malpertuis*. As soon as they check, you'll see it was *Joachim Stiller*.'

Frank kept his finger over the mouthpiece. Eventually he moved it away and said, 'Signal's going again,' moving his finger over and away from the mouthpiece as he did so. 'So you sent him the wrong tape?' he then asked.

'Yeah.'

'Why?'

'To teach him a lesson. Fuck with me, I fuck with you.'

'You vain, conceited, arrogant, malicious little prick,' Frank said, but his finger was covering the mouthpiece again. Moving it away, he said, 'I'm backing away from the river to see if the signal improves. Maybe the monument is interfering with it.'

As soon as he had withdrawn as far as the monument, he

disappeared around the back of the metal screen and ran towards the tunnel entrance. Once he emerged from behind the monument, there was a line of trees between himself and the river. He dived into the tunnel entrance, half-ran, half-tumbled down the escalator, ran straight into a cyclist the moment he turned the corner into the tunnel itself, picked himself up and ran as fast as he could, dodging on-comers and holding on tight to his phone.

He had reached the mid-point when it happened. The blow to his head could have come from in front or behind. There was no telling. Frank went down like a corpse, his mobile clattering against the tiled wall and skittering off down the rapidly darkening tunnel.

23

POINT OF VIEW

Frank came round. He was disoriented and had a thumping headache. Two people were kneeling over him.

'What happened?' he asked, rubbing his head.

The man, a middle-aged North African, shrugged; a young white woman was shaking her head.

'How long was I out?'

This time the young woman shrugged. Frank looked at his watch, struggled to make sense of the unnumbered dial. The man was trying to hand him something – his mobile phone. Frank tried groggily to get to his feet with the young woman's help. Standing, if a little unsteadily, he checked his call records and worked out from the time of his last call dialled that he could not have been out for more than a few minutes, probably less. There was a bump on his head, swelling by the second. The good Samaritans were still hanging around extending vague offers of help. Frank was looking at the floor as things suddenly started to slot back into place.

Three lines of stone flags on the left of the central panels, five on the right.

Three on the left, five on the right.

Turning and raising a hand in thanks, Frank ran.

Leaving the tunnel on the right bank, he turned and headed back towards the river. Two squad cars were parked on Ernest V Dijckkai, which was as close as they could get to the Wandelterras Zuid, where Frank ran into Detectives Dockx and Bertin.

'Why am I not surprised to see you?' Bertin asked.

'Did you get him?' Frank said, ignoring the jibe.

'Did we get who?'

'His name is Jan Spitzner. He's involved.'

'Which is more than I feel *I* am sometimes,' retorted the cop.
Dockx contented himself with looking on disapprovingly.

Frank filled the pair in on the basic facts of his conversation
with Spitzner, which excluded any mention of the videotapes, so
when Dockx finally spoke, to tell Frank that the video found
with the third girl and labelled *Malpertuis* had in fact turned out
to be *De Komst Van Joachim Stiller*, taped off Belgian TV during a
repeat transmission, Frank just nodded and stared across the river
at the jetty on the left bank where he had stood talking to
Spitzner. So any lingering doubts about the veracity of the webmaster's testimony seemed to have been quashed by this latest
revelation. Or had they? There still remained the possibility that
Spitzner had a man on the force: their partnership could account
for what Frank had just been told.

'I don't suppose you have his number?' Bertin said.

'He called me. No number. But you could always email him.
Perhaps he'll call you like he called me.'

'Oh, by the way,' said Dockx, 'we found a witness. Someone
reported a white van stopped in the middle of the road the night
Ms Marchmont went missing.'

'Where?'

'Close to the restaurant. A couple of blocks.'

'A white van. That should narrow it down a bit.'

As he walked away from the policemen, leaving them to direct
the search for forensic evidence and witness statements, Frank
wondered about Spitzner's motive for calling him at all. Pride in
his evil achievements? Putting the pictures up on the site was evidence enough of that. Remorse at what he'd done? Hardly. A
desire to set the record straight? If Frank took what Spitzner had
said at face value and accepted that he had abducted the three
girls who had wound up dead – and only those three – and that
another man was responsible for the murders, then perhaps
Spitzner wanted Frank to know that he was not involved in Siân's
disappearance. But why? Was it simply human nature not to wish

to be credited with an offence you hadn't committed? Even when you'd committed the same offence with three other victims. What about those who made false confessions? Were they likely to be offenders themselves or just harmless fuck-ups?

As Frank pictured himself leaning once more on that wooden jetty over the swirling waters of the Schelde talking on the phone to the fuck-up who claimed to have abducted the three dead girls, but not to have killed them, and not to have laid a hand on Siân, he realised he was getting dangerously out of his depth. He began to wonder if he was a fuck-up himself. The only thing he knew for certain, despite having spent ten minutes listening to Spitzner whisper in his ear and despite having then found himself near enough to the man that he could have felt his breath on the back of his neck if only he'd known he was that close, was that he was actually no nearer to finding Siân. Only if the man called him back might he find out more. But if Spitzner had wanted to carry on the conversation, why would he have smacked Frank over the head?

He made for the hotel, where he would charge up his mobile and decide whether to stay in Antwerp and wait for the phone to ring or go to Brussels in search of Vos.

Danuta, her dark roots obvious from this angle, helped Eva carry her stuff up to the tiny apartment at the top of the Last House. Dropping Eva's bags, they each, perhaps for the benefit of the other, performed a superficial inspection of the accommodation, since they were both seeing this part of the building for the first time. Neither had even known it was there, because, as the owner, I had gone to the trouble and expense of providing a separate entrance and private staircase when redeveloping the property.

I had left a key and instructions for Eva at the house.

'No cameras,' said Danuta, her gaze sweeping the walls.

Eva gave a tired little laugh. 'Good,' she said.

In the spare bedroom of the house in Sint-Jozefstraat, my centre of operations, I moved closer to the screen and switched from the smoke detector camera, which provided an overhead view, to the camera hidden in the wall clock. The pictures from these concealed devices were not as good as those I got – and those the members enjoyed – from the rest of the Last House, but they had the benefit of being taken without the subject's knowledge. This was how I had wanted to watch Eva. All I desired now was for Danuta to go back downstairs leaving Eva on her own.

That wasn't strictly true. Twenty-four hours earlier that would have been all I desired. Now there was another far more unwelcome distraction. I looked away from the screen and sat back in my chair to see if I could hear anything, but the noises from downstairs – from downstairs in the house in Sint-Jozefstraat – had stopped for a moment. I knew the respite would be brief.

I returned my gaze to the screen. Eva lay down on the bed, which Danuta took as her cue.

'I'm just going to have five minutes,' Eva said, resting her head in her hand and allowing it to sink into the pillow. 'I'll come down later.'

I heard the door close as Danuta left the apartment.

I switched to the third and final camera, the pinhole device in the bedside lamp. This angle afforded me the perfect view of Eva's lovely face in repose, like 'blanche' in Man Ray's photograph *Noire et blanche*. I watched as her muscles gradually relaxed with the occasional twitch, and then her breathing became slow and regular and she was asleep. After about ten minutes, during which time neither of us had moved and my lower back had started to ache from holding the same slightly uncomfortable position, her eyes began to sweep from left to right like twin searchlights beneath her lids.

The spell was broken by more noise from downstairs.

The source of the noise was Penny. Penny had come back. The previous evening there had been a knock on the door. I had answered it to find Penny standing outside in Sint-Jozefstraat.

'I lost my key,' was all she said. There were no explanations, no tearful reunion, no catching up on each other's news. I didn't ask her where she had been. I found I didn't want to know. I hadn't wanted to know for a long time. Instead I backed away and allowed her to enter the house. Perhaps I shouldn't have done. She walked slowly as if carrying a great weight, although she had no bag. I watched her walk into what had once been our living room, while I remained in the hall, able to see through the crack between the door and the frame. She moved around, picking things up and putting them back down, yet with no apparent purpose. She didn't appear to be looking for anything.

I withdrew, leaving her there, and went back upstairs to my room where I was running live feed from the Last House, waiting for Eva to show up. I didn't know if she would arrive that evening or the following day. I heard Penny go through into the kitchen and open the fridge. She must have dropped a bottle of something on to the tiled floor because I heard a crash. I didn't go to investigate. Later she came upstairs and pushed open the door of the second bedroom, the room I was in. My shout halted her progress through the doorway. She waited a moment, then reversed out, leaving the door open. I got up to slam it shut, hoping she would get the message. I thought if I ignored her she might go away again, but she didn't. She slept downstairs on the couch and when I went down in the morning, she was sitting there staring at the blank television screen like a long-stay patient.

In the kitchen there were slices of ham on the floor. Squashed capers and broken glass in a pool of vinegar. A pile of cut-up newspapers had been upended and dispersed on the table, some of them having fallen on to the floor.

I went back upstairs. I didn't want to miss Eva. I knew that the night before had been her last in her apartment at Groenendaallaan. Her landlord had given her notice when he had discovered what she did for a living.

As I watched Eva sleep, all I could hear was Penny moving around downstairs, bumping into things, tearing pictures off the walls and Frisbeeing them at the television, and I knew it was over. I couldn't stay. Nor was there anywhere left to go. I couldn't occupy the room above the Last House because I had installed Eva there for my own reasons.

I could hear Penny downstairs, at first just mumbling, then speaking increasingly loudly and calling out in sharp, cracked bursts. 'Who are you?' she was saying. 'Who the fuck are you? WHO THE FUCK ARE YOU?' I didn't know to whom she was addressing the question, whether to me, herself or some unknown third party.

★

Jan Spitzner was watching as Danuta re-entered the Last House. He switched from camera one to camera fourteen as she moved from the front of the house to the back to swap a few words about Eva with Nana, the Congolese girl, who was sitting reading a detective novel having, for the benefit of the members, removed her top and placed it on the seat beside her. When Danuta headed for the stairs, Spitzner flicked to camera nineteen so that he would see her reaching the landing on the second floor. He reverted quickly to camera fourteen to have another look at Nana, then switched to camera twenty-three, which was the sole camera in Danuta's bedroom, in time to see her flop on to her bed and give a long weary sigh.

Bringing up his email programme, he started to type.

Subject: Who's next?
From: jan7230@freeze.com
To: danuta@lasthouse.com

Who should be next, Danuta? Who do you think? Eva? One of the Irish girls perhaps? Or Nana? We don't want to be accused of being racist, after all. Janx

He moved the pointer over the send button and his finger hovered over the mouse. With a smile on his face he looked up from the machine and out of the window. To the left were the docks; straight on and across the river, the long timber-walled shed of the redeveloped Hangar 26, beyond which the tallest landmark was the derelict grain silo at the head of Kattendijkdok; slightly to the right, on this side of the river, the King Baudouin Monument, the wooden jetty just beyond it and back inland the entrance to the St Anna Foot Tunnel, then, across the water, the Wandelterras Zuid, the old town, the Grote Markt, the cathedral. He could make out the great humpbacked silhouette of Centraal Station, squatting rodent-like over the Diamond Quarter, the viaduct carrying the track out of the station in a wavy line like the wire out of the back of a computer mouse.

He looked back at the screen, moved his right hand, clicked and dropped the email in the trashcan.

★

Siân was in deep water, far from the light, kicking out feebly as she struggled to climb to the surface before her lungs gave out, but something was fast around her ankle, anchoring her to the bottom. Air exited her mouth in a flurry of champagne bubbles. She watched them cascade upwards, catching the light and drawing it down into the depths. The more bubbles she made, therefore, the lighter it would be, and the lighter it was, the closer to the surface she would be. Didn't that follow? It did indeed become brighter in the water around her. The bubbles tickled her face as they escaped.

She heard the sound again that she had heard previously and this time she very nearly put a name to it. But still it hung tantalisingly just out of reach. A low, mournful sound. Evocative of Clacton's bitter winter afternoons. Cold grey sea. Boats floating on the horizon. Then, suddenly, she knew what it was; she mouthed the word before she forgot it. Her lips moved but no sound came out. The word was foghorn. She seized hold of it before it could slip away into the deep water. Foghorn, hooter, klaxon. The sound a ship made. She was near water. She *was*, though. She actually *was* near water. Antwerp was a port, she reminded herself. Maybe wherever you were in Antwerp, you could hear the ships, or maybe you had to be in the docks, or close to the docks, to hear them.

She opened her eyes. All around her was as black as it had ever been. There was no light, no trick of the light, no champagne bubbles of light escaping through a liquid darkness. But she felt different, stronger. Her throat less sore, mouth less dry. She could move. Both arms were free. One hand knocked against something that then fell over. A plastic bottle. Water. She grabbed it to conserve the contents, but there was a lid. She unscrewed it and drank the sweetest – and shortest – drink she had ever drunk. Swallowing hurt and so did the fact that there was no more water to drink. But the rehydration, even if it was inadequate, did invigorate her. She felt more awake and more alive than she had done for days. Her sense of smell perked up: damp, salt, something sharp and acidic, but what? Belatedly realising that she shouldn't have been able to move both her arms freely, she tried to shift her legs, only to find that one was secured, by the ankle, and she was still a prisoner.

'Henk Van Rensbergen?'

'Yes?'

'Frank Warner. Listen, Henk. I need your help. I need a list of places to look. Abandoned places in Antwerp.'

'I got my knuckles rapped by the police for taking you to the Institut Lemaire.'

'They're pissed off because they didn't think of it first. I'm still trying to stay ahead of them. They're so far behind I've got to. Do you have any ideas?'

'Don't worry. I can handle a little attitude from the police. Otherwise I wouldn't be able to do what I do.'

'Exactly.'

'Let me look through my records.'

'You'll call me?'

'You want somewhere he can stay and keep out of sight?'

'I *know* there's a place somewhere, an abandoned building presumably, if he's sticking to the pattern, where he's holding Siân and is keeping her alive until he's got the right tape.'

'Ten minutes. Fifteen at the most. I'll call you.'

Spitzner would have preferred it to have been someone neither from the Last House, nor connected with the Delvaux film, but those were his only two links to Danuta. She presumably had family and friends somewhere in Poland, news of whose disappearance would reach her swiftly, but it was a little far to go when the same effect could be achieved here in Antwerp.

For the three successful abductions he had carried out so far, Spitzner had used hire vehicles. A different van each time, from a different rental company. Different makes. Different colours as well. He was careful.

He sat now in the fourth such vehicle at the corner of Zirkstraat and Lange Koepoortstraat, the engine running, waiting for Nana, the Congolese girl from the Last House, to appear in his rear-view mirror. If she stuck to her routine, she would walk up Lange Koepoortstraat, intending to turn left into

St-Paulusstraat and head up to the red light district, where she still worked the windows a couple of times a week. He guessed she needed the money, unless she did it because she liked it.

He spotted her and was glad to see that she was alone, as usual. Once she had passed the van, he selected first gear and checked his mirror. Slowly and quietly he moved away from the kerb. She was still fifty metres from the intersection and the only other pedestrians in the vicinity were an old woman with a bag of shopping and two youths in hooded tops. He buzzed his window down, rested his left elbow casually on the door frame and pulled alongside. As Nana turned to see what was up, his mobile rang. Spitzner received very few calls, which was how he liked it. He cursed and pulled the phone out of his pocket and checked the screen. He looked at the number displayed. It was familiar, but he couldn't immediately identify it.

You've given up on Jan Spitzner. You don't doubt he'd be able to find a tape of *Malpertuis* for you, but you no longer trust him. Pulling a trick like supplying the wrong tape was a sign that he was tired of his subordinate role and wanted more input. It wasn't about Spitzner, so he had to be left out of the picture. Taking him out permanently, of course, was an option that had occurred to you, but there seemed little point. His creative contribution had been unhelpful and in poor taste, but he wasn't a liability.

You're in an Internet café on the south side searching for a VHS of Harry Kümel's supposed masterpiece. It's not about Kümel either, but you need this tape to carry on. And then you'll need the others – *The Lost Paradise*, *The Secrets of Love*, *Eline Vere*. You have a feeling that *The Secrets of Love* will not be so hard to find, erotica never going out of fashion. As for *The Lost Paradise* and *Eline Vere*, you do not know; all your efforts for the time being are going into locating a copy of *Malpertuis*.

You get numerous links for 'Harry Kümel Malpertuis', but none offering videotapes for sale, apart from links to online stores that then tell you they can't find a match for either the title or the director's name. Adding 'VHS' to the search string takes you to a website for a Brazilian film festival, where there's a paragraph on *Malpertuis*. You don't speak Portuguese, but you can see clearly enough it's a dead end.

You try eBay without success, scan American movie sites of no conceivable interest, and end up scrolling through the message boards of a UK-based fiction magazine where you find a number of postings about Kümel's films. You send a quick email to the contributor who posts with the most conviction and apparent knowledge of his subject, a Kümel enthusiast called Michael Kemp, then give him five minutes to respond, in case he's online, before quitting, paying the proprietor and leaving. You jump in the van, keeping half an eye out for the next Internet café.

Picking up Vos's notebook, which he'd been flicking through once more while walking back to the hotel, Frank started to inspect its contents more closely. It wasn't that he hadn't already looked through the notebook several times – he had. But he had always been either chasing after someone (Siân, Vos), or trying to get away from someone (the police, himself), or he'd looked at the notebook late at night when he was already half-asleep. Some outside factor, he now tried to convince himself, had always compromised his concentration. He told himself he had to look through it once more, and to think laterally, while waiting for Van Rensbergen to call back.

He searched through the pages of notes, half-formed ideas and numerous rudimentary diagrams relating to the film Vos had barely started shooting. He reread passages, struggling with Vos's careless handwriting, looking for hidden meanings. There was a section of about twenty pages in the middle of the notebook where the director appeared to have sat down and written whatever came into his head. Whether it was stream of consciousness or automatic writing, Frank wasn't sure, but he had read bits of it before and it had seemed rather banal. He skipped through it again. The glimpses he had of the content didn't give him cause to reconsider, but when the section was nearing its end, by which time he had started to turn the pages faster, he suddenly stopped and went back, a change in the density of the writing having caught his eye. Sure enough, there was a double-page spread that did not follow on from the page before. The writing was slightly larger and did not stick to the lines on the page, drifting up at the right margin.

Frank read it.

The next page picked up from three pages before, as if the text on the spread had been written at an earlier time. As if Vos had opened the notebook at random to get some thoughts down on paper before he forgot them.

He wrote about Harry Kümel. About similarities between *Daughters of Darkness* and Resnais's *Last Year at Marienbad*. He noted that *Marienbad* was partly inspired by Delvaux's work. Lightly scored arrows established links between Robbe-Grillet, who wrote *Marienbad*, and Delvaux, the latter having produced decors for the film adaptation of Robbe-Grillet's novel *Les gommes*, which was underlined in the notebook. Delvaux and Robbe-Grillet collaborated on a book, *Construction of a Ruined Temple for the Goddess Vanadis*, which was also underlined. An observation concerning Delvaux's obsession with trains, particularly night trains, was circled in pencil and an arrow drawn back to *Daughters of Darkness*, which Frank remembered opened with a love scene on a night train bound for Ostend. Here, in parentheses, symbolist painter Leon Spilliaert was mentioned, specifically his *Woman on the Quay* (1908). Then Vos had written 'nudes/dunes – Kümel & Delvaux. Flemish tradition or Belgian?'

What did any of this prove? That Vos knew of Kümel's work and had seen *Daughters of Darkness*. Surely, one would have expected him to. His notes made explicit certain similarities between the frames of reference of the two different artists, but then both were Belgian, so both would have been influenced by the landscape in which they had grown up. Delvaux was a Walloon, but he had settled in Flanders, close to the coast, with its wave upon wave of dunes. Kümel was born in Antwerp, the Flemish capital, and had lived all his life in the city.

All it really established was an intellectual link between Vos and Kümel. The former was, at the very least, interested in the latter. There had to be some reason behind the depositing of Kümel videos with the bodies of the murdered girls. There had to be some level of interest, on the part of the murderer, in Kümel.

Possibilities raced through Frank's mind as he flicked through to the end of the notebook, finding nothing else remarkable. He opened it again at the beginning and looked at Vos's name, which the director had written on the inside front cover in fibre-tip pen: 'J. VOS'. At the bottom of the inside front cover was a phone number. When Frank had noticed it before he had assumed it was Vos's, recorded there so that anyone finding the notebook might call him to arrange its return, but now that he looked at it again, he saw that it wasn't Vos's. At least, it wasn't the number that Frank had for the director. He picked up his mobile and accessed the phone book to check. Vos's number, the one that Frank had previously used to speak to the American, did not correspond to the figures inscribed in the notebook. Could this explain why he'd had no response from Vos's phone in recent days? Did he have two mobiles, for A-list and B-list callers? Might he finally get hold of Vos by calling this number?

He punched the digits into his phone.

Nothing.

He tried prefacing them with the international code for the USA.

Still nothing.

He inserted the Belgian code instead and got a ringing tone. It rang twice. Three times. And was answered.

'Who is this?' said a voice.

Frank snapped the phone shut to end the call, his palms greasy with sweat.

He had recognised the voice instantly. The nasal quality. The unnatural-sounding American accent. He'd been talking to its owner an hour ago.

He stared at the phone in shock, waiting for it to ring. He imagined Spitzner on the other end fizzing with rage for Frank's having traced his number. Worst case scenario, Spitzner would now somehow arrange for Siân to die, if that was within his power, merely out of spite or damaged pride. At best, he was bound to withdraw the offer of help he'd been making earlier in the day.

While struggling to get his head around all the various new

implications, he realised he was staring one certain awful truth in the face: Johnny Vos and Jan Spitzner knew each other.

The phone rang. He stared at it. The number he now knew to be Spitzner's had appeared on the screen. He continued to stare at it, willing it to stop so that he wouldn't have to answer it. Insane notions flew into his brain. He thought of stamping on the phone. Or putting on a silly voice to answer it. Like he might have done if he'd known it was Siân. He'd pretend to be a Chinese restaurant or he'd answer it by saying 'Siân Marchmont's phone', which always threw her for a moment.

He flipped open the talk pad and listened.

'Where did you get this number?'

Spitzner's voice was flat, without emotion.

'Where is she, Spitzner? Where is Siân?'

'You might as well book the funeral,' he said, before hanging up.

Frank rang back, but got a recorded message, the kind of default message that you would get when someone's phone was not switched on, or had been flushed down the toilet, or thrown directly into the river.

'Fuck. Fuck fuck fuck. Fucking fuck.'

He tried the number again and got the same message. He called Henk Van Rensbergen, who said he'd been trying to get through because he'd drawn up the list Frank had requested. Frank asked him to dictate it, but Henk said it was quite long and so it might be better to email it, which he would do right away. Frank thanked him and rang off. He gave it five minutes, then went online and picked up his emails, among them Van Rensbergen's. The list was longer than he'd anticipated, including such places as Antwerp South railway station, the Astrid, Calypso, Rex and Savoy cinemas, among numerous others, a military hospital and barracks in Antwerp, a brick factory in Boom and a metal works in Hoboken, and the Kattendijkdok grain silo and Boel shipyard, both in the Antwerp harbour area. The last name on the list was Doel. No elaboration, just Doel. Frank didn't know where or what Doel was, though he guessed it would mean something to Bertin and Dockx. Van Rensbergen had added a note to the effect that he couldn't guarantee all these places were still abandoned. Some could have been knocked down and redeveloped since his last visit. But it was as good a list as he could come up with in the time allowed.

Frank quickly transcribed the list and wrote a hurried note to detectives Bertin and Dockx, giving them Spitzner's mobile number and explaining both where he had found it and why he suspected there wasn't actually much point in calling it.

He dropped the package off at the police station on Lange Nieuwstraat before jogging back to Centraal Station and catching the next fast train to Brussels.

You park the van outside a fashionable optician's on Mechelseplein and cross over the square to an Internet café on the far side. Within five minutes you are online and have picked up a message from Michael Kemp, who writes that he does indeed have *Malpertuis* on VHS cassette and would be more than happy to run off a dupe and mail it to you. He apologises for its being the butchered English-language version reviled by the director himself and goes on to say that Kümel is due to show a new print, a director's cut, at a season of his films to be held at the National Film Theatre in London later in the year.

Fortunately, in among the various irrelevant kindnesses, Kemp also gives you his phone number.

You wait until you're back outside, alone in the middle of Mechelseplein, before calling him.

'Michael Kemp?' you say when he answers.

'Yes.' Slow, slightly cautious.

'I just picked up your email about *Malpertuis*.'

'Oh right. Like I said, I'd be happy to dupe you a copy. Just tell me where to send it.' London accent, unstressed.

You give him the address of the Internet café. 'But I don't want you to post it. Please courier it to me. Obviously I will pay.'

'You're on a deadline?'

'Just please try to make sure it's here by morning.'

'It'll be there. Don't worry about it. So er . . .'

You sense he's waiting for you to explain why you want the tape and why you need it so fast. A Kümel fan, he wants to talk about the films, swap reminiscences, trade anecdotes. How often can he get the chance?

'I'll be waiting,' you say.

You're about to end the call, but Kemp remains silent and in his silence you hear doubt. Kemp is not a stupid man. He reads the papers, watches the news. He's heard about the dead girls in Antwerp, the series of Kümel tapes. If he's kept up to date, he'll have heard that the latest tape was *Malpertuis* and he won't have heard yet that it wasn't, in fact, *Malpertuis*, but *Joachim Stiller*, because they haven't released that information yet. But he's still likely to link this appeal for a copy of *Malpertuis* with the series of found tapes. He might be the suspicious type and he might not be, but you decide not to underestimate his intelligence.

'I'm a journalist,' you say, taking a gamble. 'Freelance. I'm trying to get an angle on this story.'

You wait for his response.

'I see,' he says finally. 'I understand. I'll organise a courier right now. Good luck. Let me know if you need any further help and don't forget the season at the NFT.'

He asks for a name. You give him one and repeat the address of the Internet café.

'First thing tomorrow,' he says.

On arrival in Brussels, Frank walked from the Gare Centrale to the Museum of Modern Art, where he went straight to the Delvaux collection. He studied *The Spitzner Museum* for a few minutes. In the presence of the paintings he felt as if Vos were near, but was aware that this was almost certainly an illusion. There being no actual sign of the American, he left and walked up rue de la Régence, through place Royale and into rue Royale. With the parc de Bruxelles on his right, he walked north. Government buildings lined the wide street. There were few pedestrians. At the top of the incline, shortly before Botanique métro station, a fierce wind was channelled either side of a huge tower, the Cité Administrative de l'Etat. The lights and flags of the Hotel Astoria were a welcome sight across the street.

The moment Frank entered the hotel, he realised he was walking on to the set of *Daughters of Darkness*. The reception

desk, where, thirty years previously, Paul Esser's concierge had
stood and stared goggle-eyed at Delphine Seyrig as the Countess
Bathory, unchanged since her last visit forty years earlier, was to
the left of him. Straight ahead was the ornate chandeliered
lounge where the countess had sat knitting while waiting for
Stefan and Valerie, and to the left the wide staircase where John
Karlen, playing Stefan, had paused while the concierge explained
there had been no reply on the telephone from his 'mother', in
fact an older man, played by a heavily powdered Fons
Rademakers. Frank imagined Kümel moving around this grand
space in a loud shirt and 70s sports jacket, thick sideburns and
heavy glasses, diffidently directing actors twice his age.

Frank enquired at the desk and discovered that Vos had indeed
taken a room, but that he was not in the hotel at present. The
clerk had no idea when the director might return and Frank had
to caution himself not to press his case, for fear of being asked to
leave. Instead he sat in one of the high-backed leather armchairs
with a drink from the bar. He watched the door and saw everyone who either entered or left the hotel during the course of the
evening. Vos didn't show. When it became clear that he could stay
in the lobby no longer, he booked a room. At the back of his
mind was the thought that if the cost of the room were to be
halved it would still be far too exorbitant for him ever to stay
there – under normal circumstances. Under the circumstances
pertaining, however, he didn't care how much it cost. Right then
it was the only thing he could think of to do that didn't seem
entirely pointless. He assumed the police were working on
Henk's list and would call him with any news.

During the Miocene period, the Antwerp area was a gulf in which
powerful currents stirred the decomposing carcasses of seals,
dolphins and whales into a thick soup. Sharks fed on the flesh, losing teeth to the ocean floor, where they combined with mammal
bones to form the green glauconitic sands of the Pliocene period
known locally as the Sands of Kattendijk.

Kattendijkdok, between Bonaparte Dock and the huge docks
of the main Antwerp harbour area, runs north-south and is
exactly one kilometre long, approximately 150 metres wide. At

the north end, close to Siberia Bridge, squats a disused forty-metre grain silo.

The flat roof and overall size are characteristic of a concrete silo, but the rectilinear bins would be more typical of a wooden structure. When you inspect the building up close, you see it's largely brick-built. The bins themselves may be concrete, but the lower parts, the central stairway shaft and the headhouse are all brick.

Around the back, in the lee of an abandoned trailer, one of the metal roller doors leading to the work floor curls up at the bottom corner like a can of sardines. If you pull it up further, being careful not to snag your clothes on the sharp jags of torn metal, you can slide under into the building. Once inside, you proceed to the office on the waterfront side of the building. A calendar advertising 'Central Auto' shows three months to a page, October to December 1999. A heavy circle has been drawn around 19 November – a Friday, presumably the day the silo was last operational – in red marker pen. A steep flight of concrete steps leads up from the work floor, the narrow stair-well lit by a vertical ladder of grimy windows, which offer a progression of views of Antwerp dominated by the cathedral tower. It takes about five minutes to climb up past the con-cealed bins, which account for 80 per cent of the building's height and volume, to the distributing floors, where there are windows on all sides to provide ventilation in an area prone to grain dust explosions.

The lower of the two distributing floors is a forest of thick steel pipes extruding from the ceiling at various angles before sinking into the concrete floor to deliver their grain to the bins below. The upper distributing floor is marked by a circular series of holes leading to those pipes. Three spouts, which would once have delivered the grain from the headhouse, on the floor above, hang uselessly above the holes.

You climb beyond the distributing floors to the headhouse, which contains three steel hoppers, a confusion of rusting machinery, a sequence of high windows that can be reached only by means of an unreliable-looking ladder – one of the windows on the north side, close to where the top of the ladder rests against the wall, has been smashed — and a small cabin with a blacked-out window and locked door.

The first Siân knew of her release was the rattling of a key in a lock. It sounded very close by, closer than she would have imagined possible, and so she thought she must be hallucinating. She calmly accepted that the solitary confinement and the sensory deprivation had driven her into temporary psychosis. But the rattling continued and turned into a scraping and then was followed by the unmistakeable sound of a mortise lock yielding.

A door she hadn't known was there or could be so close was suddenly thrown open and light blinded her. She shielded her eyes, but was aware of a man entering the room. Was this Frank? The police? She realised he was neither as she recognised the stench of her abductor, the acrid smells of sweat and improperly dried clothes and the foul stink of his breath. As he unlocked the chain around her ankle, she opened her eyes a crack and tried to take in the dimensions of her prison, which was unbelievably small. In the darkness she had been convinced it was bigger. On the floor in one corner she noticed a dust-furred telephone — unconnected, of course — that somehow she had failed to find with her questing fingers. She heard a sudden clattering and looked through the open door to see a pigeon flying out through a high window. The sky was a whitish blue. She could see nothing else through that or any of the other windows. She looked at the machinery in the space outside the cabin, but it meant nothing to her.

Then the man was lifting her over his shoulder. She still hadn't seen his face. Was he releasing her? Taking her somewhere else? Or was he going to kill her now? She heard another ship's hooter as he hefted her out of the cabin and started to cross the floor towards a set of stairs leading down. Wherever she was, she was on an upper level. As they started negotiating the narrow stairs she got her second real shock: the view from the window revealed them to be high above the city. She saw the cathedral in the distance, the river on the right, a long narrow dock straight ahead. Then they turned right round to descend the next flight and she couldn't see anything except the rough dirty weave of the man's coat. She thought about struggling, but knew she didn't have the strength. Where was Frank, she kept asking herself?

As they rounded the next bend in the stairs, Siân caught the heel of her shoe against the diagonal of the flight they had just descended. The shoe came off and fell on to the landing behind them.

24

MISERABLE HUMAN SKINS

Frank was dozing in a soft bed in the five-star Hotel Astoria in Brussels when his mobile rang, the ringtone being assimilated for a moment into his dream before he realised what was going on and grabbed it. As he flipped open the phone, he looked at his watch and cursed. Of all the days to oversleep, he could have chosen a better one.

The call was from the police. They had found the place where Siân had been held.

'You've found her?'

'No, we found the place. She's gone.'

'Gone? What do you mean, gone?'

'Gone. He's taken her. Somewhere else.'

'How do you know it's the place? Where is it? How did you find it? Was it on the list?'

'It was on the list. A grain silo in the docks. A patrol car called in a sighting of a white van parked outside. When we got there, the van had gone and so had whoever had been held prisoner in the building. And whoever had been holding her.'

'Why was it gone? How could they have left? What about the patrol car? Didn't they stick around?'

'No. Look . . .'

'No, you look. I don't understand. How could you let him get away?'

Frank was dressing as the conversation proceeded.

'News of the sighting came in and we got there as soon as we could.'

Dockx appeared to be holding something back.

'If I find out you sat on this sighting,' Frank said, 'before chasing it up, whether we get Siân back or not, I will fucking – fucking—' He wanted to say 'kill you', but he knew it wouldn't make any difference. They could hardly fuck it up more than they already had done. But he couldn't say it. His head had started to hurt.

'We found a shoe.'

'You found a shoe? This is what happens. You find shoes, clothes. And then you find a body.'

'It may have come off accidentally. She may have left it deliberately. You need to identify it.'

'I want to see this silo. I need to see it.'

Dockx gave him directions. Frank said he'd be there in an hour. The detective didn't ask where he was that he couldn't be there sooner.

At the front desk, Frank asked for Vos.

'Mr Vos came back late last night and left early this morning,' the clerk told him.

'Is he coming back?'

'His account was settled, sir.'

Frank spent the train journey to Antwerp looking through Vos's notebook again in the vain hope that there might be something else, some other clue he might have missed previously. He took a cab from Centraal Station to Kattendijkdok, where he was met by the now-familiar sight of squad cars and crime scene officers. Bertin was leaning against the bonnet of an unmarked car striking matches and throwing them into the dock one after another. Dockx stood by the car holding a transparent plastic wallet containing Siân's shoe.

'That's Siân's,' said Frank. 'Can I go in?'

'I'll take you,' Dockx said.

Frank glanced at Bertin, who struck another match and tossed it into the grey water, where Frank heard a little fizz as it was extinguished.

Dockx led the way across the cobblestones, past a fifteen-foot crane, to a door. There was a sign taped to the frosted glass in the door that read: 'BIJ AFWEZIGHEID TEL 233 6191 DE TROUW'. In case of absence, phone etc.

'This door was locked,' Dockx said. 'We forced it. We think he got in round the back.'

'And out again,' added Frank acidly.

Dockx ignored this and led Frank into the building. They passed into an office. There was a spiral-bound manual collecting dust on top of a filing cabinet. A hand-drawn plan of the silo stuck to a glass dividing wall. Taped to the same window, stuffed inside a plastic bag to protect it from the damp atmosphere, was a clipping from a Flemish newspaper. The headline read 'Rostelli moet stoppen met zijn hypnoseshows', but the presumed hypnotist's name had been crossed out and replaced with the name RONNY, written in black marker pen. A picture of Rostelli had been altered, too. His hair had been made to appear longer and he had been given a moustache and goatee, presumably to make him look more like Ronny, whoever Ronny was. But then Frank noticed a subhead halfway down the article: 'Dutroux,' it said, in bold type. He looked more closely at the text, which said something about a hypnotism show in Ostend having some connection with Dutroux.

Dockx looked back to see why Frank had stopped following him. Frank nodded at the press cutting. Dockx cast an eye over it and shrugged.

'Follow me,' he said.

'There were press cuttings on the wall in Ghent,' Frank said as he followed.

'This is different,' Dockx argued dismissively. 'An office joke.'

'Yeah, well, you'd know,' said Frank under his breath.

They started up the stairs and had to stand aside at the first landing to let some of Dockx's colleagues pass them on their way down.

'This is where the shoe was found.' Dockx indicated a chalk circle on one of the landings further up.

After a moment they continued their climb.

'This is where the grain came down,' Dockx said, pointing to thick steel pipes visible on an open floor near the top.

'I'll let you know if I want a lecture on industrial archaeology,' Frank said.

They climbed a further two flights and Dockx nodded towards a cabin that took up part of one side of what was clearly the top floor of the structure.

'Could you give me a moment?' Frank asked pointedly.

Dockx advised him not to move anything.

Frank stooped and went inside the cabin. There was a chain wrapped around a pipe coming out of the back wall. He picked up the end of it, felt its weight. There was a plastic bottle of Spa spring water – empty. He sniffed the neck of the bottle, but any trace left by Siân would only be discovered in the lab. On the wall near the pipe he found a number of fresh scratches on the brickwork, short shallow scars at odd angles, and he wondered if this had been Siân's attempt to leave a mark, maybe even write her name. He moved back to the door and pulled it shut to recreate the conditions in which she'd been held. It became pitch dark and he quickly began to feel claustrophobic, pushing the door open again in a hurry.

He looked round the rest of the space. Steel hoppers for grain. Machinery, valves, pipes. He looked up at the windows and saw the smashed pane and the ladder. He glanced round to see that Dockx was sitting on the top step looking out of the lower windows at the view over Antwerp. The ladder wobbled when Frank put his weight on it, but he didn't care. As he climbed, he knew that the man they were looking for had climbed this ladder before him. His hands had gripped the same metal sides. His shoes had rested on the same rungs. When he reached the top, he held on to the empty window frame, the glass having been removed with some care, and looked out.

The river was behind him, turning through ninety degrees to the west just below the top of Kattendijkdok. To the left and straight ahead, huge docks cut crazy shapes out of the matted grey-brown carpet of the port. A red freighter was moored in the foreground. Frank's eye was drawn to the north-west skyline. On the far left, some distance apart, yet of roughly the same height,

were two flare stacks. Flames spouted from the top of one, then
vanished, the action repeating itself as if the stack were breathing
fire. Beyond the flare stacks and slightly to the right were two
massive cooling towers belching clouds of steam into the atmosphere.

'What are you doing, Frank?'

Dockx's voice made him jump.

'What's that over there?'

'What?'

'Two cooling towers to the north-west, fifteen, maybe twenty
kilometres.'

'That's Doel. There's nothing there except a nuclear power
station, which you can see, and a small town that very soon will
not exist any more.'

'Why not?'

'They're extending the port, building a new container terminal. Come down. We should go.'

'So the town's just going to be demolished?'

'It's been an ongoing process for some time. People have been
leaving. There are very few left now. Most of the place is boarded
up.'

Frank delayed coming down from the top of the ladder. He
looked at the cooling towers on the horizon and he felt as certain of this as he had ever been of anything: the man who had
Siân had taken her there. He would have stood here where Frank
was standing and he would have looked out and the thing that
would have drawn his eye was the detail that had attracted
Frank's.

The moment Frank returned his hands to the ladder and
started to descend, he was going to Doel. He wasn't about to
share this with Detective Dockx, however. The police had let
Siân slip through their net here. All they had needed to do was
keep a watch on the white van while assembling a team to enter
the abandoned silo. Their having failed to do so appeared to indicate that nothing had changed since Dutroux. Frank didn't want
to find himself reading in the paper about the dead English girl
and how her murder could have been prevented but for the
bungling incompetence of the police.

'So what do we do now?' he asked the detective when he reached the bottom. 'Do you have any idea at all where to look next?'

'We have the description and licence plate of the white van. And we had a call from the English police. A film fan in Brighton answered an email from some guy in Antwerp trying to track down a video of *Malpertuis*.'

'Did he have one?'

'Yes. He made a copy and couriered it to an Internet café in Antwerp, where it was picked up this morning.'

'You have a description of the man who picked it up?'

'Unfortunately not a very good one. He was of medium build, wearing a baseball cap pulled down low.'

'That description fits half the adult males in Belgium.'

'The café owner was trying to serve another customer at the time and didn't get a good look at him.'

'So, we're fucked. We're nowhere. Meanwhile he's got the tape he's been waiting for.'

'Which is why we're wasting our time chatting up here.'

Frank followed the detective down the stairs, pausing to touch with his fingertips the damp concrete inside the chalk circle where they had recovered Siân's shoe.

When they reached the dockside, Bertin was sitting behind the wheel of the unmarked car, grimacing.

'Can we give you a lift?' Dockx asked Frank.

Frank thought for a moment, considering the wisdom of keeping them in the dark, then reached his decision.

'If you're going anywhere near my hotel,' he said.

Bertin made some bad-tempered remark in Flemish, but Frank ignored him, unfolding his map in the back of the car and covertly studying the route to Doel.

'Call me if you get anything,' he said as they dropped him off outside the Hotel Miro.

'Likewise,' snarled Bertin as he accelerated away from the kerb while the rear door was still swinging shut.

'Fuck you too,' said Frank after the departing car.

He went up to his room, gathered some stuff together and was back on the street in five minutes. He found a taxi rank, but no

one would take him to Doel. No explanations were offered, just
a variety of brush-offs. He knew they'd be unlikely to find a fare
for the return journey, but felt aggrieved nevertheless. Instead he
took the underground tram three stops to Groenplaats, then
jogged as far as the St Anna Foot Tunnel, which he negotiated at
a brisk walk, mindful of his previous experience. Emerging on
the left bank, he crossed over to a series of bus stops. There was
one bus waiting. He looked at the timetable and compared the
route number. It went to Doel via Kallo. He looked at the map.
Kallo was halfway to Doel. He stepped up and asked the driver
for a one-way ticket to Doel. She took the cigarette that she had
just lit out of her mouth and told him in a mixture of Flemish
and sign language that she wasn't going to Doel, only as far as
Kallo, but he could get another bus from there. He got on and
took a seat near the front. He waited ten minutes, constantly
turning his wrist to check his watch, looking around to see if any
more buses, perhaps going to Doel, might appear. None did. He
was just about to say something when the driver finished her cigarette, threw the still smouldering fag end out of the door on to
the pavement and gripped the big wide steering wheel with her
muscled forearms. The door closed with a wheezing hiss and the
bus set off.

Frank hoped the service might be an express and would whisk
him to Kallo in no time, but this proved not to be the case. The
bus limped through suburb after suburb. Checking to see where
Beveren was on the map, he saw they were taking just about the
longest possible way round to get to Kallo. It wasn't that the bus
kept stopping. There were plenty of stops but no one was waiting. He was on a bus to nowhere. On the outskirts of Beveren,
the bus turned right and wove a tortuous route through a
residential district where the roads were so narrow the bus was
constantly having to stop to allow cars to pass. Finally, the driver
stopped for a passenger, a woman who bore a striking resemblance to the driver herself. The women knew each other. The
passenger settled her bags of shopping on the seat in front of
Frank, then stood alongside the driver so they could chat. They
talked loudly, to be heard over the engine, and laughed a lot.
Frank began to regret not having asked Dockx and Bertin to take

him to Doel. He would have been there by now and might have already found Siân. He took out his phone and was considering calling the police when the bus rocked to a halt and the driver turned and told him that they had reached Kallo. Both the women watched him as he got to his feet and climbed down from the bus. There was no pavement and very few houses.

'So where do I get my bus to Doel?' he asked the driver, as he wondered why the other passenger wasn't getting off if this was the end of the line.

The driver pointed up ahead. A hundred metres down the road was another bus. Frank started walking and turned to glare as the bus he had been on sailed past him, the two women watching him and still laughing. When he reached the next bus, he asked the driver if he was going to Doel. He shook his head and reached for a timetable. After running a stubby finger down several columns he looked up and shook his head again.

'Not today,' he said.

Feeling close to tears, Frank started to walk. He had a map and the map showed that Doel was about five miles away, not much more. There was a road that hugged the river bank, then cut inland for a short way before reaching Doel. He thought again about calling the police but remembered how they had fucked up at Kattendijkdok. After five minutes, Frank reached a T-junction. Directly ahead, on the other side of the main road, was a turning area. The bus – his bus – was waiting there, the driver and the woman passenger still both on board, their heads thrown back as they enjoyed another joke. He turned right and walked along the edge of a wide, empty road with a railway line on his left. There were no trains and what few cars there were all came from the other direction. The drivers, all men travelling alone, looked at him as they went past. According to the map, this road would soon curve around to the left, following the line of the river, which was on the right side of the road but remained hidden by a high embankment. Frank could hear a strange sound that he at first thought might be the pumping of blood through his carotid artery, or the noise his trouser legs made as they rubbed together. Then he began to wonder if he was imagining it.

It would be quicker to cut across the industrial land on his left, but it was securely fenced off. When the road began to curve, he crossed over and climbed up the embankment. The river was wider than in the centre of Antwerp by as much as a third. A large container ship was moving downriver at what seemed little more than walking speed. Beyond the ship to his left were the twin cooling towers of the nuclear power station that Frank had seen from the top of the ladder in the grain silo headhouse. The opposite bank was entirely given over to industrial use. Dominating the view on that side, however, was one of the flare stacks he had also seen from Kattendijkdok. Every two or three seconds it blasted an orange flame into the sky as gas was burned off. The matching flare stack further downstream was not operating. Up here on the embankment the sound he had heard down below was more pronounced. He took his phone out, looked at it and put it away again. And then it clicked: the cycle of the sound, increasingly like a heartbeat, matched that of the erupting gas flares. They were merely out of synch, light travelling faster than sound.

For some reason, solving that mystery made him feel better. His pace duly increased and the cooling towers drew closer. Soon, perpendicular to his route, he could see the busy road that his map showed would come in from the left and disappear into a tunnel under the river, to emerge on the right bank where it would join the road going north to Holland. The Dutch border, he saw, was only two or three miles north of Doel. Shortly after going over the road at the point where it swept into the tunnel, he would have to turn away from the river for a short distance before the road he was on would turn right again and run parallel to the river until it drew level with Doel, where there was another right turn. He looked at his watch: 12.45pm. It should take him no longer than half an hour to reach the ghost town.

Large numbers of Antwerp fossils were unearthed in the mid-1980s when some of the later docks were being dug. Kallo became one of the most productive areas for amateur fossil hunters, and then Doel, where Pliocene sediments appear in two strata, the Sands of Kattendijk and, above them, the Sands of Oorderen.

Finds have become more common over the last few years as the land between Kallo and Doel has been increasingly transformed by the restless extension of the docks on the west side of the river. Maps of the area are worthless, becoming historical documents the moment they are printed. The people of Doel have responded to the pressure to oust them from their homes either by giving up and accepting compensation deals or digging in and mounting a campaign intended to prevent the inevitable: 'DOEL MOET BLIJVEN'. Doel must stay.

Doel will soon be buried under several metres of mud.

All that remains of Doel now, by the time you get there, are a café and a windmill, a forlorn lighthouse, a handful of diehard residents and the 170-metre cooling towers of the nuclear power station. Marching on the town from the south is a column of electricity pylons studded with warning lights that sparkle like radioactive dust. If Doel doesn't feel like the end of the earth, that's only because you know there is a place ten minutes to the north, just beyond the Dutch border, even bleaker and lonelier – the Flooded Land of Saeftinge.

On a street facing the dike that protects Doel from the river most of the houses appear empty, windows shuttered. The Hotel De Jagersrust at the south end has been boarded up for months; the house at the north end, the last house in the street, is open to the elements, its unglazed window frames dark as gouged eye sockets. Since you will not be staying long, you move the girl in here. You sense that time is short. On the drive from Antwerp you had constantly been expecting to be pulled over. The police cannot be far behind, and it would not surprise you if Frank Warner were to turn out to be ahead of them. Given this and the break in the pattern caused by Jan Spitzner's providing the wrong tape for the last girl, you feel that, while you remain wedded to the idea of ritual, strict adherence has ceased to be essential. There will be no mannequin this time, merely a ceremonial screening and then you will do it.

You unload the TV/VCR and portable generator from the van and install them in the upstairs back room of the last house. The building has been stripped, leaving little more than splintered joists and bare brick walls. The girl, obviously stronger than you thought, has managed to crawl from the back of the house to the hallway, where anyone passing in the street could have seen her through the gaping doorway.

No one is passing, but you take the precaution of fastening a plastic tie around her ankles while you drive the van around the block and park it in the next street in the shadow of a huge glittering pylon.

Returning to the house, you sit the girl in front of the monitor and insert the tape. If, as Michael Kemp informed you, this is the heavily edited English-language version of *Malpertuis*, then she has approximately ninety-nine minutes to live. The Flemish version would have extended that to a little beyond two hours. You check your watch and see that the time is just after 1.30pm.

Frank turned left where he expected to turn left, walked parallel with the R2 for a short distance, and then turned right. According to the map, it was now about four kilometres to Doel. On both sides of the road, pylons carried the electricity generated by the nuclear power station he could see in the distance. Within 100 metres, however, he found the road turning through a right angle to the left. Doel to the left, said a sign. Indeed, there was no alternative. Straight ahead, the route he had expected to take, was impassable: a chemicals factory, a fan of vertical steel pipes that looked like an oversize wind instrument. He looked hard at the map. He'd never had any problems reading maps, so how had he gone wrong? Maybe it would just be a short detour and wouldn't delay his arrival in Doel by more than a few minutes.

The landscape was bleak. There were no trees. A ditch ran by the left side of the road, its contents rust-red under a film of foamy chemicals. After a quarter of an hour the road turned to the right again and Frank speeded up, encouraged, but ten minutes later it swung round to the left once more. When he looked closely at the map he saw that this region was overscored with the warning, in red, 'Werk. In uitvoering (Travaux en cours)'. It wasn't as if Frank hadn't known there was construction in progress in the vicinity of Doel, but somehow he hadn't expected it to affect his route.

The time was 1.15pm.

The next right turn instilled more false hope, as it was followed by another left ten minutes later. The twin cooling towers
of the nuclear power station were still visible off to the right, but
they were getting further away instead of closer. Frank looked at
his watch. One-thirty. A lump formed in his throat. He pulled out
his mobile, intending to call the police and ask for help, and saw
that there was no signal. Not because his battery was flat, but
there was just no signal. To his left he could see water. He ought
to have passed Doeldok, which he had seen marked on the map,
but when he looked at the map again he saw that there were blue
dotted lines as well as red ones.

He would try to flag down a car, but none had yet passed him,
so he started to run. He knew from the signs that the road still
went to Doel, even if it took a long way round. If he scaled the
fence on the right of the road and tried to sneak across industrial
land, chances were he'd be apprehended and never make it to
Doel. A buzzing noise caught his attention and he looked round
to see a car approaching. It was still a way off, but he stood by the
side of the road and waved his arms in the air. He saw the car
slow down as it approached him, then speed up and swerve past
him when he stepped into the road. A teenage passenger yelled
abuse out of his window as the older driver grinned at the wheel.
Shouting obscenities after the disappearing car, Frank started
running again. He checked his phone. Still no signal. It was just
gone ten to two.

You watch the opening scenes. A ship arriving at a misty port. A
blond androgynous sailor, a half-glimpsed woman, two cartoon
villains – a chase through cobbled streets of gabled houses. Ghent,
Bruges, Ostend locations. Nightclub scene – Johnny Halliday, las-
civious whores, bared breasts. You look at the girl. Her curly red
hair falls across her face, and her eyes are closed. You shake her.

'Watch,' you tell her, as fear and panic begin to creep up on
your lifelong bitterness. 'I was eight when this was made. Eight.
My mother was a whore. She abandoned me. A man in a mountain stuck his cock into my arse because my mother was a whore.
Watch the film.'

★

The cooling towers seemed further away than ever. The land on the right of the road rose up steeply as if a viaduct or bridge approach were being built. Frank was still running, but more and more slowly, his breathing ragged. Tears dried on his cheeks. He howled at the skeletal pylons. If Siân survived, he would be a good man for the rest of his life. There would be no more keeping his options open, no more shopping around. He would do the right thing and Siân would never come second to anything or anyone again, whether it was the movies, a feature commission or a chance encounter in a Dean Street screening room.

As he dragged himself on, he implored a god he didn't believe in: 'Make him leave her alone. Don't let him touch her legs. Give her a fucking break, you miserable twisted fuck.'

Two-thirty.

Siân had been blindfolded during the journey. She could still detect the sounds and smells of the river. Now that the blindfold had been removed, she struggled to keep her eyes open to watch the film, desperately trying to believe that if she did what he wanted, he might let her go. Reason and experience suggested otherwise, but she wasn't ready to give in.

When she had turned to look at him, he had twisted away and told her to watch the film.

She had never seen the film before and thought it very unlikely, given the circumstances, that she would ever want to see it again − if she got the chance. The dialogue was hard to follow because of the noise of the generator, and the picture quality was poor, second-generation, the original recording taken off Channel 4, ad breaks included. The entire cast seemed to be stuck in a maze-like house called Malpertuis, trapped there by their own greed, because the will of the Orson Welles character dictated they would only enjoy a share of his inheritance as long as they didn't leave the house.

She wondered what she had to do to get out of this house. She formed the impression from what he had said about his mother that offering him sex would not be wise. She sensed that he was easily driven to anger and that antagonising him, by trying to get a look at his face, would not be helpful either. For the

time being, she would do as he asked and hope for some kind of
a break.

Outside the house, seagulls shrieked incessantly.

Another car was coming, a black BMW. Frank had a go at flagging
it down while continuing to run, so that he wouldn't be wasting
time when it didn't stop, and to his surprise it pulled over fifty
metres up the road.

'Thank you,' Frank gasped when he reached the BMW. 'I'm
trying to get to Doel.'

'You're nearly there,' the driver said. 'Get in.'

Frank tried to get his breath back.

'There's not much there,' the man said.

'Do you live there?'

'No, I live over that way.' The man waved his left hand. 'In
Holland. Beyond Saeftinge.'

'The Flooded Land of Saeftinge,' Frank said, looking at the
map.

'If you're thinking of heading that way after Doel, don't go
alone,' the man advised. 'It's easy to get lost and when the tide
comes in it's impossible to get back. Only go with a guide. Better
not to go at all.'

'I'm not,' said Frank. 'I'm just going to Doel.'

'Well, this is Doel,' the man said, turning sharp right. 'I'll take
you all the way in.'

'These roads don't seem to correspond to the map.'

'They're all new.'

Frank nodded and thanked the man when he stopped the car
in the middle of the street between a tiny church and a shuttered
café. He watched as the BMW turned the corner and was gone.

As silence fell on the street, broken only by the shriek of
seagulls, he felt the loneliness of the place. There were no cars
parked outside the houses, where no lights could be seen burning. There was a dike at the end of the street, beyond the
boarded-up Hotel De Jagersrust on the corner. He walked
towards the dike and climbed the concrete steps set into it. The
river was wide, the tide low but rising. Lights twinkled at the
various industrial complexes on the right bank. The time was

just after three. There was a wooden platform and jetty beyond the rather basic lighthouse – little more than a flashing red light on a pole. On the way to the jetty he passed a monument to the RAF and British anti-aircraft batteries along the Schelde. He walked down the inclined jetty until he was standing just above the water. Green moss grew on the wooden planks. A vertical ladder led upwards to the higher platform, but it was open to view and there was nothing to see. Retreating from the jetty, he ran along the dike towards the windmill, passing a row of houses on his left. Most were sealed. One, the last house in the block, looked ready for demolition, no windows or doors remaining. The windmill had been converted into a café, but it was closed. Across the road from the windmill was a restaurant. It, too, was shut, most likely never to reopen. Frank crossed to a street that was perpendicular to the river. There was a school on the right, houses and a few parked cars, but no sign of anyone about and no white van. He checked his watch: 3.10pm.

He started to run. He ran down the street, glancing into alleyways and unshuttered windows, looking for a light, a human figure, a white van, anything. When the houses started to thin out, he turned left and rejoined the road he had come in on, turning left at the end of that and finally reaching the point where the BMW had dropped him off. He bent double, fighting for air. The empty Hotel De Jagersrust on the corner was still quiet, although a raucous noise was being made by a flock of gulls agitating over the dike. Frank got up close to the disused hotel and peered through a crack between the boards, but it was dark inside. There was nothing to see.

The film is running late because of the ad breaks. You heard a car in the street outside and went to the front of the house to check, seeing the tail lights of a black BMW as it turned left at the end of the block.

You feel increasingly tense, jittery and frightened. You have a sense of things falling apart. A growing feeling that you will not be able to finish what you started.

In the film, the blond sailor, Yann, having vowed to uncover the secret of Malpertuis, is obsessively drawn to Euryale, one of three women played by Susan Hampshire. Throughout the film she has been the object of his gaze, which has never been returned, her eyes remaining perpetually downcast. 'We were only waiting for mortals to forget us so we could be allowed to die,' she tells him. 'The monster thought it amusing to have Philarète sew the gods into miserable human skins.' But her speech is largely drowned out by the chugging of the generator and the screaming of the gulls outside.

You turn up the volume.

'The other gods are dead because people no longer believe in them. I alone remain immortal. I am the Gorgon. I am love and I am death . . . The fruit of knowledge is bitter . . .'

I am love and I am death.

The line strikes you with almost physical force, so that you feel dizzy, as if you have risen too fast from a sitting position. You look down at the girl on the floor between you and the screen. Her eyes are closed. She looks perfect, externally flawless. For a moment you think she is someone else. For a moment you think *you* are someone else. *You are love and you are death.* You look at her again. Lying on her side, her eyes closed, she seems at peace and you have a terrifying sense not so much that she really does remind you of someone else, but that she reminds *someone else* of someone else. *I am love and you are death.*

You back away in confusion and half-run, half-fall down the stairs. The rectangle of light at the end of the hall pulls you towards it. Standing in the street, you look around, as if unaware now of *where* you are as well as *who* you are.

To the right, you see a man walking towards you, so you turn to the left and run.

As Frank turned the corner, he saw a man stumble out of a doorway fifty or sixty metres away. The man turned to look at him, then ran off with an uneven limping gait in the opposite direction.

Frank started to run, too. When he reached the last house, the building the man had come out of, he squinted into the distance, but the man had gone, disappearing beyond the windmill. Frank had noticed the house before, but it had been quiet then. Now there was noise coming from within.

'Siân,' he called out as he entered. There were no lights and darkness was gathering in the ruined house, but the noise appeared to be coming from above, so he ran up the stairs, three at a time. Upstairs there was one large room, formerly two, the dividing wall having been knocked down. Most of the noise was coming from a small generator, but next to that was a portable TV/VCR, the volume turned right up. On screen was a frozen close-up of an eye. Credits, in vivid red type, were rolling, to the accompaniment of Georges Delerue's spoof Offenbach waltz.

Frank looked at Siân's legs. They were intact. As he knelt down and put his hands to her face to see if she was cold or warm, the recording finished and was replaced by the fizz and dazzle of snow.

Part Ten

THE TUNNEL

25

FRAMES PER SECOND

'I was thinking,' said an earnest young man in the front row, 'that Delphine Seyrig was not the only thing *Daughters of Darkness* and *Last Year at Marienbad* had in common. In a sense, yours was a kind of response to some of the questions raised by Resnais's film. Or, to put it in a different way, you posed some of the same questions again in a different context.'

'Ah, well,' responded Kümel with a charmingly indulgent smile, 'I never think about that sort of thing. Just make the movie and move on. The only thing that really interests me is structure. The rest is silence.'

If there had been any worries about the wisdom of pressing ahead with the Harry Kümel season at the National Film Theatre, they had proved unfounded. NFT programmer Geoff Andrew had merely postponed the season by three months. To have delayed any longer or cancelled the long-planned event would have been unfair on Kümel and fans of his work. It was hardly the director's fault that his films had been so horribly misused by the man the tabloids had taken to calling 'the Kümel Killer'.

The interview in a packed NFT1 was going well. Kümel looked dapper in a grey suit and black T-shirt, his silver beard neatly trimmed.

Another hand went up in the audience. Documentary filmmaker David Thompson, in the interviewer's chair, gave the questioner the floor.

'You have already talked a bit about Orson Welles. Can you tell us what he was like to work with on *Malpertuis*?'

Frank squeezed Siân's hand. The interview had been preceded by a screening of the director's cut of the film in a brand-new print. Siân, although she had been with Frank to see *De Komst Van Joachim Stiller* and *Eline Vere* earlier in the week, was not ready to watch *Malpertuis*.

'You must go, though,' she had insisted.

'No way,' Frank had said. 'We'll have dinner and then go to the interview, if you're sure you want to.'

With Siân's blessing, he had gone to the matinée screening instead while she had been at work.

'In life he was a wonderful person,' Kümel said, of Welles. 'I continued to meet him right up to his death, and we talked on the phone almost once a month. But on the set he was a childish monster who had lost touch with cinema as it evolved. He would say, "I want the camera there. I am your star." All the same, he was a genius.'

'You OK?' Frank whispered to Siân.

'I'm fine.'

After being picked up from Doel by ambulance, Siân had spent a night in hospital in Antwerp, receiving treatment for shock and dehydration. She had satisfied the shrink that while she had undoubtedly been traumatised by her experience she was not a suicide risk and would seek help in London if she felt she needed it.

She and Frank had wanted to return home the next day, but the police wouldn't allow it and Siân was forced to submit to a series of interviews. Could she describe her abductor? Not to any useful degree. Had he said anything that might help the police identify him? She told them what he'd said about his mother and the abuse he'd been subjected to. Why, in her opinion, had he abducted her when she was neither a prostitute nor working on Johnny Vos's film? Although she hadn't worked on the film, she said, she had been indirectly associated with it. As for the other angle, all she could come up with was that she had been wearing new clothes that she had just bought and they were perhaps 'more glamorous' than her usual style.

They asked her if she believed Johnny Vos might have been behind the abduction. Her gut feeling, she said, was that he was not. Although she hadn't managed to get a proper look at the man during the time she had been held captive, she found it hard to believe that she wouldn't have recognised him if it had been someone she had known. But, she concluded, she couldn't swear to it.

The white van had been found in Doel, parked in a yard off one of the few streets Frank had not searched in his lightning tour of the abandoned town. In the van they had found the man's mannequin-making materials, some clothes and a very old and battered postcard of Paul Delvaux's *The Pink Bows*.

On his return to Antwerp, Johnny Vos had shown up at police headquarters on Lange Nieuwstraat and Detective Bertin had apparently slammed him up against a wall and demanded an explanation for his having Jan Spitzner's phone number in his little black notebook. This guy had contacted him, Vos had explained, saying his name was Johannes Spitz and he was an actor. He had asked to be considered for a part and Vos had agreed to audition him for the scene he was planning to shoot in Leopold De Waelplaats.

Vos had described to Bertin and Dockx how, when he met Spitzner, he had felt there was something strangely familiar about him. On the basis of which, he had cast him as Delvaux.

The detectives had asked Vos if he had had any contact with Spitz, or Spitzner, since the filming. Vos said he hadn't and he had no idea how to get hold of him.

Bertin and Dockx had continued to question Vos, giving him a hard time for his having left Antwerp when he'd been ordered not to. He'd detailed his various trips to Delvaux sites – Antheit, St-Idesbald, Brussels – and had agreed not to leave town again until they said he could.

Although the van had turned up, there was no sign of its driver, apart from a witness statement volunteered by a security guard at the nuclear power station who had seen a figure loping past the perimeter fence heading north. The only thing to the north of the nuclear power station was the Dutch border and beyond that the Flooded Land of Saeftinge. If the killer had strayed into that desolate and labyrinthine marshland, Dockx said to Frank, with the tide rising as it was that afternoon and the daylight all but extinguished, it was very doubtful he would have made it out alive.

Unable to trace Jan Spitzner using either his mobile number, email address, ISP or web page provider, the police had checked out the name he had reportedly given to Vos. They found a record of a Johannes Spitz born to a fairground couple in Eupen in 1956, which put him in the right age range since Vos estimated him to be a few years older than himself. This checked out when they had another look at Vos's tape of the scene shot in Leopold De Waelplaats.

Despite the efforts of police in Eupen, however, no further trace of Spitz or his parents could be found. The received wisdom was that fairground people tended to move around and not leave much of a trail.

A thorough search of the Flooded Land of Saeftinge with dredging equipment and police frogmen failed to produce anything. In the light of the killings, the police said, they were reopening a number of unsolved murders and missing persons cases across Flanders.

No one should hold their breath, Frank said to Siân as they finally travelled back to England by Eurostar. As they emerged from the Channel Tunnel into chilly, iron-grey Kent, a palpable feeling of relief came over them. To escape the media attention in London, they rented a cottage in Essex for a week and Siân paid a visit to her father in Clacton-on-Sea.

Under pressure to file a piece for the paper that had sent him out to Antwerp in the first place, Frank made several false starts, approaching the subject from a different angle each time. Quickly deciding he didn't have the authority to write about the killer, especially since so little was still known about him or who he really was, Frank found himself repeatedly coming back to something he had read in Vos's notebook: 'nudes/dunes – Kümel & Delvaux. Flemish tradition or Belgian?' The phrase 'Flemish tradition' brought to mind Rubens, Van Dyck, Rogier Van Der Weyden, while a Belgian tradition would necessarily be more up to date.

Belgium, Frank argued, boasted a stronger surrealist movement than that of France. Magritte and Delvaux may have been the best-known figures, but there were others: Marcel Mariën, André Souris, Paul Nougé, Henri Michaux. Add Kümel and André Delvaux and a Belgian tradition could be said to have emerged.

However, the most notorious Belgian artist at the turn of the millennium, Frank noted, was Wim Delvoye, whose shit-making machine, *Cloaca*, was exhibited at the Museum of Contemporary Art in Antwerp.

Was it possible that the Belgian tradition in art had withered, while the equally strong Belgian traditions of cynicism, corruption, misanthropy, social mistrust, racial intolerance and organised cruelty were thriving? Marc Dutroux was a sign. The scandal of Sainte-Ode, in southern Belgium, where nineteen villagers were convicted of abusing an eleven-year-old girl prostituted by her own father, was perhaps another. 'You can't just say that this kind of thing only happens in Belgium,' the state prosecutor had said. 'It happens everywhere.'

Frank eventually delivered a piece, but it was spiked. They no longer wanted a set report on Johnny Vos's Delvaux biopic, but nor did they want a discourse on the moral decay of Belgium in the twenty-first century.

While thinking about what to do next, Frank had called Danuta on the mobile number she had given him. She was in the process of moving to Amsterdam, where she had more film work lined up – in the sex industry. De Blieck had closed down the Last House on the Left before the police could close it down for him. Even before the murders, the police had been getting heavy in the red light district. Some of the red and blue lights were being extinguished. Now whole streets on the edge of the Schipperskwartier were going dark.

De Blieck, Danuta told Frank, had ripped out the cameras from the house on Moriaanstraat and was converting it into apartments to let, although the 'hidden' bedsit at the top of the house was Eva's for as long as she wanted to stay, rent free. According to Eva, De Blieck was dealing diamonds again, he and his girlfriend having declared an uneasy truce since her return from her wanderings.

Frank channelled his energies into supporting Siân. Although she had toughed it out with the Belgian authorities, she had been profoundly affected by what had happened to her. She became generally very introverted with periods of exorbitantly extrovert behaviour. Most of the time she avoided talking about it with Frank, out of consideration for him because she knew he carried around a certain amount of guilt. It was a responsibility that wasn't his to shoulder, she emphasised, but that made little difference. She talked to her GP and he recommended counselling, which she didn't take up. Her contact with the police was minimal, since she fell between the victim support networks of two countries. She told Frank that she felt she was in a tunnel and sometimes, on good days, she could see a chink of light at the end. What kept her going, she said, was that when she looked back she couldn't see any light at all.

One night, when they seemed intent on drinking every drop of alcohol in the flat, she told him that the hardest thing had been the killer's never having shown her his face. When Frank asked why, she said that Frank wasn't to take this the wrong way, but that it had meant she had been unable to build a relationship with him.

She suffered recurring nightmares set in the house in Doel. The film was always playing in the background, the volume too high, as she tried to escape from the house by crawling out of the windows, but instead of falling into the street she found herself somehow back in the house, like a figure in an Escher diagram, with the very clear feeling, not that she was about to die, but that this was the last house she would ever see.

The upcoming Harry Kümel season was always a marker. They both knew that they couldn't ignore it. When it came to the end of June, with the season only two weeks away, Siân announced that she hadn't had a nightmare for almost a month, and there still had been no more murders in Belgium. It was widely assumed, since the killer had got only halfway through Kümel's oeuvre, that he had perished in the Flooded Land of Saeftinge. Siân declared that she wanted to put the episode behind her and move on.

Frank said the season wasn't important. They could go away

and miss it completely, if she wanted. But Siân said she was coming out of the tunnel and she was determined that the season
would see her leave it altogether.

Following the interview, there was a small party in the green
room. Frank checked out the other guests, recognising a director
and a couple of producers, as he collected a glass of wine for Siân
and helped himself to a beer. When Kümel appeared, he was
bright and effusive, evidently enjoying the attention and pleased
with how the interview had gone. Frank introduced him to Siân,
and Kümel clasped her hand in both of his and kissed her on each
cheek.

'Frank is a very lucky man,' he said.

'Thank you,' Siân said, smiling first at Kümel and then turning to include Frank, who was thinking that it was a long time
since he had seen Siân this relaxed and happy.

'Your friend Johnny Vos,' Kümel said to Frank, when Siân had
gone to get a refill.

'No friend of mine,' Frank said.

'He is in Italy now?'

'Apparently. He went to Milan to try to persuade Asia Argento
to be in his Delvaux film. She has this tattoo . . .'

'Yes, I heard about that.' Kümel rubbed his beard, amused. 'He
was cleared of suspicion, was he?'

'They could have done him for wasting police time and
resources. I mean, he could have been a bit more cooperative. But
they were pretty sure he had nothing to do with what happened.'

'Even though he had Spitzner's phone number?'

'Spitzner was an actor. Or he was pretending to be. Amounts
to the same thing, I suppose. He was using an assumed name.
Pretending to be someone he wasn't.'

Siân rejoined them and Kümel beamed at her.

'So, are you working on any new projects?' she asked the
director, taking a sip of wine.

'Which one would you like to hear about,' he asked, touching
her arm, 'the Jules Verne or the Alexandre Dumas? Let me tell
you a little about both.'

After the party had broken up, Frank led Siân back through

the building out on to the South Bank. It was a warm night, so they sat for a while on one of the benches facing the river.

'We haven't done this since we first met,' Frank said and found himself having to look away.

'We should do it more often,' said Siân.

They watched as a police launch motored upriver.

'I thought I'd lost you,' Frank said.

They climbed the steps up on to Waterloo Bridge and leaned on the railing, looking back at the South Bank. The blank façades of the National Theatre, the NFT, the Hayward Gallery and the Royal Festival Hall glowed so brightly you would have thought there was a brilliant full moon hanging just out of shot. Each individual white spoke of the London Eye shone like silver thread.

'My favourite spot in London,' he said, putting his arms around her.

'Mine too,' said Siân, slipping her arm around his waist and drawing in closer.

In the black pools of Siân's dilated pupils, Frank saw a tiny white shard of light. The moon. Not a full moon, though. A crescent moon.

ACKNOWLEDGEMENTS

This book could not have been written without the extraordinary support and understanding of Harry Kümel and Henk Van Rensbergen. I am extremely grateful to them both.

I would like to acknowledge the financial assistance of the Authors' Foundation. I am grateful to the foundation's assessors and administrators.

Thanks to Kate Ryan, Jean Royle and John Saddler; to all the Chisellers and Miserablists, Mike and Paula, Conrad and Rhonda, Chris and Chantal, and Joel. Brian Radcliffe was generous with his time and his hospitality. Gareth Evans, Peter Whitehead, Geoff Andrew, Tom Charity, David Thompson, John Pym, Michael Kemp, M. John Harrison and Christopher Burns all provided advice and support. Local knowledge was garnered from Wim Verhaeghe and Eva Vermandel. Philippe Jouk, Geert Maes, Ditte Mollet, Serge Bosschaerts and Frank Van Der Kinderen provided further assistance in Antwerp; Chris and Karen Bulcaen helped out in Ghent; Dominic Ryan and Sheila Chellun were generous hosts in Brussels. Thanks, too, to Michel Apers, Olivier Fayt, Nick Ryan and Craig Taylor. Ben Slater of Sheffield's Showroom Cinema provided a kind service; Nick James and Alex Hogg were outstanding ambassadors for the British Film Institute; Peter Roberts at the BBC was generous with his time and his tapes. I'm grateful to Greg Sanders for his invaluable help in New York. Harvey Zito and Arthur Langermann, in London and Antwerp respectively, could only have been more helpful if they'd actually given me some diamonds to take home.

London's Tate Modern and the Sofitel Astoria, Brussels, both provided valuable services. Thanks, also, to Pete Ayrton and everyone at Serpent's Tail.

The lyrics quoted in Chapter 20 are from 'The Bride Came C.O.D.' by Paul Buck for 48 Cameras, taken from the album *B-Sides Are For Lovers* (1985).

The following publications were referred to during the writing of this book: *Paul Delvaux: Surrealizing the Nude* by David Scott (Reaktion Books); *Unreal Reality: The Cinema of Harry Kümel* by David Soren (Lucas Brothers Publishers); *Split Screen: Belgian Cinema and Cultural Identity* by Philip Mosley (State University of New York Press); *Paul Delvaux 1897–1994* (Royal Museums of Fine Art of Belgium); *Delvaux* by Barbara Emerson (Fonds Mercator); *Surrealism: Desire Unbound* edited by Jennifer Mundy (Tate Publishing); *Grain Elevators* by Lisa Mahar-Keplinger (Princeton Architectural Press).

Part of chapter nine appeared previously in *Vertigo* edited by Holly Aylett. An excerpt drawn from chapters two, three, four and five appeared in the first issue of *Black Clock* edited by Steve Erickson.

The views and remarks of the artist Barry Burman were illuminating and his enthusiasm encouraging. Barry died while I was writing this book, which I would like to dedicate to his memory, as well as to my wife, whose consistent support, understanding and encouragement made the writing of it possible.